A LIMEY AT GETTYSBURG

The Adventures of an Englishman
during the American Civil War

Eric B Dennison
and
Robert T Mitchell

authorHOUSE®

AuthorHouse™ UK
1663 Liberty Drive
Bloomington, IN 47403 USA
www.authorhouse.co.uk
Phone: 0800 047 8203 (Domestic TFN)
       +44 1908 723714 (International)

This is a work of fiction. All of the characters, names, incidents,
organizations, and dialogue in this novel are either the products
of the author's imagination or are used fictitiously.

Published by AuthorHouse 07/15/2019

ISBN: 978-1-7283-8909-7 (sc)
ISBN: 978-1-7283-8908-0 (e)

Print information available on the last page.

This book is printed on acid-free paper.

FOREWORD

My father, Eric, was born in 1927. He was educated at Berkhamsted Preparatory School and Brighton College, then joined the army and served until 1948, mainly in Egypt. He later graduated with a BSc in Geology at Cambridge and took a postgraduate course in Tropical Agriculture in Trinidad, which enabled him to join the Colonial Service as an agricultural officer. He served in this role in Nigeria, where he was accompanied by his wife, Brenda, whom he had married in 1954. They had two sons, Bruce and Craig. On their return to England, Eric was invited to join his father-in-law's packaging company as a director. He continued running it for many years after the death of his father-in-law.

Brenda died in 1995, and Eric semi-retired soon after. After retirement, he occupied himself with lots of hobbies, including writing stories for magazines and writing the first draft of this novel.

He was diagnosed with stomach cancer in 2008 and died at home on 23 September 2009, before the book was completed.

I recently asked my friend Rob to finish the story. The plot and most of the research belong to Eric, but Rob has written some new sections, added more research, and filled out the story. I hope that my father would be pleased with the result and that you enjoy reading it.

Craig Dennison

I would like to express my thanks to Kate, Heather, Craig and the editors for their help and advice, and to Connie Knox and James Dennison for the cover design.

Robert Mitchell

Chapter 1

February 1861

Firth Brown stood nervously before the large oak door of his editor's office. This was the seat of power, the place from where Mr William Smythe, editor and owner of *The Manchester Echo,* ruled his empire with a rod of iron, steering the paper to ever-greater profits. Smythe was not a true journalist, more a businessman with an uncanny ability to send reporters out for the best stories, ahead of the competition. Smythe was really only interested in the *Echo* making money; to that end, it was essential not only to get the best stories but also to pay his staff the lowest wages. He was well known in the trade for sending his reporters out on the most unpleasant assignments and then thanking them profusely when they came back, rather than paying them good money. After all, praise did not affect his bank balance.

Firth checked his tie was straight, wiped the sweat from his hands, and swallowed down his fear before finally knocking smartly.

"Come in!" a voice shouted from inside.

Firth opened the door, walked hesitantly into the office, and stood before the huge desk. He was only a few months short of his twenty-first birthday, but had for some time now considered himself a fully grown man. To prove it, he even sported a thin, dark moustache of which he was very proud. He was rather skinny (or "lean" as he preferred to think) and stood a full five feet, eight inches tall in his stockinged feet. Nevertheless, at that moment, he felt like a naughty schoolboy who had been summoned to the headmaster's office.

"Sit down, my boy," Smythe instructed him, without looking up.

Without any preamble, Smythe got straight down to business.

"You are twenty years old, I see here," he said, reading from a sheaf of notes he held. "And you have been with us for four years. I hope you know, Brown, that I have, for a while now, regarded you as one of our best young reporters, so you'll be pleased to know I have decided to do you a great honour by giving you one of the best assignments this paper can offer."

Firth said nothing, knowing he was about to be handed a difficult job, given Smythe's long-held reputation for this type of thing. And what timing! Firth had it in mind to ask his boss for his permission to get married. No one there would dare to wed without his consent.

"At my club," Smythe continued, "there is much talk of the Southern states seceding from the Union. I always thought that, having left the British Empire, they would squabble among themselves. The only thing that amazes me is that it has taken them so long. It's surprising that they've done so well up to now, really. You know, they've even won the admiration of the royal family! Especially Prince Albert, but then, after all, he's really a German. Thank God the states are independent now, or we'd have got involved in their vulgar arguments."

Smythe took a breath and then said, "What I have in mind is for you to go over to America and stay in Washington to be on the spot if a war starts. I've booked you a third-class passage on the next steamship, so you'll get across quickly. I've arranged for you to stay in a moderately priced hotel fairly near that monstrosity they're calling the White House."

He shook his head sadly, as if hoping the whole unpleasant business would go away.

"When does the ship leave, sir?" asked Firth, wondering what he would say to his fiancée. There was no way he dared to question the editor's wishes.

"It leaves Liverpool Docks tomorrow afternoon," said Smythe, "which gives you plenty of time to prepare. You will, of course, continue your work for the remainder of the day—I want that article on waterproof boots for the gentry finished before you go."

Smythe pondered for a moment.

"I will give you tomorrow morning off so you can pack your bags. Make sure you take plenty of our headed stationery. I want everyone to know whom you work for. I suppose you will also want to say your goodbyes to your family. Do you have one?"

Firth knew Smythe didn't really care if he had a family. He just wanted to get his poorly paid young reporter off to the Union as quickly as possible, so that he could send his dispatches about the coming war. Although it was all happening thousands of miles away, any talk of war would be of interest to the paper's readers in Lancashire because cotton for all the local mills came from the Southern states. Disruption to their supplies would cause a loss of profits and could cost a great many jobs.

"Well, what are you waiting for, boy?" Smythe boomed. "Get on your way now."

"Yes, sir," said Firth. He rose and left the office in a daze.

What rotten luck! He had at last persuaded his future father-in-law to allow him to marry his beloved daughter, Jane Mary McCormack, and now he had to ask for the marriage to be postponed.

He could hear Mrs McCormack in his mind already. *You see, Jane? Just what I expected. I told you he was no good and that he'd let you down. What do you expect from a journalist? To think, you could have chosen a professional man, and you chose … him!*

He could see the tears welling up in Jane's eyes. It would be unbearable.

Firth returned to his desk to finish his article about the waterproof boots. He was interrupted by his friend Percy, leaning across his desk to ask what the editor had wanted to see him about.

"What did he say? Has he given you a raise, or told you to find another job?"

"I'm going to America tomorrow," Firth told him. "He wants me to report on whether a war will break out. It's really come at a rotten time. Did you know Jane and I have been planning our wedding?"

4

"Ha! You lucky beggar. I'd drop any girl if I had the chance to go to America," Percy said with a wistful look in his eyes. "They say the dance halls in New York are even better than the ones in London and the girls are even more generous with their favours, if you understand me. Certainly better than this strait-laced city!"

Stroud, who was the subeditor and a petty, insignificant little man, crossed over to their desks.

"If you have nothing better to do than gossip, I'll send you two up to the editor. He doesn't pay you to waste his time."

"Mr Brown's going to America tomorrow," blurted out Percy. "He's going to represent the paper if war breaks out."

"Well," said Stroud, "that's all the more reason for *Mr* Brown to get on with his work. We want that article on waterproof footwear before we go to press this evening. If it's not finished, *Mr* Brown, you'll have to stay on late this evening, even if you are going to America tomorrow."

Firth and Percy continued working until the usual closing time of seven in the evening, when all the staff, or those who had finished their day's work, could go home.

Stroud came over again, to look at what they had done. Satisfied, he sent it down to the print room.

"All right, you two, you can go, but make sure you're in the office on time in the morning."

"I shan't be here in the morning, Mr Stroud. Mr Smythe said I was to get ready for the ship tomorrow. I need some of our stationery as well, so can I have a requisition order for that, please?"

"Did Mr Smythe tell you to take our stationery?"

"He did. He said he wants everyone to know which paper I represent."

"He's being very generous with you. I doubt whether any war in the Union will be worth the trouble. Just some minor skirmish between a load of ex-colonials. All right, come back in the morning, and I'll give you the requisition order. The editor may have thought better about sending you by then."

It was well known in the office that Stroud had only gained his lofty position by ingratiating himself with Smythe, and it was good sport to speculate on what favours he might have done for the editor. It seemed to Firth that the little man was forever attempting to justify his position in the eyes of others by always trying to be seen to be right.

Firth walked through the streets of Manchester to Cheetham Hill, the middle-class area where Jane and her parents lived. He was going over and over in his mind what he would say, but he knew that, no matter what he said, it was a hopeless situation. As he neared the house he was tempted to carry on walking and then just sail away from England the next day without seeing Jane. But no, that would be the worst thing he could do and the act of a real swine.

If there's one thing I am, he thought, *it's a decent man. All I can do is tell the truth and hope they'll understand.*

With renewed determination, Firth opened the wrought-iron gates and made his way along the footpath to the solid double front doors. They were much like the rest of the house: large and imposing, such that it overshadowed the surrounding properties. Mr McCormack was not shy in displaying his wealth and was consequently well known in the upper circles of Manchester society.

Firth knocked firmly on the door, and the maid answered.

"Good evening, Mr Brown," she said, and took his hat and coat. "The family are in the living room, sir. This way, please."

She opened the door to the living room and announced him to those present. "Mr Firth Brown, sir."

Jane looked up with a smile and rushed over to him. "Oh, Firth."

"Good evening, my love," he said. "How wonderful you look, as usual." Then, he turned his attention to her parents. "Good evening, sir, Mrs McCormack."

They made small talk by discussing the weather and the current political situation, with special regard to the events in America. But the conversation felt forced and quickly dried up. Sooner than he would have liked, Firth decided he had to face the unpleasant task of telling them of his forthcoming trip.

"Jane, my dear, do you think we could have a moment of privacy? There's something I must tell you."

"Anything you have to say to my daughter, young man, can be said in my presence or not at all," said Mr McCormack rather abruptly.

Jane was looking at Firth with questioning eyes.

"I'm sorry to say that I've come with some bad news, sir," Firth said, addressing her father. "My editor is sending me on an assignment to America, and I must leave by steamship tomorrow."

Jane's inquisitive look was replaced by one of horror. Her mouth opened and a small gasp escaped as she brought her hand to her throat. Firth thought for a moment that she might faint, but instead she burst into tears and ran towards the door, tripping on the edge of the carpet in her haste to get away. The door slammed behind her, and Firth was left facing Mr and Mrs McCormack in a hostile silence that seemed to go on forever. He thought this day would surely be the end of his happiness.

"I always knew you would be a disaster for my daughter!" hissed Mrs McCormack.

"I think you had better leave my house immediately, Brown," said Mr McCormack in a quiet but menacing voice. "You have turned out to be as big a disappointment as my wife predicted."

"But, sir, please, I shall be back soon! I'm sure this war, if there is one, won't last long."

"Get out of my house! Now! How dare you argue with me!" Mr McCormack bellowed across the room, his face changing from pink to red to a fiery purple.

Firth turned and left the room. The maid, who had clearly heard everything, was already waiting with his hat and coat. She handed them to him with a sly smile, opened the front door without a word, and then closed it behind him rather more loudly than was necessary.

Chapter 2

Firth got off the train at Liverpool Docks Station and walked the short distance to the Waterloo Docks deep in thought, his mind a jumble of emotions. Although he was excited, he was also nervous, and upset at having to leave Jane. That morning, while washing himself, he'd studied his reflection in the mirror. It showed a confident-looking young man, which was totally at odds with the way he felt. This would be his first absence from his home and family for any length of time, and he was struck by just how unprepared he was. Feeling slightly dazed, he'd dressed in his freshly laundered working clothes, put his prized silver watch in its pocket, and packed his bag with only the essentials: washing and shaving implements, two changes of clothing, his pens and bottle of ink. All the while, he'd pondered over what was to come. Every day from now on would be a new adventure.

Until a few hours ago, he'd always lived with his parents and his younger sister, Megan. It had been an emotional and tearful parting, especially as it had come so suddenly. Firth had promised to write regularly and send a posting address as soon as he could. He'd then taken one last look at the family home as he walked away. After a short stop at the paper's office, where Stroud had given him a book of headed notepaper, ten American dollars, and his instructions for his arrival in America, Firth had then gone on his way. Upon leaving the office, Firth had felt even more miserable, and he'd then started to reflect on how he'd reached this point in his life.

His father, an English teacher, had passed on his love of writing to his son. Upon leaving school at the age of fourteen, Firth had joined the staff of *The Manchester Echo*. He'd started work in the print room and, after a year of cleaning and sweeping, progressed to typesetting and learning to operate the machinery. What he really wanted, though, was to be a journalist, and seeing a finished newspaper in all its glory after his toil only fuelled his enthusiasm. His father knew a man who knew Mr Smythe, and it was arranged for Firth to start work as a junior reporter. He loved writing, even though the pay was poor at just ten shillings a week, and until now, he'd only been trusted with the most minor of stories. But now, out of the blue, he was on his way to America to cover his biggest story so far.

As he got nearer the docks, the volume of people and noise grew markedly. He could see ships' masts in the distance, one towering over all the others, most of which were cargo ships. His vessel, and the biggest by far, was Cunard's *Persia*. She was a magnificent sight: nearly four hundred feet long with two huge red funnels gently puffing thick black smoke and three fully rigged masts. The black painted sides of the immense ship seemed to rise like a cliff out of the water. She carried two 40-foot paddle wheels, and at 3,300 tons, she was one of the largest ships in the world. She was built to cross oceans, and looked like it. Cargoes of all types, including live animals, were being winched, carried and walked aboard, and a line of passengers slowly walked up a none-too-safe-looking gangplank. Firth posted a letter to Jane, then joined the queue and handed his ticket to one of the ship's officers as he reached the end of the gangplank.

"Thank you, sir. That's Deck E, bunk number eight. Turn right as you board, and follow the signs."

Firth thought this was an odd way to direct him. Surely the man must have meant *cabin* eight. He crossed the plank with some trepidation and was glad to be inside the ship. It seemed a lot smaller now, with low ceilings and narrow corridors, but he found his accommodation with little difficulty. To Firth's dismay, the officer had been quite correct. Bunk number eight was the middle one of a stack of three, and had only a curtain to provide the occupier with a small degree of privacy. There were twenty-five sets of identical bunks, all of them opening directly onto a communal area, the main feature of which was a giant table, big enough to seat all of the huge cabin's unfortunate occupiers. The space was dank, dark, and smelled rather unpleasantly of past travellers. His bunk, like most of the others, was built directly against the hull of the ship, but even so, there were no portholes. He would have to endure the noise of the sea, the thrumming of the engines, and the close proximity of dozens of strangers for two whole weeks. Firth was becoming convinced that the crossing would be an ordeal, to say the least.

He deposited his bag in a box at the foot of his bed and pulled the curtain across while the other passengers boarded. There were no women, of course; they had their own accommodation elsewhere and were strictly segregated.

The only place the men he was travelling with could meet their female companions was on the outside upper deck. While he was waiting for the hubbub to die down, he wrote another letter to Jane, trying to explain things to her and pleading for her forgiveness, then he went to find out how to post it. On deck for the first time, he was surprised to see that they had already left the docks. The engines were winding up, and the giant paddle wheels were slowly moving. He watched England recede into the distance, wondering how long it would be until he returned.

They soon cleared the Mersey and entered the open sea, the wind increasing to become a biting gale; towards the rear of the ship, there was also freezing spray from the paddle wheels to contend with. His lightweight working clothes were no protection, and he was soon chilled to the bone and had to go down below again. It was difficult to navigate, however, as the first-class accommodations were completely out of bounds to other passengers, so he had to brave the elements once more, looking for the same entrance from which he had originally emerged.

He made his way straight to his bunk, climbed inside, and pulled the curtain across. He curled up on the bed, shivering, and started planning a new letter to Jane, one that wouldn't just repeat his earlier pleadings, but it was a hopeless task. The constant rolling of the ship added to his discomfort, and he soon felt distinctly queasy. He had heard a few of the other passengers throwing up their last meal, and it wasn't going to be long before he joined them.

The first night at sea became a nightmare, with shouting and arguments among the passengers, the incessant thrash of the paddle wheels, and an atmosphere that was thick with the smell of unwashed bodies, tobacco smoke, and vomit. He had a sleepless night and, despite an empty stomach, couldn't face any breakfast. Instead, he went up to the empty outside deck. As soon as he opened the door, the icy North Atlantic winds hit him like a slap in the face, but he endured it because it was the only place on the ship he could go, other than the communal cabin. He was feeling miserable and had abandoned his original idea of interviewing some of the people aboard on their views about the possibility of a civil war in America. It would take all his strength merely to endure this awful journey.

He was sick every day for a week. During that time, he barely had a bite of food, as he had no appetite and was unable to keep anything down anyway. Slowly, though, his body adapted to the conditions it found itself in, and by the eighth day, he was feeling something like his old self again.

He found that, despite the foul atmosphere and the endless pitching and rolling of the ship, he was now sleeping soundly. His appetite had also returned with a vengeance, and he was ravenous. This being third class—or steerage, as it was better known—meant there was barely enough food to go around, especially as nearly everyone had by now found their sea legs, and what there was did not look as if it would be worth eating, having lost its freshness days ago.

He had revived his earlier idea and decided to sharpen his reporting skills by interviewing the passengers about their views on the situation in America, but he was soon disappointed, as most had no interest at all and some didn't even know what was happening. They were mainly immigrants whose minds were focused on how they were to make their new lives in America, and that was all they wanted to talk about. Only one man had any direct interest. He was a representative of a cotton company based in Charleston who was returning home after successfully negotiating a supply contract with a clothing company in Wigan. He was, though, far more interested in crowing about his success and the commission he had earned than talking about the war which he seemed to hope would just fade away.

On the ninth day, the temperature dropped further, and a new hazard emerged, one which only made things worse. Firth was on one of his regular outside excursions when he spotted the first of many icebergs. This one was relatively small, its highest point below the level at which he was standing, but it was soon followed by some true giants.

Already, four ships had been lost that winter on the crossing, all from collisions with icebergs. They ranged in size from tiny floating flakes to massive drifting islands, with sheer sides that dwarfed even this huge ship. The captain was very careful to pick his way through the ice; but, even so, it took five days and nights at slow speed before they were finally clear.

A day later, land came into sight. They passed Newfoundland and the Canadian coast and then saw the United States for the first time. As they neared the coast, the sea calmed, and soon they were manoeuvring into the docks.

Firth had his bags packed long before it was really necessary, as he couldn't wait to get off that filthy, stinking ship and onto dry land again. After what seemed like an age, they finally stopped moving, and the gangplank was lowered. He was one of the first to disembark, and at that moment, he didn't care if he ever set foot on a ship again.

His initial impressions of New York were of a vast, tightly packed and incredibly busy city, far more so than he was used to in Manchester. There were people everywhere, not to mention horses, carts, coaches, and lots of streetcars. Being back on dry land had set off his appetite again, so he looked for somewhere to eat. There were plenty of restaurants and bars, but they were all run by foreigners and nothing looked familiar. Eventually, he chanced upon an establishment run by an Irish family, where he filled his stomach with a hearty meal of meat pie and potatoes. He resumed his walk across town, feeling much better.

Firth marvelled at all the traffic and noise and the many strange-sounding languages spoken, as well as all the unusual faces that went with them. He could pick out some Italians, as there was a small community in Manchester, but there were also lots of other Europeans, Orientals, black Africans, Jews in their distinctive garb, and even one or two Arabs in head scarves. He followed his instructions, which were surprisingly easy, given the unfamiliar but entirely logical grid layout of the city, across Long Island to the New Jersey ferry terminal. A small ferry over a freezing, choppy, fast-flowing river would have terrified him a few weeks ago, but his recent nautical experience meant he could take it in his stride. He paid the fifty-cent fare and was taken across the Hudson River to Jersey City. From there, it was just a short walk to the Exchange Place Rail Road Depot. He had timed it well; the train was waiting patiently at the platform, ready to take him on the last leg of his journey to Washington.

Chapter 3

As soon as he arrived in Washington, Firth sought out the small second-class hotel where he would take up his lodgings. It was on Fourth Street, not far from the new White House, the centre of government, and it was just two blocks from the city jail. It certainly lived down to Smythe's statement that it was an "economical" residence. He had to carry his own bags into the foyer, where there was just a threadbare carpet in the centre of the room, surrounded by unpolished boards and a few tables whose tops were marked with rings. The walls were badly stained and the ceiling was a golden brown from years of smoke coming up from the kitchen. The concierge was a small, poorly dressed man of about fifty who had a shuffling gait, and the top part of his spine was bent like a question mark. He smelled of stale cigar smoke, as did the whole room. Even his desk had a dark round stain above it from the constant smoke. The smell got stronger as Firth approached the desk.

"Have you got a reservation?"

"I have," answered Firth.

"Name?" asked the man.

"Firth Brown. My newspaper, *The Manchester Echo,* booked me in."

Firth was already starting to dislike the man, what with his shabby appearance, and not even a hint of politeness. No "sir", no "please", nothing.

"Ah yes. Here we are, Mr Firth Brown of *The Manchester Echo*—just like you said. We've been expecting you," intoned the little man. "My name is George Hammond, and I run this hotel on behalf of the owner, Mr Dayton, who is currently ill. We charge $1.50 a night, including meals. Now then, this is a respectable establishment with no drunkenness, and don't be bringing any women back to your room. Understand? We only have well-behaved male travellers here. Well brought-up they are, and mainly passing through the capital on business, so most only stay for a few days. Journalists," he said with a sneer, "tend to give even the best places a bad name."

"Oh really? And why's that?" asked Firth. "Have you any other journalists like myself here?" He was thinking, with increasing conviction, that no one with any sense would stay in this fleapit for a second longer than was necessary.

"No, we have no others," said Hammond blithely.

Firth decided that he would find new lodgings as soon as possible, but he knew it wouldn't be easy. Smythe had given him very little money and had arranged for him to receive his salary at a local bank. His keep would be paid out of the newspaper's funds, and a small amount would be put into his bank in England for when he returned. He was, after all, expected to leave and sail home in a few months, at the most.

He signed the hotel register and, following Hammond's directions, went up to his room to unpack. The room was small with poor-quality furniture and had little space to spare. Only the essentials had been provided: a washstand with a basin and water jug, a small chest of drawers, and a rickety wardrobe. As he opened the wardrobe door, a shelf fell out. Firth looked around in dismay. The only other items were a lumpy-looking bed, an oil lamp on a small table, and a hard wooden chair. He sat on the bed and, using his suitcase as a desktop, wrote yet another letter to Jane—his sixth since leaving England.

At one o'clock, Firth went down to the reception from his second-floor room to ask Hammond about meal times. He was told that lunch was already being served in the dining room along the passage.

"There is also a lounge which our gentleman can use, but no visitors, mind you; they have to stay out here at all times. In fact, we don't encourage visitors at all. I particularly make that point, what with you being a journalist and all. I've heard your lot can be very free and easy with your ways."

Firth made his way down the dingy passageway to the dining room. He wasn't expecting much, but he was pleasantly surprised. The room was completely different to the rest of the hotel, with big bay windows and crisp, clean, white tablecloths. There was a neatly dressed maid standing by a large trolley next to a door on the other side of the room.

"Good afternoon, sir," she greeted him. "Would you like to sit here?" she asked, then showed him to a table next to the main window.

"Very nice, thank you," he said with a smile.

Firth looked around at his fellow residents. There were five other men, three of them dressed in dark business suits; the other two were in rough travelling clothes, perhaps farmers who had come to town to buy provisions.

"What would you like to eat, sir?" asked the waitress. "We have meat and beans with bread; butter can be supplied, but it's extra."

"Anything else?"

"I'm afraid we only offer the one dish, or you can have soup as an alternative." She then said quietly, "I wouldn't advise the soup myself, but if you like, there's a small eating house on the corner of the block. Many of our guests eat out."

"Thank you. I'll have the meat and beans, please."

"And bread?"

"And bread—without butter." He smiled.

He had to at least sample the hotel's food before spending extra on something that wasn't an essential expense, as short of money as he was.

He soon realised why most of the guests took their meals elsewhere. The meat was stringy and the beans were like stones; while the meal might have once been hot, it wasn't now. Unfortunately, and unsurprisingly, Smythe had taken the cheap option of full board at the hotel with no allowance for eating out, but this was too much! He would have to find some way to have his food somewhere else for little or, preferably, no cost.

After he had finished his lunch, Firth went back up to his room and started writing his first report. He described how he had left the steamship at the docks in New York and made his way by train and ferry to Washington. He mentioned how surprised he had been that some of the people he had met on his journey did not seem to care whether the Southern states seceded from the Union or not. The few who had shown any interest had been very much for President Lincoln. Nearly all these in the second group had, most reluctantly, concluded that war was inevitable.

Having written his report, he left the hotel and walked to the post office that would send off his dispatches. It was a small place on Indiana Avenue, just a few streets away. It had a creaking sign outside that announced to the world that letters and parcels could be posted to anywhere in the states of America, and across the sea to Europe. Firth noted that it also offered a telegraph service. He joined the short queue inside. When his turn came, he paid the fee and left his report with the clerk, then decided to go back to the hotel.

The wooden sidewalk was bustling with people walking in both directions, and some who seemed to have no direction at all. Just in front of him, a girl of about nineteen was strolling with her mother. The lower half of her body was obscured by a voluminous light-blue dress, but he was captivated by her bouncy walk and a blonde ponytail that swung from side to side in time with her steps. Firth was smiling, admiring the view, when her carefree afternoon was suddenly interrupted as she tripped over a loose board and fell into the road, right into the path of a fast-moving horse and cart. Firth leapt into the road without hesitation and, grabbing the girl's arm, pulled her out of the way with only inches to spare. He gently helped her to her feet and then onto the sidewalk.

"Are you hurt?" he asked with concern.

"N-no, I'm fine, thanks to you, sir. You saved me from being trampled under the horse's hooves," replied the young woman.

Her mother rushed forward to hold her daughter in her arms.

"Oh, darling, darling, are you all right?"

"Don't worry, Mother, I'm perfectly well, thanks to this gentleman."

The lady turned to Firth with a relieved smile. "That was very brave of you, young man. What's your name?"

"Firth, madam. Firth Brown."

"Well, Firth Brown, my daughter and I would like to show our gratitude by asking you to call on us this evening. I'm sure my husband would wish to thank you as well. Here is my card."

"You will come, won't you?" asked the woman's daughter.

"I would be delighted, ladies. Thank you very much."

"Wonderful. You British have such nice manners, and here I am, forgetting mine. My name is Elizabeth Burkett," she said, with a small bow of the head. "Until this evening, then. About six o'clock if that suits?"

"Please call me Firth. I look forward very much to this evening. It's been a pleasure to help, ladies." He doffed his hat and took his leave.

Firth could hardly believe his luck. On first leaving England, he had not been able to get Jane out of his mind. Now her memory was fading fast, and the pretty face of Elizabeth Burkett was there to replace it. Elizabeth was a beautiful girl. When she smiled at him, he felt he would willingly risk his life for her all over again. He had even glimpsed her legs up to her knees when she fell over, a part of a woman he'd never had the good fortune to see before. Her legs, he thought, were very beautiful too. He was delighted with the way events had unfolded, and now his imagination was running wild with possibilities. His excitement was such that he couldn't concentrate on anything else that day

21

and found himself constantly checking his pocket watch, waiting for the evening to arrive.

Eventually, five o'clock came. He could wait no longer, so he set out to find the address given to him by Mrs Burkett. It wasn't far away, and he arrived well before the appointed hour. The house was a white, wooden, two-storey construction that looked as if it might have four or five bedrooms. It was on the sunny side of a tree-lined street, with detached houses of a similar size on both sides. It could have been one of the better areas of Manchester, except the houses were of wood rather than brick.

Firth consulted his watch again. He waited until two minutes to six, then walked up to the front door. A young black maid opened it at his knock, and he was shown into a small reception room containing a table, two armchairs, and an unlit fire. The weather was still chilly, and the room was obviously not used much. Either from apprehension or cold, a shiver went down his spine.

"The master will see you now, sir," the maid informed him. "Please follow me to the sitting room."

"Mr Brown, I presume. Welcome!" boomed a large man standing with his back to a log fire. "I believe I owe you my thanks for saving my daughter from being run over today."

They shook hands.

"I was pleased to help, sir." Firth nodded to Elizabeth and Mrs Burkett.

"Good, good. I don't know how it is in your country, young man, but here, people of standing don't generally invite strangers into their homes. My wife is rather overly enthusiastic where visitors are concerned, but under the circumstances and as you are new to our country, I am happy to break the usual rules."

"Thank you, sir" was all a somewhat puzzled Firth could think of to say.

"Will you have a cup of coffee, Mr Brown?" Mrs Burkett asked. "Sugar?"

"No sugar, but I would like some milk please."

There was a slightly awkward silence.

"We don't usually have milk in our coffee—especially the men," Mr Burkett said, emphasising the last three words.

"I'll have it as it comes, then. Thank you," replied Firth hastily.

The maid knocked and came back into the room.

"You have another visitor, sir."

"Who is it, Martha?"

"It's Mr Burrows, sir. I've shown him to the reception room."

"Please excuse us, Mr Brown. I must see this fellow. Come along, Marg; we don't want to keep him waiting."

Firth could not believe his luck. They had left him alone with Elizabeth! He would only have a few minutes, so he decided, against all convention, to act quickly.

"Elizabeth, I know this is very forward of me, but perhaps we could meet up sometime. I expect I'll have to leave Washington for my work soon, but I won't be away for long. I have to interview some soldiers about the coming war."

"You seem to be very sure there will be a war," replied Elizabeth.

She hesitated then added, "Yes, it *is* forward of you Firth. However, and luckily for you," she said with a smile that was growing wider with each word, "I walk my dog each weekday morning between the hours of ten and eleven. We go to the small park opposite the house, so it will not be hard for you to find. Mother sometimes comes along, but usually it's just me and Rufus. That's my dog's name, by the way. Perhaps we may see each other if you happen to be taking a stroll at the same time."

"I'll see what I can do," he said with an equally wide smile.

At that moment, Mr and Mrs Burkett returned, and Firth and Elizabeth immediately assumed straight faces, all the while threatening to burst into laughter at any second.

Firth dared not look at Elizabeth, so he just stared at his shoes until order was restored.

"Our visitor has left," Mr Burkett announced.

Firth took the thinly veiled hint—he didn't want to upset the Burketts by outstaying his welcome.

"I must also go now. It has been most kind of you to receive me," he said.

"Perhaps you would like to come to a little tea party I'm giving on Saturday, Firth. It's for a few friends, both gentlemen and ladies," said Mrs Burkett. "That will be all right, won't it, George?"

"It's your party, my dear, but he seems a respectable-enough lad," said Mr Burkett, in a rather offhand manner, and left the room without another word.

Firth thanked Mrs Burkett and assured her that he considered it a great honour to be invited to her house once again. He had decided that the best way to see more of Elizabeth was to be as gracious as possible to her mother. It was obvious her father was the master of the house but regarded the day-to-day affairs as beneath him.

"We would be delighted if you came, wouldn't we, Elizabeth?" said Mrs Burkett. "Washington society is very interested in the views of the British, especially concerning the possibility of a war in the Union. A knowledgeable journalist will be very popular indeed."

"I, too, will be very interested in their opinions. It has been a great pleasure to see you again, Miss Elizabeth," continued Firth. He wanted to tell her how lovely she looked but felt it was too soon, especially as her mother was well within earshot.

Firth walked into the hall, where Martha handed him his hat and coat.

"What time do guests usually arrive for the mistress's tea parties?" he asked the girl in a low voice, for he was not sure if it was considered good manners to speak to the maidservant.

"About three o'clock in the afternoon, sir."

"Thank you," he replied.

Turning towards the door, he saw Mr Burkett looking sternly at him from a nearby doorway.

"You don't ask the servants anything regarding the running of this house!" Burkett bellowed. He turned to the maid and, for a second, seemed about to cuff her.

"I'm very sorry, sir," said Firth. "I'd neglected to ask the time for the party and didn't want to worry Mrs Burkett, or yourself. I'm sorry, sir."

This effusive apology for such a minor misdemeanour seemed to have the desired effect, as Burkett merely stared hard at him, then went back to his room.

The maid, Firth noticed, was quite flustered, certainly more than he would have expected. After all, in his mind, she had done nothing wrong.

CHAPTER 4

Firth was awoken the next morning by the early spring sunshine streaming through the cheap brown curtains drawn across his window. He rose, then washed and dressed quickly, cheerfully anticipating the day ahead.

At five minutes to ten by his watch, he was waiting just inside the gates to the park Elizabeth had mentioned. He certainly didn't want Mr Burkett to see him. A few minutes later, she walked through the gates with a small spaniel on a lead, which was keeping obediently to heel.

Firth walked up beside her.

"So, this must be Rufus. Aren't you going to introduce us?"

Elizabeth did not seem in the least surprised. "Of course, Firth," she said with a pretty smile. "Rufus. Rufus, look at me. This is Mr Firth Brown. Mr Brown, this is Rufus."

The dog looked up at him, its tail wagging. Firth dropped to his knees and held out his hand.

"Delighted to meet you, Rufus."

To Firth's amazement, the little dog gave a small yap, then sat down and held out its paw.

The dog's approval was a great start for them, and eleven o'clock came around all too quickly. Elizabeth insisted she had to go, so Firth said his goodbyes with a promise to meet them again the next morning.

Firth spent much of the rest of his time writing articles for his newspaper. He was kept extremely busy, as events were starting to move quickly. On 15 April, the fall of Fort Sumter to the Confederate army was confirmed in Washington. Initially, most of the city's citizens were stunned by the news. This feeling was soon followed by the realisation that war was now very likely, and the flames of popular outrage were fanned when it was learnt that the Union flag had been attacked and taken down. News then came in that, surprisingly, no soldiers had been killed at the fort during the thirty-three-hour cannon duel. This information gave the peace contingent in Washington and New York the chance to insist that the Union should not be hasty in declaring war on the Southern states.

The day before the fall of Fort Sumter, Firth had received a telegram from his editor. Smythe wanted him to return to England, as it seemed to him that there was not going to be a war after all. Firth was equally convinced that events would prove Smythe wrong and sent a very polite, but short and expensive, cable saying so. A week later, he received another terse wire demanding that he should stay and report on events until the war ended. It seemed Smythe had heard the news. Furthermore, his pay would be increased so that he could travel to the sites of the battles Smythe hoped would occur.

Firth was overjoyed to know that he would be staying in America for many weeks, possibly even months, but he also knew that he would have to send as much detailed information to Smythe as he could to justify his continued assignment. The best way to do this, he thought, would be to seek out a local bar and meet some of the regulars. Such a place would be full of gossip, speculation, and hopefully some real news as well.

On his first visit to the Bell Coffee House and Bar, he befriended a local man, an immigrant from Ireland by the name of Joe Higgins. Firth's first impression of this fellow was that he was a rather odious but talkative character who was willing to part with his information for the price of a drink. Firth had the feeling that Higgins was a loudmouth who was making up stories to impress anyone who would listen. Before dismissing him altogether, though, Firth decided to put him to the test.

"Tell me, Joe, have you heard anything about Fort Sumter lately?"

"I can tell you there was a big battle there last week."

"Anything else?"

"Plenty now me friend, but such info don't come free, ya know," he said with an expectant smile.

"Fair enough," Firth said. He crossed to the bar and returned with two beers.

Joe proceeded to reel off an account of the battle which corroborated every detail Firth already had and added a few more besides. Firth was surprised, but he was also pleased to realise he'd found a reliable source. They met every day, and as he got to know Higgins better, the man became keener to impart more-detailed information, including news of skirmishes and battles he had heard from his own secret sources.

On 20 April, the day of the tea party, Firth made sure not to arrive early at the Burketts'. He was unfamiliar with

American etiquette; besides, he wanted there to be plenty of other guests to talk to. He had already discovered that Mr Burkett, in particular, was not given to small talk, and he didn't want to be seen talking to Elizabeth all the time whilst under the gaze of her parents.

He waited until his watch showed ten past three, and then he knocked on the door.

It was a lively affair, with around thirty men and women gathered in the garden, conversing in small groups of four or five.

Firth spotted Elizabeth with her mother, talking to two other women. As he knew no one else with the exception of Mr Burkett, he went up to the ladies.

"Good afternoon, Mrs Burkett, Miss Elizabeth."

He and Elizabeth had agreed to make it seem as though this was their first meeting since Firth's last visit to the house earlier in the week.

"Mr Brown!" exclaimed Mrs Burkett. "We are *so* glad you could come. Aren't we, Elizabeth?" She then proceeded to recount to her companions Firth's gallant rescue of her daughter from almost certain death.

"Come, let me introduce you to some of our guests." She took Firth by the arm and guided him around the garden. Most of the guests were factory or other business owners and their wives, and they all seemed to be of similar opinions regarding a war. It would be a disaster for both the Union and the Confederacy, he was told. Most wished the Southern troops would just pack up and return home, leaving them to get on with the serious business of making money.

One of the guests, though, was of particular interest to Firth and the only one with a different view. He stood out from everyone else, being clothed in the full-dress uniform of a Union officer. He was introduced to Firth as General Alexander Dyer, the newly appointed Head of Ordnance at the federally owned Springfield Armoury in Massachusetts. He told Firth that the factory was now supplying the army with the latest weapons, further discussing his plans to design a completely new type of gun, one that would combine the muzzle-loading musket and the pistol, having the bullet and powder in one self-contained cartridge. It would be loaded by a simple movement of the hand, first backwards and then forward.

"It will be easier to use, quicker to load, and more accurate," Dyer concluded with pride.

"It sounds extraordinary, General. I'm sure my readers will be very interested to hear of this. When will the army start using them?"

Dyer looked a little startled, realising that he'd said too much.

"Well, my boy," he said, clearing his throat, "it's just an idea at the moment, you understand. We won't be starting the serious design work for a while yet. We're just too busy for now." He pondered for a second. "I must swear you to secrecy concerning this, Mr Brown. I shouldn't really have told you so much. It's very important that the rebels know nothing of our plans."

"Well, I am a journalist, sir," Firth reminded him.

"Quite so, young man, and a very good one too, no doubt. How about this—you say nothing of what I've told you, and I'll make sure you are the first to get the story when we're ready. Do we have a deal?" Dyer asked, offering Firth his hand.

"You have my word, General," Firth replied with a smile, shaking his hand. "And here's my card."

On 22 April, at the Bell, Joe Higgins was even more talkative than usual.

"Blood has been drawn at last!" he raised his voice as if he were proud to be proved correct. "I knew it wouldn't take very long for them Southerners to lose their tempers!"

"Tell me everything, Joe. When did it occur, and what exactly happened?" asked Firth. This was news indeed.

"It was two days ago, in Baltimore, Firth, in the state of Maryland. Some rebels attacked the troops of the Sixth Massachusetts Regiment. Four men were killed, and thirty-nine were injured. The outskirts of the town have been burned, and the authorities in Baltimore have sealed the rail bridges to stop any trains from the South entering the city unawares." Joe suddenly stopped and looked hard at Firth. "If you want any more information, it'll cost you more than a cup of coffee. Dollars will be required, my son, and the amount will depend on the importance of the story."

Firth was disappointed—what he gave Joe would have to come out of his own money. However, he wasn't surprised. Joe had reeled him in like a fish on the line, and now he was well and truly hooked.

He bade Joe farewell and returned to his hotel to write a long and involved report of the incident, giving it the heading "The Battle of Baltimore". He wrote it as if he were actually there, witnessing the event.

The next morning, he walked to the post office and sent off his report. It wasn't until two weeks later that he received a telegram from his editor:

To: Mr Firth Brown
6 May 1861
Impressed with report, brave man. Send
more. Be concise.
Wm. Smythe, Editor

Firth was amused to receive this abrupt message, as it would make his life much easier. He could send short reports with next to no detail and yet make it look as though he was rushing about getting news while really spending his spare time between gathering information from Joe at the bar and meeting Elizabeth in the park.

Elizabeth had managed to get away by herself nearly every day. Her mother had developed a severe chest cold, and the doctor recommended she stay indoors and rest as much as possible.

It seemed as though fate was on his side, not only where work was concerned but also in the more exciting arena of romance. Elizabeth now occupied most of his thoughts during the day and certainly before he fell asleep at night. Jane had been all but forgotten.

One day, Elizabeth ran out of the house and straight to him on the other side of the street without her usual caution and with tears in her eyes. He rushed forward and grasped her hand.

"What is it, Elizabeth? Has something happened?"

"I'm so upset, Firth. It's my father!"

"Is he all right? What's happened?" he asked again, all the while thinking that this was an opportunity he could not miss. He let his hand run to her elbow and put his arm round her shoulders. She didn't push it away, so he let it slide down to her waist. It was such a wonderful feeling to hold her in his arms that he found it difficult to concentrate on what she was saying.

She wiped a tear from her eye and looked up at him.

"When Mother went upstairs to rest, I went to Father's study to get some writing paper. As Father is usually at work in the morning, I didn't knock." Elizabeth stopped to regain her breath and control her sobs. "I heard a noise coming from the room, so I opened the door. We've had some trouble with rats coming up from the drains recently, so I thought it might be that. But then, when I looked round the door, I saw Martha bent over the table with her skirt up round her waist. And Father was … was—" She stopped herself, unable to find the words.

There was no need for explanation. Firth had a pretty good idea of what her father had been doing.

"Crikey! That must have been an awful shock for you," Firth said, and he tightened his hold on Elizabeth to comfort her.

He gently kissed her on the cheek, and she laid her head on his chest. She had stopped crying but made no effort to stop him kissing her.

"I would not have you distressed for anything in the world, my darling!"

She looked into his eyes, and he kissed her tenderly on the lips. He could not help thinking that one man's bad luck is another man's good fortune. Elizabeth responded to his kiss, and they lingered in each other's arms. He took the opportunity to confirm what he had always suspected: that she did indeed have a lovely figure. Mr Burkett had inadvertently done him a great favour.

CHAPTER 5

Firth was sure he felt not only a strong passion but also true love for Elizabeth. However, a darker side of him also realised he could be on to a gold mine. With a bit of luck, not only would he get his girl, but he might also be able to persuade her father to give her a dowry. Love followed by marriage was much more than he could afford without help.

The next day, as they were walking Rufus in the park, Firth waited until they reached a secluded spot away from any prying eyes. He stopped Elizabeth with a little tug on her arm, then turned to face her. As he looked into her eyes, he lowered himself to one knee.

"Elizabeth," he began, "I know we haven't known each other for very long, but I have truly never felt this way about anyone before. I love you, and I want you to marry me. Will you?"

Elizabeth looked stunned. After a few seconds of silence, Firth reached out for her hand.

"Elizabeth?" he pleaded.

"I will marry you, Firth. I love you so much, but we will need my father's permission, you know."

"I'll go and see him tonight." Firth had committed himself now and didn't have time for any nervousness. That would come later.

At seven o'clock that evening he knocked at Mr Burkett's house.

Martha opened the door, surprised to receive an unexpected caller.

"Is Mr Burkett in?"

"Yes, sir."

"May I see him?"

"I'll go and find out, sir. One moment, please," she replied, turning on her heel and leaving the front door open. He could hear her speaking to Mr Burkett in the study and his loud reply.

"He's come without an appointment? It had better be something important. All right, let him in!"

The maid came back and closed the door.

"This way please, sir. The master will see you in the study."

"Mr Brown!" Burkett exclaimed. "You're becoming a regular visitor. What is it you want?" His gruff voice was getting ever louder, as it did when the man was agitated.

"I have come on a very delicate mission, sir. I would like to request your daughter's hand in marriage. A request I hope you will consider carefully and look upon kindly." The words rushed out more quickly than Firth had intended.

"My God! *You*—my son-in-law?" Burkett was shouting now. "Never in a thousand years! Have you made her pregnant? That's it, isn't it, you bastard! You've taken advantage of our generosity in letting you visit us, and you've taken advantage of an innocent young girl!"

As if Burkett had not just spoken, Firth blundered on. "I am aware that you love your daughter, sir, and I will always love and protect her. We would like to ask you, though, if you could lend us enough to buy a small house. We will pay you back at regular monthly intervals." Firth had never before been so direct with an older and richer man, but love spurred him on.

Burkett was turning a violent shade of purple.

"What do you mean?" he exploded. "How dare you! You goddamn British still think you own us! How stupid do you think I am? Pregnant or not, she will never be your wife!"

"Please, Mr Burkett, will you let me explain? I love Elizabeth, and I will cherish and look after her. If that's not enough to make you agree, may I explain that the reason I wish to marry her now is because she is so unhappy, not because she is pregnant."

"Unhappy? What the blue blazes are you talking about?"

Firth took a deep breath before looking Burkett straight in the eye as he dropped his final bombshell.

"She saw you with the maid, I'm afraid. It seems that you and Martha are more than friendly with each other. Elizabeth loves her mother, and she loves you, but now she's confused and feels betrayed."

"Enough!" cried Burkett. "How dare you discuss my family so intimately! Get out! Out!"

Although Firth was shaking with fear inside, he remained outwardly composed and continued speaking quietly but forcibly.

"May I put it more plainly, sir? If she is able to live with me, away from you and in a house of her own, neither she nor I will let anything slip to your wife or to your friends.

As you are a church elder, don't you think that this would be for the best—for your reputation, I mean, and of course for your daughter's peace of mind?"

Firth watched Burkett closely. He glared back, silent for a long moment while he gathered his thoughts. This young man was obviously not one to be intimidated by shouting and bluster.

"My God, you're nothing but bold, Brown!" he said in a quiet but menacing voice.

Firth, too, spoke in a low voice, using an expression he had picked up at the tea party.

"How about it, Mr Burkett? Do we have a deal?"

The older man took a minute to control his emotions.

He replied slowly, "It appears I have no choice. Very well, Brown, you may marry Elizabeth, and I will help you with a house. But heed this, you little runt. Blackmailers never win in the end. You can be sure I won't ever forget this, mister. Now leave before I change my mind!"

Firth smiled, relieved that the worst was over.

"Thank you very much, sir. One last thing, if I may? I think a quick wedding would be best, say in two weeks' time? Let us say 2 June, a Sunday. I would not suggest it be so soon, except that war seems to be certain and may last longer than we originally expected. As her husband, I would naturally wish to protect Elizabeth."

Burkett looked long and hard at Firth.

"I've already said that you win this time. There's no need to keep going on. I will request the date you want at our church. I assume our local church is suitable for you?" he added sarcastically.

"Thank you, sir, I would be honoured. Naturally, I won't be including any of my family on the guest list, as they are all in England. Anything you suggest will suit me." Firth was acutely aware that he had made a powerful enemy, but he couldn't leave without at least making a gesture towards peace. "I can assure you, sir, I shall make a good and obedient son-in-law. Elizabeth and I are both grateful to you, and we will endeavour to make you proud of us."

Firth was being as obsequious as he dared. In doing so, he discovered that he had considerable acting abilities.

Burkett had calmed greatly by now and looked hard at Firth.

"You are brazen, my lad; ill-mannered too, but with guts, to be sure. Maybe I can make some use of you after all. If you want to redeem yourself, you'll have to follow my instructions. You do want to redeem yourself, don't you?"

"Er, yes, sir, of course," Firth answered, wondering what scheme the man had thought up.

Burkett paused, then continued slowly and deliberately, emphasising every word as though he wanted Firth to understand that what he was saying was of great importance to both of them.

"The mission I want you to undertake is vital to both of us. To me, because a great deal of money is involved. To you, because you need to prove to me that you are going to be a reliable son-in-law and an asset, not the liability I had initially imagined. I have agreed to your marriage to Elizabeth, but do not make the mistake of underestimating me. To be of use to me, you must know when to speak, what to say, and to whom. Go now, and we will speak soon."

"Thank you, sir. You won't regret it!"

With that, Firth took his leave. After the door had closed behind him, he heaved an almighty sigh as the tension left him at last. He was, nevertheless, curious and not a little apprehensive in wondering what the old man had got lined up for him.

He thought that he would always remember this day, 20 May. It was a day that would change his simple, carefree existence into one of complication and intrigue. Even his wildest exaggerations to his editor would one day seem tame in comparison.

CHAPTER 6

Firth now saw Joe nearly every day at the Bell. As the war seemed to have slowed down, he needed all the Irish blarney his friend could muster to help fill out his reports. On 24 May, he received a wire from Smythe who once again demanded that he come home to England. The war seemed to be a fiasco, and the whole affair looked as if it would come to nothing. Smythe, in his wisdom, had concluded that the American Civil War would be a one-day wonder.

Fortunately for Firth, Colonel Elmer E. Ellsworth, an attorney and a great friend of President Abraham Lincoln, as well as commander of the New York Zouaves, was killed by a hotelier. The brave colonel had been trying to remove the Confederate flag from the roof of the man's establishment when he had shot and killed him. With Joe's help, Firth made a great story of this event and sent it to Smythe as soon as he could. Looking back on it afterwards, he thought it had probably saved his employment in America. Smythe agreed to extend his stay at least until mid-June, and Firth was relieved as well as very happy. He was sure something would happen with the war by then.

Firth became a regular caller at the Burkett mansion but was still in the dark regarding the mission Mr Burkett had in mind for him. However, he was gradually winning Mrs Burkett over by carrying out small errands for her. She was not very mobile now, and so she began to welcome his visits. He only visited when Mr Burkett was not in, so there could be no embarrassment concerning the housemaid. He was always very well behaved, and the entire household, including the servants, came to regard the charming young Englishman with favour, which had the effect of making Elizabeth depend on him and love him more and more.

After another week had passed, Mr Burkett came home one day and asked Firth to join him in the study. Mrs Burkett had no doubt told him that he was a frequent visitor; hopefully, she had emphasised how much she liked him.

"I have arranged the wedding and discussed the guest list with my wife. I assume that there is no one in Washington, or indeed the whole of America, that you know, but I guess I have to ask: is there anyone you wish to invite?"

"I'll have to think about it, sir. Can I let you know?"

"Humph! Make it soon, then!"

"Yes, sir."

The only person Firth knew was Joe Higgins, and he certainly would not be an appropriate guest. Inviting such a man would only confirm Burkett's suspicions about Firth.

Burkett gave Firth one of his disconcertingly long stares. "Don't forget, Brown, that you owe me a favour, and I shall call on you immediately after the wedding. Don't even think of letting me down. I've bought you a house, but I hold the deeds and will do so for many years to come!"

Firth could not help speculating about the favour his future father-in-law would demand. Would it be dangerous? Probably. Illegal? Surely not! *Why won't he just tell me?*

As May became June, the weather continued to improve, and the young lovers spent more and more time together in their hideaway in the park. It was bliss, and Elizabeth occupied all of Firth's thoughts. Jane McCormack had become a faded memory.

"I'm glad that things have quieted down a bit," Firth said when he met Elizabeth.

"Hmm?" she asked, far away.

"The war. It's all gone quiet. I think about you all the time, you know. I couldn't bear to be sent away now!"

But Elizabeth was more concerned with events at home. "I saw my father with Martha again. How could he betray Mother in this way? You would never do anything like this to me, would you?" she pleaded.

"Of course I wouldn't, Elizabeth. I love you and could never do anything to hurt you," replied Firth, putting his arms round her.

They were very comfortable with each other now and would lie down together on the grass behind the evergreen bushes that shielded them from the pathways.

"We will soon be married, my darling. We have only to wait a few more days. Then, we'll be wed and have our own little house down the road. Near enough to see your mother, but far enough away that you can avoid seeing your father if you want to."

"I can't wait," she replied in a breathy voice, holding Firth even tighter and making no objections to his advances.

Firth could see how unhappy she was about her father's behaviour, but he also felt that she was becoming more compliant as the day of the marriage drew near. He had an overwhelming need for her that he could no longer contain.

His hands again worked their way under her skirts and started moving upwards as he kissed her passionately.

Elizabeth, despite her desires, tried to deny him. She gently pushed him away. "Oh, Firth, we mustn't continue. Please, let's wait until we're married."

"Don't you love me? I love you, and I want you; I want you so much!"

Firth could feel her resistance weakening. The warm weather, the grassy embankment, and the persistence of his firm but tender hands conspired to break down all her defences. Every day, he imagined what it would be like to make love to her, but he also knew that it shouldn't happen until they were married. Now his arms were holding her tightly, he was kissing her warm, soft lips, and he felt her melting. Slowly he ran his hand up her long, smooth thigh. He was gently caressing her skin, exploring every inch as he moved towards his goal. She gave up all pretence of modesty and began to unbutton him. The cool grass and the sun's warm rays added to the experience, and the knowledge that there were walkers only a few yards away gave an element of risk that was truly erotic.

It was the first time for both of them, but with a lot of fumbling and suppressed laughter, they each found what they were looking for. Elizabeth took him in her hand, a bold move which both surprised and delighted him. He in turn felt her wetness, and he knew what it signalled. He could contain himself no longer, and they made love. Elizabeth was making small noises that only spurred him on to even greater heights. Firth had never experienced such ecstasy. A number of people walked by, but the young couple were well hidden and so carried away that they were oblivious.

43

It was over all too soon, and they each made themselves respectable once more. After a long final kiss, they brushed the grass off each other and returned to the house hand in hand, both unable to contain their smiles. They went round the side of the house to the rear door and into the sitting room, where they could hear talking. It seemed that her father and mother were discussing the wedding arrangements but were obviously not in agreement.

When Elizabeth and Firth entered the room, Mr Burkett addressed them both. "We have decided to put the wedding off until 15 June," he announced in his abrupt manner.

"But why, Father?" cried Elizabeth, her happiness gone.

"We have our reasons, girl. As I am paying for everything, I don't think I have to explain myself to you!"

Elizabeth started to sob quietly, and Firth passed her his handkerchief.

"Oh, for God's sake, stop crying, will you?" Burkett scolded her. "All right, all right, anything for a quiet life. One of the main reasons is that some of your mother's family can't come down from Boston until then. They're all busy preparing for this damned war, which everyone keeps talking about but which never seems to start. It won't hurt to wait another few weeks, will it?"

"If there are any battles, Firth will have to go away to report on them!" exclaimed Elizabeth.

"Pah! Nothing's going to happen! Have you seen any real fighting yet? Anyway, it might do you good to wait a little longer. Maybe you'll come to your senses and not marry this fellow," he said, as if Firth were not there. Without another word, he strode imperiously out of the room.

"How could your relatives let us down like this, Mamma?"

Mrs Burkett was quiet. After a moment, she said softly, "I don't like to be disloyal, dear, but I'm afraid what your father says is not quite true. The delay is because of him, but he won't tell me why. He used my family as an excuse, Elizabeth. He seems adamant, and you know he never does anything without a good reason."

Mrs Burkett looked down at her knitting. Murmuring to herself so that the young people could barely hear, she said, "He tells me less and less. He's no longer the man I married!"

CHAPTER 7

Firth was concerned that the war was not proceeding at a fast enough pace for his editor in England. Smythe had sent another telegram repeating his previous instructions telling Firth to pack his bags and be ready to come home. But, once again, fate intervened. News came of an impending battle just in time for his return to be postponed.

The forces of the Union and the Confederacy were amassing at Bull Run, near Manassas, and there was also some fighting at a place called Fairfax Court, just sixteen miles from Washington. Joe had told him that the Confederates had a detachment at this location, and Firth thought this information would make exciting news, written up in the right way.

He wrote his piece under the headline "Confederates only 16 Miles from Washington. Union Doomed?" He knew the Lancashire readership of the *Echo* would be cheered by this news. He knew by now that it was always wise to emphasise how well the Confederacy was doing. What he didn't mention was that the Confederate troops were small in number and well ahead of their main force, very exposed to any attack.

The circulation of *The Manchester Echo,* of course, depended on its popularity, which in turn affected Smythe's wealth. Ultimately, this was what Firth's continued stay in America depended on.

Fortune continued to favour Firth. On 3 June, he learnt that there had been some fighting the previous day at Philippi village, a small clump of houses in West Virginia. A Confederate force of only 773 men, under the command of Colonel Porterfield, were surrounded by a Union army of more than three thousand, led by General William Rosecrans. A terrible rainstorm broke out, and the poorly disciplined Confederate sentries left their posts, looking for cover. When an advance guard of Union troops under Colonel Kelly struck at daybreak, the rebels were taken completely by surprise. Luckily for them, the colonel was wounded in the melee, causing confusion among his men and allowing many of the Confederates to escape.

Firth wrote a long, critical piece under the headline "Union on Top—Confederates Routed". The local newspapers in Washington were even more scornful, describing the action as a farce. Indeed, so intent were the rebel troops on escaping their attackers that one paper referred to the incident as "The Philippi Races". Firth received a message from Smythe saying he was delighted and that the newspaper's circulation was steadily increasing.

On 10 June, another battle occurred. For Firth, this was great news; he now knew the war was heating up, and his editor would not consider bringing him home for some months.

This new battle on the Virginia peninsula was called Big Bethel. Federal forces under General Pierce advanced on the Confederates, in the dark of night, but they were poorly trained for night fighting, and the battle plan was badly executed. This led to two columns firing at each other and killing twenty-one of their own men. They also lost the chance of a surprise attack, allowing the enemy to be thoroughly prepared by the time the battle really started.

Abram Duryee commanded the Zouave soldiers, who made up about half of all the federal forces at the time. He told General Pierce it would be folly to continue, but he was overruled. The Confederate forces took full advantage of the Union leadership's incompetence and were well dug in, ready to face the advancing troops. At the end of the short battle, Major Theodore Winthrop, military secretary to General Butler and commander of the Union troops, led a charge against a fortified gun emplacement. He was killed, leaving his men leaderless. It was the final straw for the Union forces, who were forced to retreat, leaving eighteen dead soldiers for only one rebel. Many of the Yankees were also wounded, and Firth managed to get lots of gory accounts of lost limbs and other injuries from Joe, who had a friend at the army hospital.

Firth was caught in a dilemma. Sure, the war seemed to have started properly now, meaning he would be staying in America for the foreseeable future. The problem was that, with so much happening, it was making it difficult for him to see Elizabeth. Consequently, he was delighted when there was a lull in the fighting. He had hardly seen her at all in the past week, and there were only four days left until the wedding. She was overjoyed when he met her in the park after she'd spent many days walking Rufus alone.

"I've missed you so much, Elizabeth. But it's been so busy, I just haven't had any time to see you. I'm so sorry."

"I thought you were having second thoughts about marrying me. You know, since we—" Elizabeth's voice trailed away, and she blushed.

"Nothing could be further from the truth. I can't wait for the wedding," he assured her.

"But you've been so preoccupied when we meet. Some of my friends have told me that when a man has had his way, he's no longer interested. They say he loses respect for a girl once they have—" Her voice trailed away again, and she dabbed her eyes with a lace-edged handkerchief.

"Not this man. There truly has just been so much to write about, I couldn't find a spare moment. After all, it *is* my job."

"I know. I'm sorry. I'm just being silly."

He put his arms around her and kissed her, feeling the warmth of her lips.

"Elizabeth, I'm worried that I will have no one at the wedding, not even to be my best man. Your father, of course, has already pointed this out to me; he just couldn't help himself. I'm sorry I haven't seen you so much, but I can tell you that my mind has been full of thoughts of you, so much so that I'm finding it difficult to concentrate on my work."

"Well, that's all right then," she said, brightening considerably. The handkerchief had disappeared. "Have you no one at all?"

"There is someone I've thought of, actually. I think he may cause quite a stir." Firth abruptly changed the subject. "I'm also worried about this favour your father wants me to do for him. I promised him I would help him in return for his permission for us to marry. He told me he'd speak to me soon after the ceremony, but I still don't know what it is he wants me to do!"

Firth left Elizabeth at her home and made his way back to the hotel. He wrote a letter to a Major Finlay, a well-known figure at the British Embassy. The major was an imposing man with a beautiful wife. When Firth finished the letter, he left his room and walked to the Embassy. He knocked at the door, which was answered by a servant in livery.

"Good afternoon, sir."

"Good afternoon. Please give this letter to Major Finlay. I would like to wait, as he may wish to see me after reading it," Firth said, handing him the letter.

"Very well, sir. May I have your name please? The major doesn't see anyone without an appointment."

"He may change his mind once he's read that," Firth insisted.

"Your name, sir?"

"Brown. Firth Brown. I'm a journalist, and I'm in America covering the war for *The Manchester Echo.*"

"Very well, sir. This way, please." The servant ushered Firth into a pleasant waiting room and went away, bearing his letter on a silver tray.

A few minutes later, a tall, well-built man with red hair and a handlebar moustache with waxed tips appeared at the door.

He could only be a Scotsman, looking like that, thought Firth.

"I am Major Finlay of the Highlanders, military envoy here at the embassy." It was obvious that he always introduced himself in this fashion. He had a clipped military accent, but no amount of army training could cover his Scottish upbringing.

"This is a rather strange request you have made, young man. You are British, though, so I feel I may be able to help you out. I'll need a wee while to think about it."

"Well, thank you for considering it, sir. Let me see if I can persuade you before I go, if I may."

"Go on."

"You see, sir, I've met the most wonderful girl here, but all my family are in England, and it's far too expensive for them to come here, so I have no one to invite from my side at all. I will of course ensure that the wedding will be reported in my paper at home, including a full description of yourself and how you have supported a British subject alone in a foreign country. It would give me great pleasure to reciprocate your kindness if you could see your way to agreeing. I would also be delighted if your lady wife could attend."

Firth could see that the major was beginning to understand that there could be advantages to this situation. What he had initially thought of as a chore might just be worthwhile.

"Very well, Mr Brown, I will come. I have the date from your letter. Leave some details with the doorman. I need to know the address of the church and what time I should arrive. I hope there will be a reception to which my wife and I will be invited."

"Of course, sir. Thank you very much. Until Saturday then."

Firth returned to his hotel in time for the evening meal and went into the dining room. He asked the waitress if she had any news and paid her for some small snippets of Washington gossip. She also provided him with a good meal, and some of the other guests had since noticed that his plate always had the best meat and the largest portions. He liked to think they assumed he was tipping her for better meals.

The next day, he called at the Burketts' house. He was shown into the sitting room by Martha. Was it his imagination, or was she thickening at the waist? It certainly looked as though she had been crying. He would have to speak to Elizabeth later, to see if she could shed some light on the situation; at the moment, though, he had other business to attend to.

"Mr and Mrs Burkett. I'm pleased to see you on this beautiful day," Firth said brightly.

"You are rather early to call, even if you *are* marrying my daughter," barked Mr Burkett. He was damned if he was going to be polite just because he had received a little flattery from his insufferable future son-in-law. "What is it you want?"

"Well, sir, you asked if there was anyone I wished to invite to the wedding. I'm pleased to say that my very good friend Major Finlay of the Highland Regiment and the British Embassy has kindly offered to stand in for my father," said Firth, enjoying himself immensely as he watched Burkett's face drop. "I would like to know what time his carriage should arrive at the church, and also the exact address. His wife, a very striking lady by all accounts, will accompany him. I would also be obliged if Mrs Burkett could send a written invitation to the major and his wife, as is customary on these occasions."

Mr Burkett was, for once, speechless.

His wife, though, took it in her stride and gushed, "How *wonderful!* I've heard he is a great favourite with the ladies of Washington. I didn't know you knew anyone at the British Embassy, Firth. I'm so pleased you have some friends here. I hear he looks quite magnificent in his uniform. I do hope he will wear full dress. Oh, my dear Firth, this is wonderful news." It was the first time he had been referred to so affectionately.

"Thank you very much, madam. I'm most grateful to you." Firth was smiling broadly. "I don't believe you have met the major, Mr Burkett. I think you will find him a fine fellow indeed. He says he has heard of you and is looking forward to meeting you."

Chapter 8

At last, the day of the wedding arrived. Mr and Mrs Burkett had arranged for a smart carriage to take Firth and his best man to the church. The guest list included a great number of relatives, friends, and business associates of the bride's family. Firth would have felt overwhelmed and insignificant if it were not for the fact that his best man was by far the most conspicuous and best-dressed fellow in the entire wedding group. He looked outstanding in full regimental regalia. His uniform included a kilt, sporran, white ruffle, and a dirk, and he even had a large claymore, which hung from his belt. Mrs Finlay drew plenty of attention of her own, clad as she was in a long white dress with a Finlay tartan draped across her ample bosom. They were the best-dressed guests at the wedding.

Elizabeth looked ravishing in her wedding dress of white silk adorned with pale-pink bows. Two of her cousins acted as maids of honour and wore long pale-pink dresses, and the flowers that decorated the church were of the same shade. Mrs Burkett had gone to a great deal of trouble to make the wedding of her only child a memorable one.

During the ceremony, it appeared to Firth that the Finlays were of more interest to the guests than the bride.

Mr Burkett found this a little irritating, but Mrs Burkett was pleased with the attention they were getting. The presence of these eminent guests would make a great talking point in salons all over Washington.

When the service was over, they all went back to the Burketts' residence, where a large marquee had been erected in the back garden. It was obvious that Mrs Burkett had spared no expense with the arrangements, leaving the bills for her husband to deal with after the event. He would certainly have been less generous, especially with Firth as the groom. He had lots of other more rewarding projects in which to invest his money.

Elizabeth went upstairs with her maids of honour to freshen up, while Firth waited for her. They would soon go around to greet all the guests, many of whom Firth had yet to meet.

But, before anything could happen, Mr Burkett strode over to him and whispered in his ear, "Come into my study."

Firth followed him and was offered an upright wooden chair in front of the desk, while Burkett went to the other side and sat down in a plush leather seat.

"Well, you've got what you wanted," said Burkett. "You know that I was not pleased at first, but now I think we might work together. I want you to leave the reception in an hour, as soon as the speeches have been made."

Firth looked at him in astonishment but kept quiet for the moment.

"I will give you train tickets to Philadelphia, along with a letter of introduction. You will see a man by the name of Swinton. He owns an ironworks in the town, and iron will be a big seller in the war."

"But today is my wedding day, and Elizabeth expects me to be with her tonight. You can't do this," Firth told him with a note of horror in his voice. "It's our honeymoon night."

"I know it's bad timing, but you will only be away for a few weeks if all goes well. Work comes first, and you promised you would do this favour for me in return for my consent for the marriage. I'm calling in that favour." Burkett smiled. "Anyway, it's no bad thing for you to hold your horses for a while. You young people are so impetuous nowadays; you always want everything when you want it. Wait a little. We don't want Elizabeth to have a child before she knows how to run a house, do we?"

Firth was amazed that the man could be so callous and cruel, but he had known for some time that every move his father-in-law made was to his own advantage. Firth would have to think quickly to swing the situation his way.

"I don't think this is fair. Not in any way. You're taking out your dislike of me at the expense of your daughter's happiness. However, I am a man of my word." Firth paused for a moment, and Burkett leant back with a smile, sure that he had got his way. "But I'm not leaving until the morning."

"Today!" Burkett thundered. "I've already arranged for you to be met this evening when the train arrives. You'll do this for me, my lad, or I'm going to make your life hell!"

They stared at each other for a few long seconds.

"Very well. I'll go today, but I want you to sign the deeds to the house over to us and give them to Elizabeth for safe keeping. Call it a wedding present."

Burkett's smug expression changed swiftly.

"That is not part of our agreement. I won't do it."

"Then I'm not going."

Burkett slowly shook his head. After a moment, he said, "Very well. I'll sign the deeds. I have your word you'll leave today?"

"You do, sir. And I'll do you one extra favour. Martha could become an embarrassment to you now that she is with child. I heard that the last of your maids who allowed herself to get into this condition had to be sent off to live in Ohio, at some considerable expense, no doubt. Elizabeth and I will need a maid, and we're willing to take her on," Firth said quickly, giving Burkett no time to interrupt.

Burkett looked thunderstruck. "How the hell did you know she was pregnant? Of course, I've no idea who the father is; but, as you say, she can't stay here." He paused. "Very well, I'll accept your offer, for the poor girl's sake. No one's going to marry her now that she's carrying a baby."

He got up from his leather chair and walked over to an oil painting on the wall. He moved it to one side and opened a small safe, taking out a parchment with bold black writing on it. Sitting down again, he made a note at the bottom.

"These are the deeds to your house. I've written a note and signed the bottom to verify that I have handed them over to you."

"Thank you, sir. Would you also state that if I die from any cause, the house will become the sole property of my wife?"

Burkett snatched the deeds back with a scowl. "You drive a hard bargain." He wrote another sentence at the bottom and signed it again.

"And please date it, sir."

He did so, asking sarcastically, "Anything else?"

"I don't think so, sir, thank you," Firth said, and put the deeds in his pocket. Both men got up from their chairs, still warily watching each other, and went their separate ways at the study door.

Burkett went to talk to the guests, and Firth went over to the stairs to meet Elizabeth, who was just on her way down. She reached the last step, looking beautiful in her wedding dress, just as he arrived.

"Darling, I must talk to you urgently."

"Too late," she said with a smile. "Here comes Mamma."

"Come along, you two." Mrs Burkett smiled as she reached them. "You mustn't neglect your guests."

Elizabeth took him by the hand and circled the room, introducing Firth to as many of the guests as she could. Everyone was in a jolly mood and wanted to talk to him. He tried over and over to draw Elizabeth to one side for a moment. He had to talk to her before her father made his speech announcing that Firth was leaving. It was obvious to him that Burkett's idea was to get him away before they could sleep together and consummate the marriage. They finally came to a quiet corner of the room. No one was looking, so Firth got hold of her arm and gently pushed her through the doorway and outside to a small side garden.

He held her arm tightly and whispered in a commanding voice, "Come behind the bushes; it's very important."

"What *are* you doing, Firth? Surely you can control yourself until tonight?" Elizabeth giggled. "I don't want to get grass stains on my dress."

"I have to speak to you. It's absolutely essential that we speak now!" He quickly explained how her father had made him promise to leave as soon as the speeches were finished.

He told her about the deeds, and where he intended to leave them so they were safe.

"Your father also wants to stop us sleeping together. I'm sure he must have some plan up his sleeve. But, listen, what if you're already pregnant? We have to make it look as if the marriage has been consummated. Do you follow me?"

"The scheming … I *can't* be pregnant!" she said, thinking out loud. "But how can we make him think we have, you know—" Her voice faltered. Then, she understood what Firth was proposing. "In the garden?" She giggled, more from embarrassment than amusement.

"Yes, it's the only way," he said urgently. "There's no time for anything else. We'll have to put a little dirt on your hem and pinch a little colour into your cheeks. Do you think you can do this?"

"We don't have any choice, do we?" she said, quickly becoming angry.

Firth opened the door slightly. "Your father is just inside the reception room. We'll burst out, so that he's bound to see us."

Elizabeth and Firth pushed the bushes aside noisily when Mr Burkett came near the open door while talking to one of his friends. Firth made sure that he kicked the step at the entrance to the house as he burst into the reception room. Everyone looked their way, and Firth could see that Mr Burkett understood the situation exactly as he had intended. Burkett made a slight move forward, then thought better of it. He looked furious. If there had not been a roomful of guests to deal with, Firth doubted he would have been able to control himself. Firth was pleased his plan had worked out so well. Hopefully, he had thwarted whatever scheme Burkett had cooked up. Other guests, including an astonished Mrs Burkett, had also seen them come in from the garden.

"It's not polite society manners," Firth said quietly to Elizabeth, "but it's done the trick. Look at them all—we'll be the talk of the town!"

The speeches went well, especially Major Finlay's. Mr Burkett had told everyone beforehand that he intended to give the last speech and that he wanted the others to cut theirs short.

"I am pleased to welcome Mr Firth Brown into our family," he started, showing a great deal of false bonhomie. "We can all see how happy he has made my daughter." Firth was amazed at how convincing he was. "I'm sorry to inform you, however, that he has been called away on business and must leave immediately. This is very upsetting for Elizabeth, but he won't be away for long. We're going to see him off now, but please, everyone, carry on drinking! The food will soon be brought in, and the band will start playing in a little while."

All eyes were on Firth as he and Elizabeth made their way through the tables, curious looks and muttering following them all the way.

Burkett hurried Firth to the door and down the steps to a waiting carriage. He gave him the train tickets and an envelope addressed to Mr Swinton.

Firth refused to be hurried in this manner. He took Elizabeth in his arms and kissed her passionately. "I'm sorry" was all he said.

"Hurry home, my love," she said, choking back tears. She deliberately avoided looking at her father.

Burkett, on the other hand, did not even have the good grace to let them have a single private moment. As Firth let her go, Burkett impatiently started up again. "This is your introduction," he said, indicating another envelope. "The driver will take you back to your hotel to get your cases, then he'll take you to the railroad station. You have a little time to spare in case of any hold-ups. You'll be met at the other end. There's some money and your instructions in this bag. Anything you don't spend, I shall expect you to return to me. Now get going." He closed the door of the carriage and slapped the horse, sending the cab forward with a jerk.

Firth leant out the window to see Elizabeth receding into the distance, dabbing her eyes with a handkerchief. Her father had already gone back into the house.

Chapter 9

"Stop here, driver!" shouted Firth.

"I'm meant to take you straight to the station," replied the sullen cabbie.

"If you don't stop, I'm getting out anyway. What's it going to be?" asked Firth.

The driver didn't reply, but the cab slowed.

"I'll only be a few minutes. Pull up at this corner. There's still plenty of time to get to the station."

Firth ran across the sidewalk to the Columbia Bank, narrowly missing crashing into a young lady. Inside, he stopped the first clerk he could see, asking, "May I see the manager, please?"

"Do you have an appointment, sir?" asked the sallow-faced man.

"Yes, I do. I've had business with him before, and he's expecting me. My name is Firth Brown."

The clerk went to a door with "Mr Edward Saxon, Manager" painted on it in large black letters. He was only away for a few seconds.

"This way, sir. Mr Saxon will see you now."

The clerk raised the hinged flap at the end of the counter so that Firth could enter. He crossed over to the manager's office and was shown into a large, comfortably appointed room.

"Come in, sir. I'm pleased to see you again."

Firth was offered a plush chair, which he declined, instead standing in front of the desk, across from the manager.

"I can't stay long, Mr Saxon. I just want to deposit this sealed envelope with you. It's the deeds to my house. My signature is on both ends, and the joins are sealed with wax. I want no one to have access to this envelope except myself."

"Very well, sir." The manager wrote out a receipt and made an entry in a large book.

"I'm sorry you're in a hurry. Perhaps next time you'll be able to stay a little longer."

"I hope so too. Good day, sir."

They shook hands, and Firth left the bank. He ran further along the road and turned up an alley to the right. At the end was the Bell, where Joe was sitting in his usual place. He smelled strongly of whiskey, even at this early hour.

"Drink will be the death of you, Joe."

"Good day to you too," he replied.

"Listen carefully; I haven't got long," Firth said and then told him about his forthcoming trip to Philadelphia.

"Every day, or better still, twice a day, go to the office which receives my letters from England, and see if there are any cables. If there's one for my wife, take it to her at our new house." Firth handed him a few coins and a piece of paper with his new address on it.

"If there's news of any fighting, or a battle, send me a telegram. I'll pick it up at the station."

"Look here, I'm not one of your slaves. I'll need more money than this; there's nowhere near enough here. It's just as well I like you, 'cause you're not the most generous fellow I've ever met. Don't know why I got mixed up with a Limey in the first place," Joe muttered.

"Probably because I pay for you to sit here all day."

They smiled knowingly at each other.

"All right! Is *that* enough?" Firth asked, laying out a few more coins.

"That'll do," replied Joe.

"Thanks, Joe. I must be off now. Look after yourself, if only for my sake. Don't let me down."

Firth ran back to the cab. "Right, let's go. Mr Burkett won't forgive you if I miss my train."

"It won't be my fault," replied the driver in a gloomy voice.

"Maybe not, but I'll blame you anyway. Who do you think he's going to believe? So, come on, let's have more driving and less answering back."

The driver whipped the horse into a trot, and the cab flashed past other vehicles on the road. Pedestrians were forced to jump clear, and he left a trail of frightened and angry people behind him. Soon, he pulled up sharply outside the railroad station. Firth grabbed his bags, jumped out of the cab, and ran into the station.

"No tip? You might give me something for that driving!" shouted the cabby.

But Firth had already disappeared inside. He ran down the platform and jumped onto the steps of the Philadelphia, Wilmington and Baltimore railroad coach, just as it started to move. He hauled himself into the carriage as the train started to gather speed, and put his bags up on the rack, then settled into a seat next to the window. He noticed that his train had few passengers on it, in contrast to a train from Baltimore that was just pulling into the station, full of Union troops.

When the ticket collector came along, Firth asked that he should be woken up when they reached Philadelphia.

"I'm sorry, sir, we don't offer those services now that the war has begun. There just isn't the staff anymore. I myself have come back from retirement."

Firth slipped him a coin.

"But, in your case, young man," he said with a wink, "I'll make an exception."

The man was as good as his word, and he woke Firth from a dreamless sleep just as the train started to slow down, before stopping at Philadelphia Rail Road Depot right in the middle of the city.

As Firth got off the train, he was surprised when a rough-looking man with a limp approached him. Despite his injury, he looked very fit and was well built, with the body and face of a boxer, but he had the dazed look of a man with only half his intelligence left, the other half having long since been punched out of him, never to return.

"Are you Firth Brown?" he asked, showing gaps in his mouth where teeth were missing. The scar on his chin grew more inflamed when he spoke, as if it were a strain for him to move his jaw.

"I am."

"I've been sent by Mr Swinton to pick up you and your baggage and take you to your hotel. He doesn't usually treat visitors so kindly, so I guess you must be important to him. Who are you?" asked the man, rudely.

"What's your name?" asked Firth.

"Lew Todd."

"Well, Lew Todd, we'll get on a whole lot better if you take me to where I'm staying and keep your questions to yourself," Firth snapped. He had surprised himself with how tough he had become in recent weeks. This new attitude was now brought to the fore, as there was something about this visit to Philadelphia that he didn't like. "I suggest we be polite to each other, and then we'll be fine. Why am I going to a hotel and not staying with Mr Swinton?"

"How would I know?" he asked aggressively, but then thought better of it, deciding that this young Englishman was not one to be pushed around. It might be advantageous to him to be a little more attentive. "He said he's having some repairs done to his house and is short of room."

"Is that so?" asked Firth.

Todd was surprised by the unexpected question. "Hey, that's all I know, all right?" He paused for a second. "Look, I haven't seen anything going on at his house. I'm just telling you what he told me to tell you."

"That's better, Lew. I think we're going to get along just fine." Firth handed him a dollar. "That's for being good enough to meet me. And there's more where that came from, if you help me some more. I'll also pay you for any information you can give me. How's that?"

"That's generous of you," said Todd. "Old Swinton only pays me the minimum since I had to give up boxing. Do you know what he paid me to get you? Ten goddamn cents is all. He takes advantage of me now that my memory ain't so good."

"Well, now that we understand each other, I'll treat you with respect and pay you for your help while I'm here."

Firth had realised that he was in a strange town, with no friends; the sooner he found an ally, the better. It looked as though simple-minded but strong Lew Todd would fit the bill nicely.

"Let's go to the hotel."

"Yessir," said Todd, whipping the horse into a trot.

They soon arrived at a small hotel that had seen better days. Firth was shown into a room that was not filthy but certainly not clean. He felt the bed and asked for a warmer to be sent up. The place did not inspire much trust in the staff, and so he vowed to leave his bags locked.

He went back downstairs even though it was late, because Todd had also told him that Swinton wished to see him right away. They continued their journey through the dingy streets, to a small hill overlooking the city, where there were much larger and better kept houses. Swinton lived in one of the biggest houses, on Vineyard Street, but it looked slightly shabby compared to its neighbours. It had a look of faded grandeur. An equally shabby maid answered the door.

"What do ya want?" she asked in a broad accent that showed she had come from the wrong side of the tracks.

"I have come to see Mr Swinton. I believe he is expecting me. My name is Firth Brown."

"Oh yeah. Come right on in."

The maid took his coat and hat and hung them on a tall stand. Inside the house, the paint was old and stained with tobacco smoke. Everything gave the impression that the house and the people in it had once been rich but had fallen on hard times.

A short round man of fifty or so, with small, deep-set eyes and a blotchy face put his head round the study door.

"Come on in, Mr Brown. I believe you have a letter from Mr Burkett for me." He spoke in a wheezy voice that portrayed severe illness.

"Right here, sir," said Firth, handing him the envelope.

"Thank you," Swinton said, looking Firth up and down a little more closely than seemed polite, almost as if he were wondering what Firth might be hiding. He put on some glasses and read the letter slowly, then looked up with more interest at the young man standing before him

"Thank you, Mr Brown. This is most interesting. Come back and see me tomorrow at the factory. The man who brought you here will pick you up at nine o'clock."

He hesitated. Then, just as Firth thought he would be dismissed, Swinton seemed to change direction.

"Come and sit down. I'd like to have a little chat with you."

He started to go over to the drinks cabinet, then thought better of it, as though that was taking his hospitality too far. They talked about several matters, but the conversation soon turned to the war. Swinton told Firth how sorry he was that he could not volunteer for the army. His age and his bad chest would make him unsuitable, he said, but he was still going to help by providing as much metal to the Union as he could. "I feel that's the least I can do for my country," he said.

"I expect you'll make a good profit, as plenty will be needed."

"I'm not doing it to make money, dammit! It's my patriotic duty to do the best I can," he rasped, rather pompously.

The door opened then, and the maid shuffled in. "Lew is ready to go. He told me to tell you."

"Well, I shall see you tomorrow," Swinton said with a wheeze, seemingly pleased that his guest was leaving.

It now occurred to Firth that he hadn't really wanted to talk at all, just to delay him. Why, he had no idea, but he expected to find out shortly.

Firth went out into the hall, where the maid handed him his hat and coat. As he put them on, he noted that she made no effort to help him, merely watched him sullenly. He absently felt his coat pockets and realised, with a jolt, that his keys had been moved from the right, where he always kept them, to the left side. Someone had been going through his pockets!

The maid opened the front door and hustled him out. As he walked towards the carriage, Firth thought that Swinton must have asked him to wait to allow time for his coat to be searched. They probably wanted to see if he was carrying a weapon, or maybe to take wax impressions of his keys—or both.

Firth was worried and thought to himself, *That's why he inspected me so closely. He was looking for any bulges, to see if I had a gun.* This was getting more puzzling by the moment. Why would Swinton think that Firth might want to kill him? Whatever was going on, he thought he should get some protection, so his first step in the morning would be finding a gun shop.

"Mr Brown, your carriage is waiting, and so is your tired driver," grumbled Todd. "I don't know what you're thinkin' about, standin' there, but if it's all right with you, I'd like to go now."

"Of course, Lew. Let's go," Firth said, climbing into the carriage.

At that moment, a young girl ran out of the house and down the steps, pushed Firth the rest of the way into the cab, and then climbed in behind him.

"What ya doin', Miss Swinton?" Todd shouted, surprised. "Does ya father know you're out?"

"Shut up, Todd! Take me to the Pembrokes'," commanded the girl.

"So, are you the English reporter?" she directed to Firth, with a hint of mockery.

She was small, like her father, and had a nice, slightly plump figure. Fortunately, she didn't have his piggy eyes. Hers were large and round, with long lashes. She had pretty lips that carried the hint of a smile. Her mouth also carried stubborn lines that she had obviously inherited from her father. She seemed confident enough and knew her own mind. Firth thought she was a woman not to be underestimated, despite her lovely light-blue eyes.

"I am, miss. From *The Manchester Echo.* My name is Firth Brown."

"I am Daisy Swinton," she said, and held out her hand as if to be kissed.

Firth was quite willing to obey, and he noticed that she left her hand in his for longer than was necessary. He hoped he had found another ally, but he was unsure yet if he could trust her.

CHAPTER 10

At nine o'clock sharp, Todd picked up Firth from his hotel and took him to Swinton's ironworks. The gun shop would have to wait for now. A clerk showed him to the office, and Swinton offered him a seat.

Leaning back in his chair, a large ornate affair, Swinton wheezed, "Even my own chair is made of iron. It's probably the only one like it in the world." He paused and stared at Firth as though he were something unpleasant he had found stuck to his shoe.

Firth was immediately put on alert, but he remained outwardly calm.

"So, you met my daughter last night?"

"Yes, sir."

Firth had come to realise that Swinton talked and asked questions in short, sharp bursts, often unrelated. He seemed to want to catch people unawares. He did not shout like Burkett; rather, he hissed his words. Firth made sure he didn't get too close, lest he catch whatever was ailing the man.

"You leave her alone. She's not been born for some goddamn Englishman to get his filthy hands on her," Swinton said vehemently. The effort caused him to suffer a spasm of spluttering and coughing.

When his fit had abated, he changed his tack again. "My friend, Mr Burkett, and I want you to visit Mr Jeremy Kearney, the owner of a metalworks on Mulberry Street, a mile from here. We want you to offer to buy his workshop. We know he's old and wants to sell, as he has no one to pass it on to, but he won't sell to us. He will, we hope, sell to you if you say you are representing an English company that wants to export arms to the Union to help in the war effort. Tell him your firm would like his workshop for repairs and finishing work. There is the added advantage to us in that he has a university-trained inventor on his staff who is designing some original guns." Swinton stopped, perhaps regretting his last remark. He hesitated, then decided to continue. "Mr Kearney is very patriotic and is a friend of the president. He thinks Mr Burkett and I want to buy his company just to make money out of the government's gold reserves."

"He'd be right, wouldn't he?" asked Firth.

Swinton started at him. "You're a mite too forward, Mr Brown. You speak before you think. That's the sort of thing that could land you in trouble." He paused to let his threat sink in. "Todd will take you to see Kearney now. Find out how much he wants for his company, and whatever he says, just look amazed and shake your head. Say the price is too high."

"What about the money?"

"Come back here with his final offer, saying you must go away and think about it. I will then discuss with you how we can pay him." Swinton wheezed again and went into another spasm of coughing. Once he had recovered, he continued, "Do your work well, and get a low price. If you don't, your new father-in-law will not be very pleased. I know George Burkett well. He's not a man you want to annoy. From what I hear, he's not too fond of you, anyhow."

Swinton shuffled across the room and opened the door. He called Todd over and instructed him. "Todd, take Mr Brown here to Mr Kearney's. Drop him off round the corner so no one sees you. When he's finished, bring him straight back here."

They mounted the carriage, and Todd whipped up the horses over the rough stone roadway. It was obvious he had no feeling for animals and probably little more for his fellow man.

Firth made a mental note not to trust him or get too near those large fists. He sat back in his seat and considered Swinton's comments about his intentions towards Daisy. Women were definitely one of his weaknesses. He seemed to find all of them attractive and most irresistible. He was loyal to those he admired, except where love was concerned. It was not that he didn't cherish women when he wasn't with them. They were hardly ever out of his thoughts; but, in their absence, he fell in love with others too easily and too quickly.

How could he possibly desire the delectable Daisy Swinton so soon after his marriage to Elizabeth? Firth thought this was his Achilles heel. The trouble was, the world was full of lovely women. To a young man, they seemed to come out of every doorway.

In the case of men, it was different. If he liked a man, he would be honest and trustworthy unless he was let down. Jeremy Kearney seemed, from what Swinton had said, to be a man to be respected. Firth was not pleased that Burkett had put him on the side of the devious Swinton. He thought Swinton was one of the last people in the Union he would trust.

His thoughts were interrupted when the carriage pulled up near a beer hall on Second Street.

Todd turned to him and said, "Mr Kearney's workshop is just round the corner there. I'll wait here for ya. If I'm not here when you get back, I'll be in there." He pointed to the bar across the street.

Firth went through the doorway and into Kearney's small ironworks. The premises were neat, tidy, and freshly painted. The place had an air of prosperity, completely at odds with what he had expected. He asked the nearest man if he would take him to see Mr Kearney. He was shown to an office at the rear of the building, where a tall, thin man of about seventy was looking through some papers. He looked up as Firth approached.

"Can I help you?" he asked.

"I'm Firth Brown, sir. I think you're expecting me."

"Yes, I had a letter a few days ago telling me you were coming. I believe you wish to buy my company for a firm in England."

Firth found that he liked Kearney immediately, which made him even more annoyed with his father-in-law for using him like this.

The two men discussed the factory and walked round the building, looking at the obviously well-maintained machinery.

"This machine makes a unique, long-lasting gun barrel that I invented," said Kearney enthusiastically. "We have a lot of specialised machines here that make high-quality arms and ammunition." He paused for a moment, then quietly added, "What I manufacture here is going to help Abraham Lincoln win the war."

"What do you want for the lot as it stands?" asked Firth.

"I want eight thousand dollars," Kearney said.

Firth sighed and shook his head. "That's rather high, Mr Kearney. We were thinking of somewhere nearer five thousand."

"I'm sorry Mr Brown. You've seen what's here, and I think it's worth every penny. The price is eight thousand— take it or leave it."

"Very well, sir. I'll tell my people and come back to you in a day or two. Is that acceptable?"

"It is, sir. Good day to you."

Firth left the little factory and set off to find Todd. He wasn't with the carriage, so Firth went into the bar, where he found Todd slumped on a bench in the corner, already drunk. Firth decided to leave him; this was his opportunity to find a gun shop. He got up on the carriage and carefully drove it onto the main highway. It had been a long time since he had handled a horse, but it quickly came back to him. He soon found what he was looking for and pulled the carriage to the side of the road. The shop was sparsely stocked. There were some rifles and shotguns, but only three revolvers, the cheapest of which was a Colt, priced at twenty-five dollars—well out of his reach. Finally, he spotted a single-shot 0.36-calibre pistol, which was more affordable at twelve dollars. This also allowed the purchase of a box of twenty bullets for two dollars and fifty cents. This small gun had the added advantage that it would be easily concealable.

He drove the carriage back to Swinton's house and told him that Todd would be walking back, and probably not for some time.

Firth told Swinton how much Kearney wanted for his business. Swinton simply grunted and told Firth to go back to his hotel and await instructions, which would come in three days' time.

"Three days! What am I supposed to do until then?"

"I don't care what you do, as long as you stay out of trouble," he said gruffly.

"What am I to do without money? Mr Burkett only gave me a train ticket. I can't go three days without cash."

Swinton reluctantly took out a few dollars and handed them to Firth. When he did not retract his hand, Swinton slapped a few more into his palm.

"That's all you're getting. Now go," he said.

As he walked down the front steps of the house, Firth suddenly became aware that Miss Swinton was standing behind a nearby bush.

"I have something important to tell you," she said quietly. "Can you meet me in Jane's Tea House tomorrow morning? It's on the main street. I'll be waiting in a small room upstairs at ten o'clock. Don't be late!" She turned and disappeared along the side of the house before he could reply.

Firth spent his afternoon wandering around the town and found Jane's Tea House. It was a pretty little establishment in the centre shopping area, intended for well-to-do ladies who called in to exchange all the latest gossip. Here, they could talk openly without being overheard by their husbands or servants. The few men who did venture in tended to go upstairs, where there were discreet alcoves in which clandestine meetings between unmarried couples took place.

The next day, a little after ten o'clock, Firth entered the tea house. He had decided to be a few minutes late so that he wouldn't have to wait alone. Miss Swinton was sitting by herself at a table for two, in a little alcove in one of the small first-floor rooms.

"I hope I haven't kept you long," he said with a smile as he approached.

"No. I expected you to be a little late. You wouldn't want to be on your own surrounded by all these ladies, would you? I know men never like that sort of thing." She waved him to a chair. "Sit down, do. You can call me Daisy, unless we're in front of my father, then it's Miss Swinton."

Firth made a mock salute. "Got it, milady," he said and sat down. "What shall we have?"

They made their order.

As the waitress turned away, Firth asked, "Why did you invite me here?"

"Please! Keep your voice down," hissed Daisy. "I want us to be friends and to trust each other. Only friends, mind," she said, looking at him directly. "I know many people in Washington, Firth Brown, and I'm fully aware that you are married, as well as a flirt. I am not going to become romantically involved with you, so get that out of your mind right now!"

Firth smiled but couldn't help feeling a little disappointed.

"But I do like you," she added, with a smile of her own.

"Good. I like you too. Are you going to tell me why we're here now?"

"My mother died recently. Father treated her rather badly. But, now that she's gone, I think he wants to keep me at home to do all his cleaning and cooking. I'm not going to be his skivvy for the rest of his life. I want to leave home and become independent, and I want you to help me."

"Me? I hardly know you, Daisy. Why me?"

"I have some information that will be of great interest to you. This will be your way of paying me for it."

"What information?"

"Will you help me?"

"I'll try, but I don't really see what I can do."

"Leave that to me. Just be ready to help when I ask. Promise?"

"I promise. Now, what were you going to tell me?"

She took a deep breath and let it out slowly. "I overheard a conversation between my father and Todd. He wants Todd to kill you once you have bought Mr Kearney's factory for him. Didn't you realise? Your father-in-law would get both his daughter and the house back."

Firth's jaw dropped open. He'd expected some deviousness, but to have him killed was, he thought, going too far, even for Burkett.

"Really, you men are so naive sometimes!" Daisy laughed mockingly. "You're either romantic fools or ill-mannered thugs—rarely anything else."

"You may think I'm a soft touch, and maybe I didn't fully understand the plot. I'm not a complete fool, though. I've made arrangements for Elizabeth to keep the house if anything happens to me. I always had the feeling that this trip would be bad for my health. He is a callous swine." Firth's voice grew louder. "God, how I *hate* that man!"

Other customers turned and looked at him.

"Ssh. Keep your voice down," she hissed again. "Well, at least you've taken some precautions. That's better than I expected. Now, here's what we're going to do. Remember I told you I want my independence?"

He nodded.

"We're going to take the factory from under their noses! I want to own that place, and you're going to help me get it."

"I am?"

"Yes. Don't worry. You're going to benefit from this as much as me. First, though, we've got to deal with Todd. Tell me when you're next going to the factory, then get Todd to drive you back the long way round. I'll meet you on the bridge over the river."

"Then what?"

"Enough questions. Will you do it?"

"I'll do it, but how will I get him to come back over the bridge?"

"You'll think of something. Tell him you're meeting me. That'll set off his imagination!"

Firth smiled. "Goodbye, Daisy. We'll meet here every day until your plan is accomplished. I just hope you know what you're doing."

With that, their discussion was completed. Daisy suggested that he leave first.

"I hope you have a gun," she said as he got up, and then she added, "And that you know how to use it."

CHAPTER 11

Firth took Daisy's warning seriously. Todd would be a formidable opponent, and he needed any advantage he could get. It was just as well he had a few days, because he now needed the time. On leaving Daisy, he went back to the gun shop and asked the owner where he could go to practice with his new pistol.

"If you'll come this way, sir," said the man. "We have a short-range shooting gallery right behind the shop."

It was indeed short range. The targets, rough, man-shaped wooden cut-outs, were variously placed, but the furthest was only about twenty yards away. As Firth couldn't imagine having to fire at anything like this distance, he practiced on the nearer targets.

He pointed the gun and squeezed the trigger. The recoil slammed his hand upwards, and the sound exploded in his ears, making him jump and break into a sweat. The power of the thing! His hands were shaking, making him fumble his first reload. With a little guidance from the shop owner, he soon calmed down and got used to the gun, steadily improving his aim. He left after an hour of practice, pleased with his progress, and arranged to come back the next day, just to ensure he'd learnt everything he needed to, and also to buy some more bullets.

He continued his dispatches, stretching Joe's information to its limits, and added in some local gossip. He knew Smythe would sack him if he ever discovered that he had been pretending to report from the frontline as a witness to battles he had never seen, and he knew he'd never work in the newspaper industry again if he was ever found out.

Firth was also growing tired of Philadelphia. He was missing Elizabeth badly and wanted to return to Washington. He quieted his conscience by saying to himself that it would be impractical to travel to the sites of battles and skirmishes because, by the time he reached them, the fighting would be over. Luckily, his editor and all the staff were thousands of miles away in England.

Two main events occurred at this time. The first was on 11 July at Rich Mountain, where the Unionists, under Rosecrans, beat the Confederates. Two days later, Union forces commanded by General McClellan beat them again at Carricks Ford. Both these battles were in Western Virginia, and although short in duration and few in casualties, they resulted in part of West Virginia being held by Washington. Firth put forward some of his own views in his dispatches, pointing out that these defeats were a bad blow for the Confederate army. He promptly received a telegram from Smythe, reminding him that many Lancastrians favoured the Confederates. In other words, Firth's views were wanted only if they helped sell more newspapers.

Firth saw Daisy each morning in Jane's Tea House, and she kept him informed of her father's actions. On 11 July, she warned him that Todd would be coming to his hotel that afternoon. She also reminded him, to the point of annoyance, about their pact and how the alternative could mean his downfall, or even his death.

At three o'clock that afternoon, Todd arrived at the hotel, just as Daisy had said. He asked the hall porter to tell Firth he was downstairs and that his carriage was waiting.

"Mr Swinton wants to see you," he said in his ill-mannered fashion.

"Fine, let's get going," replied Firth.

Twenty minutes later, Firth walked up the steps to the faded front door of the Swinton's house. At his knock, Daisy opened the door.

"How nice to see you again, Mr Brown," she said, as though they hadn't met since his last visit. "This way, please. My father is in his study."

"Welcome, Mr Brown," said Swinton in a congenial tone. He got straight down to business. "I want you to go to Mr Kearney with this bank draft in his name. It's for the full eight thousand dollars he wants. Get him to hand over the deeds to his property. You will ask him to make them out to Messrs Ashton & Co. of London.

"Just between us," he continued, "Mr Burkett has arranged for a company called Ashton & Co. to be established in a little Ohio hamlet that goes by the grand name of "London". Kearney will naturally assume that it is your company, with a head office in London, England. Clever, eh?"

"That's one word for it," Firth said quietly.

"Humph. Anyway, when we sell the firm, Mr Burkett and I will each get 50 per cent of the proceeds. After you've got the deeds, bring them straight back here, then Todd will take you to the railroad station. You should be there in time to catch the late train to Washington, barring accidents. And that's it! Your part in our little enterprise will be complete. You can forget all about Philadelphia—wipe it from your mind."

Swinton handed over the envelope containing the bank draft. "I will expect you back in about an hour." He then waved Firth away like an annoying fly. Obviously, he wanted the transaction to be completed as soon as possible.

Todd and his carriage were waiting as Firth left the house. He drove to the pub round the corner from the metalworks, as before.

"I'll wait for ya here," he said, even more sullen than usual.

"Don't get drunk again."

"I've already had a lecture from Mr Swinton—I don't need one from you as well," he replied, making no move to get down from the carriage.

Firth walked round the corner to the front door of the factory.

Kearney called him into his office.

"I'm pleased that your firm has decided to buy the factory from me, Mr Brown. Ashton & Co. from London, I have been informed in a letter from England," said Kearney.

Swinton has been busy, thought Firth.

"The following day, I received a second letter saying that the company had changed its name to Ashton, Brown & Co., after an amalgamation." Mr Kearney looked up at Firth in a questioning manner.

This was the plan that Daisy had devised. She had arranged for a firm to be created in a barber's shop in the same hamlet of London, Ohio. Firth would own a quarter of the shares, and she had the remainder. They had agreed that she would carry on the running of Swinton's ironworks, with Firth as a sleeping partner. Daisy would be free of her father and have her own, thriving business. Firth would receive some of the profits too, making him more independent of his salary and his father-in-law. They had calculated that neither Swinton nor Burkett would want these new arrangements to become public, as their own dubious dealing would also be exposed. Nevertheless, Firth was aware that this would be the second time he had got the better of Burkett, and Swinton would be out of pocket too. He was piling up trouble for the future, he knew. He hoped that Swinton would be mollified by the fact that his own daughter was the main beneficiary of their deviousness and, therefore, not seek revenge. Before any of that, though, he had to conclude the business with Mr Kearney—and deal with Todd.

"Yes, sir. I've been made a partner in the firm in recognition of my part in our negotiations. As you can imagine, I'm extremely pleased to be rewarded in this way. As it's only just happened, the bank account is still in the name of Ashton & Co., out here. Perhaps you could change the name on the sales transaction to Ashton, Brown & Co., and sign the alteration?"

Mr Kearney looked up at him. "It's a little irregular, but I can't see why not." He bent over and carefully signed the document. "And congratulations, my boy. I'm sure you'll take good care of my, sorry, *your* company."

"I will, sir. Thank you."

They shook hands, and Firth left. He had the deeds of the factory and other papers relating to the transfer of the business and the machinery to Messrs Ashton, Brown & Co. of London safely tucked away in an inside coat pocket. As he reached the carriage, Todd was snoring gently on the passenger seat, which suited Firth's plans just fine. He climbed up onto the driver's seat and whipped the horses so they galloped off down the road.

"Stop! Stop! What d'ya think ya doin'? I'm in charge of this carriage! Stop!" Todd yelled, from inside the cab.

"Whoa there, whoa," Firth shouted as he reined in the horses. "Sorry, Todd, I didn't know you were in there," said Firth, as they came to a halt.

Todd hauled himself onto the seat beside Firth and grabbed the reins.

"You're going the wrong way. We're supposed to be goin' back to Mr Swinton's house," Todd shouted angrily.

"I know that," Firth replied calmly. "I was going the long way round, over the bridge. The evening sun is lovely, and I've arranged to meet Daisy."

The excuse sounded feeble, but Todd seemed to accept it.

"We're not on a sightseeing trip here! We're still on Mr Swinton's business. I guess we may as well go over the bridge, now you've brought us this far," Todd said grudgingly.

Firth was relieved. Everything was going well so far.

The carriage started across the bridge. The plan was for Daisy to wait at the far end. Suddenly, Todd brought the carriage to a sharp stop, which caused Firth to be heaved out of his seat. He landed heavily and awkwardly on the sidewalk.

"What did you do that for, you idiot?!" He got up, more angry than afraid, now that Todd had made his move. Todd had stepped down from the carriage and was towering over him.

"Mr Swinton asked me to bring back the papers—but not you. Now hand them over, and I'll be on my way."

"No chance, Todd. If you want them, you'll have to come and get them," Firth said with a show of bravado.

"Come on now. I quite like ya, but I've got to keep myself in Mr Swinton's good books. Give us the papers."

Firth watched the big man coming towards him. There was no easy escape, but he realised he had two advantages. He was quicker than the slow-minded Todd, and he had a gun that the other man had no knowledge of. Firth pulled out the gun and pointed it at Todd, who stopped in his tracks.

"Hold it right there, Todd. I'm going to see Swinton and finish our business with him myself. Now back off!"

"You gonna shoot me, Limey? I don't think so," Todd said, as he took another step towards Firth.

"One more step, and I'll fire!" he warned.

Todd just made an ugly grin and came closer.

Firth fired and hit Todd in the belly, blood seeping through his waistcoat. He let out a tremendous bellow, looked down at his wound, but remained standing.

"You'll need more that little peashooter," he grunted, and started his advance once more. "I'm gonna kill you, you little Limey runt!"

Firth ducked just as the big man threw a tremendous punch that surely would have taken his head clean off his shoulders had it landed. Firth kept low and charged at

Todd's injured belly. Todd, already off balance, staggered backwards with the force of Firth's charge and landed heavily on the sidewalk, a look of hurt and surprise on his face. He heaved his bulk upright by pulling on the ornate ironwork on the side of the bridge. It seemed an age to Firth before Todd was standing again. He was breathing heavily, and his front was covered with blood. A weaker man would never have managed it. Firth stood watching him, transfixed by the sight, as though hypnotised. He gathered himself and turned to mount the carriage, but he wasn't fast enough. He felt Todd grab his coat tails. If only he had moved more quickly. Todd grunted with the effort.

"Ya may have got me with ya one bullet, but that's not enough to stop ol' Todd—no, sir! I'm too tough for that, an' I'm too tough for you. Come here!"

He pulled Firth off the carriage and aimed a swinging blow at his head. He managed to duck, but Todd had hold of him now. Todd drew back his arm to smash his fist in Firth's face. Firth thought he was finished.

There was a loud explosion, and a flash of light. Todd's fist disappeared, to be replaced by a bloody mass of pulp. Todd looked at it in his slow way. He just couldn't understand what he was seeing. For a second, neither could Firth. Then, there was another shot, this one to Todd's chest. It was too much for him; this time, his legs buckled under him. Somehow, he kept a tight grip on Firth, and as he finally collapsed, he brought the smaller man down on top of him.

Firth rolled off Todd's dead body as quickly as he could, trying to avoid getting any blood on his clothes. He looked up as a shadow fell over him. Daisy was standing there holding a large revolver. Smoke was still coming out of the barrel.

"My God, Daisy," Firth said with relief. "You saved my life. I don't know how I'll ever be able to thank you." He was shaking now, as the enormity of what had happened began to sink in, and he had to sit before his legs gave way beneath him.

"Well, partner, I'm glad I could help. I always hated that man anyway." She seemed to be no more worried than if she had just killed a rabbit, even though she had killed a man she'd known for many years. "He insisted on treating me like a child and would tell tales to my father. I'm glad he's gone."

Firth gathered his strength and got to his feet. "Let's get him into the river before anyone comes."

"Us? You'll have to do it, Firth. I am a lady, after all," she said with a smile. "I don't want to get blood on my dress. A little bit more on your clothes won't make any difference."

Firth leant down to pick up Todd.

"Wait!" said Daisy. "Let's look through his pockets first. I'll do it; you've got blood on your hands. Move over."

Todd had only a few coins in his coat pocket, but round the back of his jacket, there was a small bulge. Daisy pulled a tiny knife from a pouch that hung from her belt. She cut open the jacket seam and pulled out a small metal box.

"Now push him over," she instructed Firth. "I think that's everything."

Firth heaved the body up onto the parapet, a task made far more difficult with Todd's arms flopping about and getting caught in the ironwork. Using all his strength, he finally pushed the corpse over the edge. A second later, they heard the splash as it hit the cold, dark water of the Chuylkill River.

"Let's get out of here," Daisy said, climbing onto the driving seat of the carriage. "We'll get you to the railroad station before the train leaves. The sooner you're out of town, the better. If they find the body, they may suspect you, but never me."

Firth had been impressed with Daisy's cool composure throughout the evening's events. It was just as well he liked her, he thought. He certainly wouldn't want to get on the wrong side of her. The best thing he could do was to be absolutely straight with her in business matters and never give her any reason to question him. He thought she could be devastatingly ruthless if circumstances called for it, contrasting with her normally kind and considerate demeanour.

"Well, now you know how I treat my enemies," she said. "But, on the other hand, I'm loyal to my friends." It was as if she could read his thoughts. "I have my father's determination and my mother's compassion. I know what I want, and I'm going to get it! Give me the documents now, and I'll put them in our bank for safe keeping. The box is in both our names. It'll stop Father getting his hands on them. There's no knowing what he'd do if he did."

Firth had not considered a joint bank deposit box. Obviously, Daisy had thought of everything. She seemed to have no doubt that they would be successful. Only one thing remained before Firth could leave. He had to find somewhere to wash the blood from his hands, and he needed a new, clean coat. At this hour, the only place to do both things safely was to return to Daisy's house on Vineyard

Street and "borrow" one of her father's coats. Fortunately, he was out when they arrived, so Firth rushed to the bathroom, while Daisy went to get one of her father's coats. It was a little small for Firth, especially across the shoulders, but it would do the job. They ran out of the house to the carriage, and Daisy drove them to the Broad Street railroad station as fast as she could.

Firth turned to Daisy. "Goodbye, Daisy. I'll be in touch as soon as I get back." He climbed down from the carriage.

"Don't worry about anything. I think we've got it all covered, and you know you can trust me." She handed him her revolver. "Take this—I don't think I'll need it again. There's four bullets left."

She waved the whip at him in a salute and brought it down with a crack that made bystanders look up and the horses rear. They started off at a brisk trot.

Firth tucked the pistol into his belt, even though he thought it was a pointless gift. Time was short, so he ran through the station to the platform where the train for Washington was waiting. In his haste, he failed to notice the two men standing by a large pillar, one of whom pointed him out to the other. They immediately jumped onto the train, one carriage behind Firth, just as there was a loud whistle and the train began to move.

CHAPTER 12

Firth sat back in his seat and relaxed. After his recent exertions, he felt the need to close his eyes for a short nap. As he unwound, he idly watched other passengers walking up and down the central aisle of the carriage, talking to friends and stretching their legs before sitting down as the train gathered speed.

His attention was drawn to two men who passed by, looking hard at each passenger as they passed. When they came level with Firth, they stopped for a second before continuing. They were both badly dressed and had the sour faces of poverty. Their most noticeable features were their cold, hard eyes that looked at the world without compassion. Firth thought that perhaps his troubles were not over after all, and any thoughts of sleep were forgotten as he watched them take a seat at the back of the carriage. He nicknamed the tall one Bean Pole, and the shorter man, Cannon Ball—he was overweight, with a large stomach that hung over his ill-fitting trousers, restrained only by an iron-studded leather belt.

The train entered a wood where the shadows made the evening seem darker. Firth could see a guard in the next carriage lighting oil lamps, but his own compartment was still in comparative darkness.

The train slowed down, and a woman in the next seat said they should take precautions—Confederate troops were said to be in the area, but most of the travellers agreed that this was highly unlikely so far into Northern territory. Firth, to the amusement of his fellow passengers, slid from his seat, and made his way on all fours along the carriage to the door at the end. He quickly opened it and leapt out, dropping to the ground. He rolled down an embankment and stopped at the foot of a tree. As he looked back at the train, he saw a man looking out at him.

The train started to pick up speed again, but it didn't stop Bean Pole jumping out of the door. Cannon Ball wasn't so brave—he was far less athletic than his companion and frightened to take the plunge. The train disappeared into the distance.

Firth crouched low in the undergrowth and drew the revolver that Daisy had given him. There was a rustle coming from a little further up the track, and then Firth heard footsteps coming towards him. He took off his hat and, using a long stick, raised it up above the undergrowth. A shot rang out, and Firth felt the hat move as it took the impact of the bullet. A neat round hole had appeared in it. Firth yelled out, as if he had been hit, and Bean Pole came running over. As he came closer, Firth took careful aim and shot the man in the chest. Bean Pole tottered and fell to his knees. He dropped his gun and raised his hands to the wound. Blood oozed between his fingers, and a look of utter disbelief crossed his face. He hadn't expected Firth to be armed.

Just as he thought the man was finished, Bean Pole moved like lightning. He reached out and grabbed Firth's arm, pulling him off balance. As he stumbled, Bean Pole wrapped his arm round his neck and quickly had him in a stranglehold. Firth could feel the warm blood of his opponent soaking into his shirt, and he was already becoming short of breath. He knew he had to act quickly, so he stopped trying to break Bean Pole's hold and instead rammed his elbow backwards, directly into his midriff. Bean Pole instantly released his grip, gasping for breath. Firth crawled away, regaining his senses, when another shot rang out. The bullet sliced through his coat and grazed his arm. The pain burned into him like nothing he had experienced before, and he could feel the blood running freely down his arm. He turned, ready to fire at Bean Pole again, but he was already dead. It seemed that his last, deadly action had been too much for him.

Firth was taking no chances this time. He kicked the man hard on the leg, but there was absolutely no response. Relieved, Firth removed the gun from his hand and took off his belt, which was full of bullets fitted into folds of leather. He put on the belt and stuck both his and Bean Pole's guns into either side. From being a man who had never even seen a gun until a few days before, he was amassing a collection rather quickly. He looked around the area of their struggle and noticed the letter he had seen Bean Pole with earlier. This he carefully tucked away in an inside coat pocket, and then he pulled the body by its boots into the undergrowth. Satisfied that Bean Pole was well hidden, he made his way down to a small stream where he washed off as much blood as possible.

He was contemplating a long walk along the tracks when he heard a train rumbling along in the distance. As he reached the line, he saw the reason trains slowed down here—some work was being done on the track. A freight train soon came into view, slowing down almost to a walking pace as it passed the track repairs. Firth ran forward, heaved himself onto an open truck, and crawled under the tarpaulin. Exhausted now, he fell asleep, despite the still-burning pain in his arm and the hardness of his new bed. He didn't wake up until the following morning, when the train slowed with a screech of its brakes. Bewildered for a moment, Firth looked out to see they were entering a freight yard. His arm injury made its presence known with a fierce throbbing. On inspection, Firth could see that his shirt was stuck to his arm by the copious amount of blood, which had now dried. He had to ignore his pain for now and get off the train without being seen. There was a sign on a large warehouse informing anyone who happened to be passing that it was the Wilmington Merchandising Store. Firth could see Wilmington Station about a hundred yards away, so he slipped out of his hiding place and ran from one freight truck to the next, gradually making his way to the platform.

"The war hasn't even started, and the trains are already late."

Startled, Firth looked around to find that an elderly man with a large, drooping moustache, was addressing him.

"Well, it's as good an excuse as any, I suppose," he said, recovering his composure. "Is it the Washington train you're waiting for?"

"No, that goes later. This next one is the slow train that turns around at Baltimore. Didn't you know?" The old man looked at him more closely. "You don't look well, young man. Where did all that blood come from?"

"I had an accident."

"Well, you'd better see a doctor. It looks pretty bad to me."

"Later. I've got things to do first."

"If it gets infected, you'll really regret it. Get it seen to; that's my advice. Anyway, what happened?"

"Oh, it's a long story."

"I got nothin' but time," he said with a rueful smile.

"All right, I'll tell you. A horse threw me, and I landed on my arm in the road. I suppose a stone gashed it. I think the blood loss must have tired me, and I woke up over there." He pointed vaguely in the direction he had come from. "How long will it be before the Washington train arrives? And where's the nearest pharmacy?"

"The nearest what?" asked the old man.

"Pharmacy. You know, a chemist, a, er, drug store."

"Well, why dincha say so? Lemme think a moment."

"I've got to get home as quick as I can," Firth continued. "My wife's expecting our first baby any time now."

The man seemed satisfied with Firth's explanations and was now eager to help this wounded stranger.

"The Washington train ain't due for another hour, and there's a doctor just up the road. I'm sure he'll be able to bandage you up and give you some ointment to stop it going septic. It'll be better than trying to do it by yourself."

"You're right, there. Where is it?"

"Turn right out of the station, and he's about a hundred yards up the road, on the right. There's a nameplate on the wall. It's Dr James."

"Thank you so much. I'll go straight away and get it seen to. Bye now."

He followed the man's directions, stopping at a general store to buy a new shirt on the way. At the surgery, he knocked on the door.

"Yes, sir?" asked a small woman as she opened the door.

"I need to see the doctor," he said, indicating his arm.

"You certainly do. Wait a moment, and I'll tell him you're here."

A few minutes later, she returned. "The doctor will see you now, sir."

She showed him into a room with a sign on the door "Randolph James, MD." Behind the desk sat a grey-haired man, who looked up as he entered.

"Please sit down," he said. "Tell me what happened."

"It's a little embarrassing, Doctor. Completely my own stupid fault. I was cleaning my gun when it went off. I should have checked it wasn't loaded, I know, but—" His voice trailed away, and he shrugged his shoulders. "Can you help me? I must get home to Washington, as my wife is expecting our baby soon, and I want to be with her."

"Well, let's have a look at this first. It depends how deep the wound is."

"Just some basic first aid will do for now, Doctor, just so I can travel, and then I'll see my regular doctor in Washington."

"I'll see what I can do." He poured some rye whiskey and told Firth to drink it all. "You're going to need it," he said grimly.

The doctor set to work and peeled the clothing from Firth's arm. The pain was excruciating, and Firth had to clench his teeth to avoid crying out. As he examined the wound, Dr James told Firth he'd been lucky.

"It's just a flesh wound. Quite deep, and you'll have a scar, but it should heal nicely." He looked puzzled. "I can't understand how the blood's got all over your other clothing. You haven't been in a fight, have you?"

"A fight?" Firth laughed. "Of course not! It happened last night, and I think the blood loss must have made me pass out. I woke up on the floor, and I think it must have bled during the night. I'm still wearing the same clothes."

"I really should report this to the authorities, you know. We've been told to report anything unusual. Wait here a minute."

The doctor left the room and Firth could hear him talking to someone. He dressed hurriedly, deciding it was time to leave. The last thing he wanted was to be held in Wilmington. He put on his new shirt and left some money for the bill. He quietly slipped out of the house, and ran back down the road, despite the pain in his arm, to the railroad station. As he turned to enter the station, he looked back at the surgery, where he could see two soldiers in blue uniforms talking to the doctor. They left the house and started walking towards the station.

The Washington train came into view, and Firth hoped desperately that it would arrive before the soldiers did. He was sure they would arrest him; or, at the very least, ask him lots of awkward questions and make him miss the train. To his relief, the train finally stopped, and he jumped onto the nearest carriage. He slammed the door closed behind him, quickly sat down on the far side, and turned to look out of the window to admire the view.

The soldiers were running towards the station, yelling. Luckily, the driver couldn't hear them over the noise of the engine, and the train slowly pulled away. One of the soldiers raised his gun as if to fire, but no shot came, and the train continued to gather speed.

"Did you see that?" one elderly lady asked her companion. "What *are* they doing?"

"Too much drink, I expect," said the other.

"How disgusting. And at this hour of the day as well!"

For the first time that day, Firth relaxed a little. He remembered the letter he had taken from Bean Pole, and took it out to read. He unfolded it and quickly scanned its contents. He couldn't quite believe what he'd just read, so he settled down to read it more closely, amazed at the lengths some people would go to in the pursuit of power and money. He read it a third time to fix it in his memory, saying the words quietly to himself. It read:

Clements,

I have another job I want you and your partner to do for me. An Englishman, by the name of Firth Brown, is an enemy of mine. He will be leaving Philadelphia for Washington on the late train on 20 June. He must not reach Washington. You may see Brown at the station if he gets past the trap that has been set for him in Philly. I don't have much faith in their abilities, so be ready. Brown is of medium height with dark hair. Quite unremarkable, but he will be wearing a long dark-brown coat and lighter-brown trousers. He will be carrying a small green holdall made of cloth, with a leather handle. It has a raised design on the side and two crests in faded yellow. He also wears a round hat he calls a bowler. You should be able to pick him out as he doesn't look quite American. He is in his early twenties, but he already has a slightly florid complexion. Probably a drinker. He has a thin moustache, and his hair is short.

Make sure he never reaches Washington. I'll pay you when you get here. Usual rates. Meet me by the ticket office at the station.

Firth noticed that the letter was unsigned, but unfortunately for the writer, he guessed who it was from its style and from the writing paper itself, which was of an unusual texture that he had seen before.

"Not bad news I hope?" asked one of the old ladies, who wore an elaborate feathered hat.

"No, but I must get home quickly," replied Firth. "I wonder if you know what time this train will arrive in Washington?"

"We have been told it is going to stop to pick up some troops, so it'll be a little later than usual," said the other lady. "About midmorning tomorrow, I expect. This war is making everything late."

"I suppose it can't be helped. They've got to get the troops to where they're needed. My brother says it will all be over in a month or so, and that there will be a truce," said the lady in the hat. "After all, the rebels only have their cotton. They live off slavery, so they're already damned in God's eyes, before they even start a war."

"I'm sure you're right," Firth agreed. He had no energy to argue but couldn't help adding, "I'm afraid they, too, believe they have God on their side, and they do have a lot to lose. All their wealth is tied up in their land and their slaves. Without the slaves, their cotton would cost too much to compete with foreigners."

The ladies looked at him suspiciously.

"I hope you're not a rebel supporter, young man," said the second lady.

"No, no. I'm a reporter, actually, from *The Manchester Echo,* in England. Like you, I hope there's a truce so I can go home." It occurred to him that there was very little chance of that happening now that he was married to Elizabeth. In fact, he realised that he was unlikely to see England ever again.

"You must excuse me, ladies. I have had a hard day and need to recover my strength before we reach Washington. I'd like to rest."

"Of course. You must sleep. You go ahead, and we'll tell you when we reach Washington."

"Thank you, ladies."

Firth leant back in his seat, and despite his throbbing arm, he was asleep in seconds, but it was not a peaceful sleep. The noise of the train wheels' rhythmic clickety-clack hammered into his head, he kept hearing the incessant chatter of his two companions, and his dreams were filled with the ugly images of his two assailants.

CHAPTER 13

Hours later, Firth was awoken as the train shuddered to a halt. Light was breaking over the buildings of Baltimore. The platform was crowded with soldiers whom Firth looked out at with interest. This would make a good story to send home, he thought. The soldiers boarded special carriages attached to the train from a siding, an operation which took quite some time.

A few officers got into Firth's carriage. One sat next to Firth, and two more sat opposite. Some others spread themselves around the carriage, leaving the two ladies to sit by themselves. Firth overheard the soldiers say that they were on their way to join Major General Irvin McDowell and his army, near Washington. There were reports that a large force, led by Confederate General Beauregard, was advancing on the capital.

"So, you're not in the army yet?" asked the captain, sitting next to Firth.

"Not me, sir. I'm an English journalist, over here to cover the war for my newspaper in Manchester," he replied. "I'm returning to Washington now. I gather you gentlemen think there could soon be a major battle? So far, there have only been small skirmishes. I was beginning to think I could go home soon."

"Alas, I think that is a forlorn hope, sir. According to our information, the rebels are moving a large force up towards Washington. We have to protect our capital," said a young lieutenant sitting opposite.

An older major interjected gruffly, "General Beauregard won the battle for the Confederates at Fort Sumter. That's where the war really started. Let's hope that this time we can give them a hiding and send 'em home with their tails between their legs. Maybe then they'll come to their senses, and we can all go back to our families."

"I fear that may not happen, sir," replied Firth. "The Southerners have their backs to the wall now. I think they know they can't win, but they're fiercely loyal to their cause, and they see no reason why they shouldn't make a break from the Union. They may not have weapons as good as yours, but they'll fight tooth and nail—you can bet on that."

"You sound as if you're on their side," said the major. "You are a journalist, aren't you—not a spy?" He laughed.

"Yes, as I said, I'm a journalist. For *The Manchester Echo* actually."

Firth's attention was then momentarily diverted, making him miss the major's next words. He thought he'd just seen Cannon Ball walk along the platform, past his window. Surely not.

He heard the major's voice again. "I said I was glad to hear it. Are you all right, young man?"

"Yes, I'm sorry. I haven't eaten for some time, and this train seems to be taking forever," said Firth. "I'm really feeling the cold now, and my concentration keeps wandering. Please go on."

"I'd like to offer you my overcoat," said the captain, but I don't think I can, what with you being a civilian."

"Give it to him, Captain," said the major. "It won't hurt."

"Thank you, Major. I'm extremely grateful," said Firth.

"Pleased to be of service. Just make sure you write up our side as the winners," said the major, with a smile. "And I want the captain's coat back when we get to Washington. We don't want a Britisher to lead us against the rebels, do we?"

The other officers laughed, and the captain put the coat round Firth's shoulders.

"Here, you may as well have my hat as well." The captain laughed, setting his cap on Firth's head.

The captain had done Firth a great favour without knowing it. Cannon Ball would never recognise him in the uniform of a Union officer.

At that moment, Cannon Ball came down the central aisle, obviously looking for Firth. Somehow, he had discovered that he hadn't been killed, probably because his partner hadn't shown up at the prearranged meeting point. He scrutinised all the male civilians, but he passed by what were apparently four army officers, not giving them a second glance. Firth turned away and breathed a sigh of relief as the thug carried on down the train.

At last, the train moved off, hissing steam and straining from the extra weight of the troops. It would be a long and slow journey to cover the relatively short distance to Washington.

"Do you play poker?" asked the major. "We all play, but I hear you do it differently in England."

"Sorry, I've never played," replied Firth.

"Don't worry, we'll teach you. Won't we, boys?" said the major. "We've time for a few hands before it gets dark."

This familiarity suited Firth. If he appeared to be part of the group, Cannon Ball was even less likely to identify him. They showed him how to play and explained the finer points of a straight flush, a four of a kind, a full house, and all the other hands and ways of scoring. The major wanted to play for a dollar a hand, but it was agreed that this was rather high. Firth was relieved to discover that the young lieutenant was not rich and could not afford to lose money any more than he could.

They played until dusk, to the disapproval of the two old ladies, who could be heard tut-tutting and whispering to each other now and again. The major eventually scooped up most of the money on the table, which was probably just as well, as Firth thought he would make a sore loser.

Later, Cannon Ball came back down the coach, still looking for Firth. He was an even more unpleasant-looking character than Firth had originally thought, with crooked brown teeth, stained by his habit of constantly chewing tobacco. He was walking slowly, studying the features of all the men. Firth pulled his cap well down, tucked his chin into his overcoat, and pretended to be asleep. He heard him speak to the two ladies opposite, asking if they had seen anyone get on before Baltimore.

"Just the man over there," said the lady in the hat, pointing.

"You mean one of those officers?"

"The man by the window. He's not an officer; he's just borrowed the captain's coat and cap."

Cannon Ball looked in Firth's direction, an ugly smile spreading across his face, and Firth knew he'd been recognised.

"I represent the government of the Union, and I have reason to believe that you are a spy," said Cannon Ball, loud enough for all to hear.

Everyone in the carriage looked up to see what was happening.

"Don't be ridiculous," Firth protested. "I'm an English journalist."

"We in Washington have been looking for this man for some time," Cannon Ball said, in a voice that he hoped carried some authority. "I'm arresting you on charges of espionage. Come along with me."

Turning to the officers he added, "This fellow's a bad lot. He's passed on lots of information to the rebels already, but we've got him now."

"Hold it, fella," said the major. "I can't just let you drag him off. Let me see your identification first."

Cannon Ball hesitated, then pulled a gun out and pointed it at Firth.

"Get over here *now!*" he said menacingly.

Firth got up carefully and walked to Cannon Ball, who grabbed one of his arms and stuck the gun into his back. Together, they walked backwards towards the exit, to the astonished looks of the other passengers. Cannon Ball hustled him out of the carriage and then through to the next one.

"Keep calm, folks. This man is a wanted spy, and I am arresting him. Please, keep calm. Come on, you, keep moving," he said, digging the gun barrel painfully into Firth's kidneys.

Firth was then pushed into the guard's van, which was full of trunks, crates, and boxes.

The train swayed as it negotiated a bend in the track, and Firth took the opportunity to turn on his captor. He whipped round, breaking Cannon Ball's hold. The man was taken completely by surprise and fired his gun without thinking. The bullet ripped through a flap of Firth's coat and buried itself in the wall of the carriage.

From behind a pile of sacks the guard appeared. He'd obviously been sleeping on duty and was rather upset at having his nap so rudely interrupted.

"What's going on here?" he demanded.

Firth was still wearing the borrowed cap and coat. His departure had been such that the captain had been unable to ask for them back. Firth now used them to his advantage.

"This man is trying to rob me, an officer of the Union," he cried. "I am carrying important documents on behalf of the government."

At that moment, a trooper and a sergeant entered from the opposite end of the guard's car, no doubt drawn by the gunshot. Seeing an officer being held at gunpoint, they demanded to know what was going on.

Firth repeated his request for help, but this time he made it a command. "Arrest this man, Sergeant! He has tried to rob me of the troop orders I'm carrying!"

Cannon Ball knew the game was up. As the two soldiers came forward to arrest him, he raised his pistol to fire at them. Firth pushed him off balance, just as he fired. He missed again, the bullet burying itself in a sack of grain which streamed its contents to the floor. The sergeant charged forward and threw his considerable weight into Cannon Ball, who stumbled and landed heavily.

Firth pulled open the sliding door, and leaning against some trunks to get leverage, he slowly pushed the dazed Cannon Ball along the floor, towards the opening. The train was going at some speed now, and the rushing wind helped Firth heave the thug out onto the track before he could recover. He desperately tried to hold on to the edge of the door, but Firth kicked his hands away. There was an anguished yell, and the hands vanished. Firth rushed over to see his adversary lying on some rocks at the side of the track, blood running profusely from his head.

"You saved my life, sir," said the sergeant.

"Should you have got rid of him like that?" the guard asked anxiously.

"Of course he should have!" the sergeant replied. "That's the only way to treat our enemies. We shan't win this war by being soft!"

"Well done, men. I shall inform the major of your bravery," Firth said. He saluted the trooper and the sergeant. "I have to pick up a box from the rear guard's car. Will you two escort me through the troops' carriages?"

"Certainly, sir."

They set off to the rear of the train, passing through the ranks of nervous-looking young men in blue who were destined to fight in the first real battle of the civil war. Among the troops were one group stood out. Firth recognised these as New York Zouaves, a volunteer regiment dressed in baggy blue pants, with turbans of white cloth bound tightly on their heads. Even though these were mainly North Africans, they were regarded with respect by other Union troops because they were better trained and prepared, and they had a reputation for being fearless in battle, unlike the majority of the army, who were mainly raw recruits.

On reaching the guard's car at the end of the train, Firth turned to the two soldiers and thanked them.

"Return to your seats, men," he said in his best military voice. "And I must order you to keep this affair quiet. We don't want to spread alarm. I'll report what happened later, and they can decide what further action to take then."

"Yes, sir, we understand." replied the sergeant. He turned to the trooper and commanded in the half-shouted speech used by all noncommissioned officers when speaking to the lower ranks, "You heard what the captain said, Trooper! Make sure you keep your mouth shut!"

"Yes, Sergeant," replied the soldier.

With that, they left the car.

The guard's car at the end of the train was filled with the paraphernalia of war. There were piles of uniforms, boxes of bullets, food, medical supplies, and everything else an army needed.

The guard here was wide awake and alert.

"Where have you come from? I have orders to let in only authorised officers," he said.

"Well, you can see I'm an officer," said Firth. "I've been sent by the major in charge to see how many cases of bullets we have stored in this wagon. He thinks we may not have enough."

Firth started counting the ammunition boxes and reading every detail printed on them.

The train was finally approaching Washington and starting to slow down.

"Are we coming to the main station?" Firth asked the guard.

"Not yet. We always slow down here in case the station master has some mail to throw into the guard's wagon. There are never many letters, but I have to open the door to check."

Firth noticed there was the usual small balcony at the end of the car. Whilst the guard was occupied, he went outside and stood at the rail. The train had slowed down almost to walking pace, ready for the mail. There was only one bag. While the guard's attention was distracted, Firth jumped onto the platform. As the train disappeared into the distance, he could see the guard staring at him in bewilderment.

"Hello!" Firth called out, startling the station master. "I have been ordered to get off the train here. There's someone I have to see here about army business. Where's the main street?"

"It's behind the station. There's not much of it, mind. Just a store, a livery stable, and a dentist who also acts as a doctor as long as it's nothing too serious."

"That's fine. Thank you," said Firth.

He walked through the station and down onto the street, towards the livery stable. He entered the premises and went through to the back, where a man was carrying some hay.

"Well, well," the man greeted him, adding sarcastically, "An officer of our glorious Union army indeed. I am truly honoured by your presence, sir."

"I need your help," said Firth.

"My help? I thought the army was gonna wrap this little war up in a few weeks. That's what everyone says. What do you want from me?"

"I take it you're not in favour of the war then?"

"You're goddamn right I'm not. It's costing us all a lotta money. Why not let 'em break away if they want to? In any case, I got relatives in the South, and I don't want my own flesh and blood to be shot. I'll ask you again—what do you want here?"

"I want to hire a horse and trap," said Firth. "Have you got one, and how much will it be?"

"Five dollars, plus ten as a deposit, to make sure you bring it back."

"That's a lot of money. I only need it for a few hours."

"That's the price, mister. Take it or leave it."

"Very well. Here's the money," Firth said, laying the cash on a bale of hay. "Is it ready to go?"

"Hey, just wait a minute. I'm not one of your private soldiers, Major, Captain, or whatever you are. I need to go and get it ready," he said sullenly.

He was obviously not a man to be rushed.

"Captain, actually," Firth informed him, throwing a salute.

Ten minutes later, the man returned. He had a horse in the shafts, and he handed the reins to Firth.

"You take good care of this trap, mister. It's the only one I have."

"I will; don't worry."

Firth cracked the reins, and the horse set off at a quick trot. He soon arrived in Washington and guided the horse and trap through the streets, to the Bell. He walked in and hung his hat and coat on a stand in the corner. No one took any notice of him. Firth looked around and found Joe at his favourite table.

"Well, hello, Joe," he said. "Fancy finding you here!"

Joe grunted. "Always the comedian, ain't ya?"

"Pleased to see you too. Listen, Joe, I need a favour."

"Oh, I see. Is that all I'm good for, to do you favours? You haven't even offered to buy me a drink yet."

"Do this for me, and there'll be a nice fat bonus for you at the end."

"How much?"

"First, I need to know if you'll help me."

"You know me. Always willing to help a friend." Clearly, Joe could already smell the money.

"I want you to take my trap back to the stables and drop me off at Mr Burkett's house on the way. You can get back here on the train, or even walk; it's not that far. It'll probably do you good to walk off some of that booze you've had while I've been away."

"The things I do for you," he grumbled. "Is that all?"

"When you get to the stables, you'll get the deposit back. Ten dollars, so don't let him try to tell you it was anything else. Half of it's for you, for doing this for me. Oh, and don't tell the chap anything about me—he thinks I'm an army officer."

"He does?"

"Yes, he does. Come on, let's go. I'll tell you all about it on the way."

The journey passed quickly as Firth regaled Joe with his exploits. By the time they reached the Burketts', Joe regarded Firth in a different light, and with more than a little respect. Three men he'd killed, and made himself rich in the bargain!

Firth climbed down from the trap, and Joe continued down the road. Firth watched until he turned the corner and was out of sight, then he went up to the front door and knocked.

A different maid answered.

"Good morning. Is Mr Burkett in?"

"Yes, sir. Come in, please."

Firth was shown to the dining room, where the master and mistress of the house were eating their breakfast.

Burkett looked up and, on seeing Firth alive and well, went pale. His food stayed on his fork, getting only halfway to his mouth. How could this have happened?

"Oh, you're back, Firth! Elizabeth will be *so* pleased," gushed Mrs Burkett.

"My God," blurted her husband. "Where did you come from? How did you get back?"

There was a mixture of shock and disappointment on his face, in contrast to his wife, who made a big fuss of her son-in-law.

"Do have some coffee, Firth. Do you want some breakfast?"

"Just some coffee, please."

"It's wonderful to have you back. Have you seen Elizabeth? She's already made your new house really homey, and she's got Martha to help her as well."

"Yes, good to see you back," Mr Burkett managed with great effort. "I must get to work."

"So soon, dear?" said Mrs Burkett. "Never mind. I shall have Firth all to myself over breakfast."

Firth chatted to Mrs Burkett about his trip to Philadelphia, omitting the fact that her husband and his business partner had made three attempts to have him killed.

"But, really, Mrs Burkett, I have to go. I just wanted your husband to know I was back, but now I can't wait to see Elizabeth."

"Of course, you must go, dear. It's been lovely to have this chat with you. I do so seldom see you. But I know Elizabeth's been missing you terribly, so off you go. One thing before you go, Firth," she added quietly. "She's told me that she thinks she's expecting a child. It's only been a week, so she can't possibly know for sure, but she's very excited. As I said, it's early days yet, but I'm so pleased for you both—I shall be a grandmother!"

Firth was stunned. Thank God they'd had the foresight to cover such an eventuality at the wedding, when they disappeared into the bushes.

"It will give us all something else to talk about other than this terrible war," she continued, oblivious. "Do you really think it will happen? Surely those people won't be silly enough to fight among themselves!"

"I'm afraid it might come to war; things are getting quite bad," Firth replied.

He made his farewells as quickly as he could, without seeming rude. He must get to Elizabeth!

Chapter 14

Martha, now Firth and Elizabeth's maid, saw Firth walking quickly towards their new home on East Sixth Street. He heard her call Elizabeth.

"Ma'am, Mr Brown is coming down the road. He's nearly at the gate."

Elizabeth rushed out, flung her arms round him, and kissed him all over his face.

"Firth, I've so missed you. It seems like you've been gone forever."

"And now I'm back. You look absolutely wonderful, my darling," he said, wrapping his arms tightly round her.

Elizabeth was indeed glowing, and Firth knew why.

"Now don't be mad at me, but before I came here, I had to stop at your parents' house just to wrap up my business with your father. While I was there, your mother let slip about, um—" He stopped, placing his hand gently on her tummy.

"I'm about six weeks gone, I think," she said as she held his hand, keeping it gently pressed it against her stomach. "It's just as well we put on that little act at the wedding. You know, I had a feeling even then that I was—"

"Anyway, let's go inside," said Firth. "You can tell me all about what you've been doing while I was away."

They turned and walked to the house hand in hand, satisfied, at last, just to be together. They talked right through the rest of the day, Elizabeth telling of her purchases for the house. She took Firth on a guided tour, pointing out various items on the way.

"It's not all new, of course. Mamma let me have my dresser and my bed, which Martha's using. We've still got a lot to buy, though, especially with two babies on the way.

"Two?" Firth asked, feigning surprise. "You don't mean, er, twins, do you?"

"No, silly! Martha. She's expecting too, remember? And sooner than me. December, it looks like. You don't mind, do you?

"I don't mind at all. I think the least we can do is to care for her, after the way your father's treated her. Don't you agree?"

"Of course I do. Thank you, darling. I knew you'd understand."

"Whatever makes you happy makes me happy, you know that."

Elizabeth called Martha in, and together they told her the news. Tears welled up in the girl's eyes. All she could do was nod before running from the room, in tears.

"Does that mean she's pleased?" asked Firth with a smile.

That night, Firth and Elizabeth made passionate love three times. The first was a quick, explosive affair. But, on the two following occasions, they took their time, starting to learn each other's bodies, and discovering what they liked and did not like.

When Elizabeth discovered the bandage on his arm, Firth shushed her.

"It's nothing, honestly. I'll tell you about it in the morning," he said.

The house was well and truly christened that night, and it wasn't until the small hours that they fell asleep in each other's arms.

The following day was a lazy affair. Firth told Elizabeth of his adventures, including how he'd acquired a quarter share in the metalworks, as well as the attempts to kill him, although he didn't reveal her father's role in things.

He explained that his arm injury was fairly minor, but he told her that the dressing would need regular changing until it was properly healed. His tale ended where it had started, with his description of his visit to her parents' house, "just before coming home," as he put it. He let his voice linger on the last word, relishing all that it implied.

"I've missed a lot of the war news while I've been gone, so I must see Joe tomorrow. My editor must be wondering what's happened to me," he told Elizabeth.

Joe was nothing if not a man of habit. He was at the same table in the Bell again. Firth glanced at the coat stand in the corner and noticed the captain's coat and hat had gone.

"Did you get the horse and trap back all right?"

"I did, and here's your four dollars and fifty cents," Joe said, slapping the money onto the table.

"Maybe your maths abilities aren't too good, Joe. I make half of ten, five. Where's the rest?"

"Well, I considered your kind offer to walk three miles home, but I decided to take the train instead. I knew you wouldn't mind paying for it."

"Quite right too, Joe. What are friends for, eh?" Firth laughed. "Now, down to business. I met some soldiers on the train coming back, and they told me there would be a major battle soon. What do you know?"

"You're right; it's going to be a big one. It looks like it will happen tomorrow or the next day. The rebels under General Beauregard are advancing on Washington. The government can't ignore them; no way. McDowell is leading the Union army, but neither side has much experience, so there's no knowing what's gonna happen."

"A lot of undisciplined men with guns, all of them ignorant of military tactics. It could be a bloodbath," Firth thought out loud.

"Me, I'm glad I have my papers to prove I'm Irish. I'm not having them dragging me off to be enlisted. I bet you're glad you're English, eh? Even being a Limey's better than joining up!"

Firth gave him a wry smile. "I'll have to go to the front to write a report for my paper. I can't give a second-hand report on such a large battle. It's not *that* much better than being in the army, you know. I could get shot, and which side would care, or even bother to give me medical aid?" Firth was suddenly feeling a little worried. "Mind you, from what I hear about the standard of care, I'd probably be better off without it."

This battle would be the first time he would actually see fighting in progress, and he certainly was not relishing the prospect.

"If I don't return, Joe, keep an eye on my wife, will you?"

"She has her father, doesn't she?" asked Joe.

"That's what worries me," Firth said grimly.

CHAPTER 15

Elizabeth had passed on to Firth that a neighbour of her parents, a Mr Peters, was going to ride out in his carriage on the morning of 20 July, to get as near as possible to the site of the coming battle, which was expected to take place by the Bull Run River. Peters, a spectacled, bookish-looking man, thought it would be an event he could boast about to his grandchildren in years to come. Firth wasted no time in visiting Peters at his home to ask if he might accompany the man to the site of the upcoming battle. When Firth told Peters that he was an English journalist, the man did not hesitate to offer a place in his carriage.

Firth met Peters at his house at five o'clock in the morning, just after sunrise, and they set off to the Bull Run, Peters driving. While they travelled over the bumpy roads, he told Firth about the various troop movements that had led to the current state of affairs. Firth would have liked to take notes, but the constant rocking and bouncing of the carriage made that impossible. He'd just have to try to remember all the information and hope he could recall everything when he came to write up his report later.

Peters seemed to enjoy imparting his knowledge, as if it made him feel important. He explained that the Union's

General Tyler had led his troops against the Confederate's General Longstreet, without orders. He had managed to overrun their positions, and then, because of his inexperience and enthusiasm, had been routed soon after. General Longstreet had pushed home his advantage and given the First Massachusetts Regiment a good mauling, sending them away with a great number of casualties.

"I'm afraid our troops are in complete disarray down there, running all over the place like frightened rabbits," Peters said. "Not a good start, is it? If I were you, I'd make sure I could get away from the battle quickly, in case our side has to make a sudden retreat. I hear these rebels are a trigger-happy bunch; you don't want to get left behind."

"Being a journalist, and an *English* journalist, means I'm officially neutral," Firth pointed out.

"They may not bother asking before they shoot you. Soldiers aren't inclined to stand around asking polite questions in the middle of a battle," replied Peters. "I was in the war against Mexico, and I know what these things are like."

"Thanks. I'll bear it in mind. I'm not planning on getting that close, though. I need to be able to see everything in order to get a good overview. I don't want to get in amid the fighting."

They duly arrived at their destination, the headquarters of General McDowell. A large party of onlookers were already assembled there, perhaps three to five hundred people. There were congressmen, traders of all kinds, even ladies with picnic baskets. The crowd seemed to have come for an afternoon's entertainment, a change from a day at the races.

There were train whistles blowing at the station, which was held by the Confederates at Manassas. No one seemed to care about the arriving trains, even though they were obviously bringing in reinforcements for the rebels. General McDowell seemed happy to wait in Centreville for some divine inspiration.

Luckily for the Union army, and unknown to McDowell, General Beauregard was giving confusing orders to his various units.

On the morning of 21 July, the Union troops were awoken early, but no one had told them where to report. They were looking in all directions, some even stumbling over the tent ropes in their confusion.

Firth was going to move up with the soldiers to Studley Ford, which General Beauregard had failed to cover with his troops. At the last moment, Firth decided to join with the impetuous General Tyler to cross Stone Bridge against a force led by the Confederate Colonel Nathan Evans, and Major Roberdeau Wheat, commanding the so-called Wheat's Tigers. Firth thought crossing a bridge would be easier than a ford; this was going to be an uncomfortable enough day as it was—he didn't need to make it worse.

Firth went with the lead brigade under Brigadier General Robert Schencke. He crossed the bridge with an advance party of troops. There was no resistance; in fact, everything looked peaceful and calm. He had no way of knowing there was a company of South Carolinian troops hidden in the shrubs, just ahead of them.

"We'll be all right if it stays like this," said a young trooper next to him. "I'm not looking forward to meeting these rebels. I hear they can be a bloodthirsty lot."

"I'm glad it's quiet too," Firth told him. "I just want to watch the action, not get too near it."

"It's fine for you. A friend of mine was in the Battle of Big Bethel, and he told me they fight like madmen. I just want to finish this war and go home to—" There was the crack of a firing gun, and he stopped in midsentence.

Firth looked in horror as the boy slumped to his knees, blood oozing from his chest. The bullet had entered his heart, and he was dead before he fell face down to the ground.

Firth knelt down by the soldier, but he knew there was nothing he could do. Suddenly, there was a searing pain across the top of his head, and blood began to run down his face. Feeling weak, he got up and ran towards the edge of the river, but the sudden spurt of energy was too much for him. His legs gave way, and he slithered down the bank, where he collapsed with his feet in the water. Above him, Firth could hear the battle start, the rebel yell coming clearly to him. The blood was running freely now, and all his strength had deserted him. Slowly the world seemed to recede, the sounds of battle growing quieter.

"Elizabeth," he murmured, and he slowly closed his eyes.

CHAPTER 16

The local charge of the Fourth South Carolinian Regiment stopped at the river, and then they returned to their positions behind the shrubs. All except for Charles Fisk. He slid down the bank of the Bull Run and found himself by a low bush. Next to the bush, he found the body of a man dressed in civilian clothes, with a bloody head wound.

He shook the body. "Hey, buddy, can you hear me? Wake up!"

There was no response, and Fisk realised this was his chance. He'd been forced into the Confederate army by the pressure put on him in his home village. He didn't agree with war—not this war or any other—and he wanted out of the Fourth Carolinian Regiment and out of the army. He wanted to return to his studies. He'd just passed his final examinations in American history and wanted to teach the subject. He knew, though, if he was a deserter, he could never return home. He would go to one of the big cities where no one would know him.

Here, he thought, was just what he needed. He stripped Firth of his clothes and took his wet shoes, leaving him in just his underwear. He took Firth's clothes and left his own uniform where it fell as he removed it.

He hurriedly pulled on his new trousers. Money spilled from the pockets. He gathered it up and put it into a leather purse, together with his own. He took possession of all Firth's documents and his notebook. He buttoned the shirt and put on the coat and a strange hat, the likes of which he'd never seen. Finally, he put the shoes on, but they didn't fit, so he pulled his army boots on again. He tied the laces of the shoes together and flung them far out into the river.

Dusk was falling now. Fisk crept along the riverbank, making sure he kept low so he couldn't be seen, and then made his way into the shrubs and eventually to trees, never to be seen alive again.

The Confederates waited until dawn came and they were sure the Union army had withdrawn before venturing out to collect their wounded comrades.

"Hey, look down there!" a trooper called to his companion.

"What's happened to him?" asked the other. "He's not wearing his uniform!"

"Maybe he's a deserter. Took his uniform off so he could get away."

"Sure, and no one's gonna notice a fellow in his underpants, now are they?"

"Well, how do I know? They don't pay me to think! We'd better take him in. He's still breathing. Come on, man, help me pull him up the bank."

It was a great effort, but they managed to heave Firth's inert body onto a makeshift stretcher, and they carried him back to their medical tent.

Two days later, Firth woke up in a large old building that looked like a warehouse. There were wounded soldiers on beds all around him, groaning in pain or snoring in their sleep. He had a terrible, burning, throbbing pain in his head, and he instinctively put his hand up to touch it.

"Hold it there, soldier," said a gentle female voice with a Southern accent. "Don't touch your head; you've got a nasty wound there."

"What happened?" he asked the pretty, dark haired nurse who stood over him.

The woman looked at him curiously. "Well, we were kinda hoping you could tell *us* that. You're lucky to be here at all. No one else thought you would survive, but I've prayed for you every night. What's your name?"

Firth opened his mouth to answer, but nothing came out. He couldn't remember his name, who he was, or where he came from. He desperately tried to remember something, however trivial, but there was nothing: the past was a complete blank. His only consolation was that he appeared to be in a safe place, and he had here a guardian angel. The nurse tending him seemed the only bit of normality in an ugly and hostile world.

"Where am I?" he asked quietly.

The nurse didn't hear him, so he made a great effort to stretch out his arm and grab her skirt. "Don't leave me. Take me away from here. I don't remember anything."

The nurse, once again, looked at him in puzzlement. "Well, I'll tell you one thing. You ain't from around these parts. That's an English accent you got there, soldier! How did you get into the army?"

"I don't know. I told you, I don't know."

"Well, I'm not going anywhere for now, my poor unknown soldier. I've got all these other men to attend to. But we're gonna have to give you a name. How about Frank? That was my late father's name. We'll call you Frank English. Yes, I think that'll do nicely until we find out who you really are.

"Frank English. Hmm," Firth said, trying the name for size. It suited him well enough, especially since he couldn't remember his real name.

Smiling at the nurse, he asked, "And where am I?"

"This is a temporary hospital in Richmond, the capital of the new Confederate state. I want you to get some sleep. It's the best thing for you for now."

"Thank you, Nurse. What's your name?"

"Cooling. Nurse Cooling. But you can call me Angela. Sleep well, Frank."

Chapter 17

Angela had taken a shine to the injured young soldier, Frank English, and she made sure he received the best possible attention. Other than the loss of memory, his wounds were superficial. She bathed them constantly to prevent infection, something which was already rife among the soldiers in the ward. She felt a little guilty at giving him more attention than was strictly necessary, but she had grown quite fond of him. All the nurses knew they shouldn't have favourites, but they were only human, after all, and it couldn't be helped.

Frank returned to reasonable health within a few days of arriving at the hospital. He volunteered to run errands for the staff or to clean up parts of the place, anything to make himself useful. It wasn't entirely selfless on his part, of course. Anything he could do to help relieved the boredom and got him away from the constant cries of men in agony, and the smell of death and decay.

Soon they entrusted him with feeding the very weakest soldiers, who were not expected to survive and were kept in a side ward of their own. He soon became well known in the hospital among the doctors and nurses, as well as the other patients. He was a constant source of gossip and speculation, as everyone wondered how this Englishman had come to be there.

The local ladies visited regularly and passed around cakes and sweets to the troops. Frank took on the task of passing on treats to men in "his" ward, as well as talking to the patients and writing letters for them. Most of them were too badly injured to put pen to paper, and some were not literate enough to write a reasonable letter. Many of them were country lads with very little or no education. Before the war, some had never even left home or ventured beyond their village boundaries.

"You're so good with them," Angela said one day while putting a fresh dressing on his wounds. "You know, they're starting to call you a saint! Don't let it go to your head, will you?" She laughed, then inspected his wounds closely. "These are coming along very well, Frank. They're almost healed. What are you going to do next?"

"What do you mean?"

"Well, like I said, you're nearly ready to go. The doctor will want to discharge you soon. I could ask them to let you stay on here, to carry on helping us. After all, you're still injured in a way, what with your memory loss. We don't know which army unit you're from, or your rank, and none of your family has come forward. I'm sure the doctor would appreciate having a man about the place who understands nursing and can help out with some of the heavier work. Some of it's very taxing for us girls!" Angela said breathlessly.

She looked at him expectantly.

"Yes, I think I'd like that, Angela. I feel like I'm doing some good here, and it certainly beats fighting," he said, warming to the idea. "But where would I stay? I can't keep occupying a bed here."

"You could stay with us in Richmond," said Angela, trying to keep her enthusiasm under control. "My mother and I live alone, and we could do with a man about the house. I'll ask her about it when I get home. The rent won't come to much, I'm sure."

"Rent? I hadn't thought of that. I have no money, Angela. Nothing."

"If I can get the doctors to take you on as staff, they'll have to pay you the going rate. In fact, you'll need a rank—corporal maybe—just to give you a little authority over these men. They can become a real handful once they start feeling better, and they need to be kept in line."

"So how do we do this?"

"Wait here!" she said.

With that, she promptly set off down the main gangway, headed towards the senior doctor's office. Angela was full of enthusiasm for her idea and decided to ask the doctor to speak to the colonel in charge of the hospital. She thought she'd got it all worked out. If she was successful, she would then have the much more difficult task of persuading her mother to take Frank in. She reckoned that if the doctors would take him on, it would give her a little ammunition when the time came to talk to her mother. Hopefully, she'd see that his employment was crucial to the war effort.

"Doctor Robinson, may I speak to you for a moment?" asked Angela.

"I'm about to go on my rounds, Nurse. I've got to get some of these soldiers discharged and sent back to their units as quick as I can. Can't it wait?" he asked impatiently.

He was not a man who liked having his routine altered, especially by a nurse without an appointment.

"I think it would be best to talk now, Doctor. It concerns one of the patients. It might be too late after your rounds. I'm sorry I didn't request an appointment."

"If it's that important, I guess I'd better listen. I know you're not one to waste my time, unlike some of your colleagues," replied Dr Robinson. "Close the door. Now, what is it you want? And make it quick!" he barked, just to let her know who was in charge.

"It's about the soldier with the memory loss. We're calling him Frank English," she began. "His wounds are just about healed now, but there's no sign of his memory coming back. The thing is, he's real good with the wounded men, sir, and he helps out with lots of other jobs about the place. We really need him, sir. Could you ask the colonel to enrol him in the nursing team? We need a male medical orderly, someone to help out with the heavy lifting. I could arrange lodgings in town." The words tumbled out, gathering speed as Angela got more excited.

"You're a persuasive girl. Pity some of our politicians aren't like you," Robinson said, and then he laughed at his own joke. He could see the good sense in the suggestion and it served to reinforce his own feelings on the subject. There was no way he could release an unknown soldier with an English accent without knowing more about him. "This is all in the call of duty, I suppose?"

Angela flushed slightly. "Of course it is, Doctor. Whatever do you mean?"

Robinson held up his hands as if to ward off an attack. "I don't mean nothing, Nurse," he said with a laugh. "I'll see what I can do. No promises, mind you."

Angela got herself under control and thanked the doctor politely.

That afternoon, Dr Robinson called Frank into his office. "I've spoken to the colonel, and he's agreed to take you onto our medical staff. You'll be promoted to corporal and permanently transferred to medical duties."

"Thank you, sir, I am most grateful."

Frank walked quickly back to tell Angela. Running was forbidden in the hospital, except in the direst circumstances.

"That's wonderful, Frank. I'll talk to Mamma tonight," she told him.

She left the hospital as soon as her shift ended and hurried home to the little house on Twenty-Third Street, on the edge of the city. Ever since her father died, money was tight and they'd had to dismiss their house staff. Now the small yard and exterior of the house were deteriorating from neglect, and the home looked a little shabby next to its smart neighbours.

"You're home in good time, child. They running short of injured soldiers for you?"

"No, Mamma. Just finished on time for once," said Angela.

"Why? You caught some disease off one of them? Or got hurt? Some of these soldiers ain't been brought up too good, you know," said her mother as she entered the sitting room.

"Don't worry, Mamma. It's nothing like that. We've got a new staff member at the hospital who needs somewhere to live. The colonel has said that it's everyone's duty to help in the war effort, and so I thought we could rent out our spare room. It would bring in a bit more money and maybe some help around the house. We could really do with a little help. The yard is looking real bad. I even heard some of the neighbours talking about it the other day."

Angela had so far managed to avoid mentioning that the lodger would be a man. She hoped the lure of extra money would be what made her mother agree.

"Yes, Angela, you're right. Bring her around."

Angela's mother was a tall, large-chested, big-boned woman who wore her hair in a bun. She carried a lot of weight and was inclined to sway from side to side as she walked, reminding onlookers of a carthorse. She had long ago lost her looks and now gave the appearance of being a formidable woman indeed. Under her tough exterior, though, there lurked a kindly heart, one she seldom showed to anyone other than Angela, her only child.

"Thank you, Mamma. I think it's the right and proper decision. All of us will have to do what we can if we're gonna defeat these terrible Yankees. I'm going to go back to the hospital to help with the luggage."

Angela ran down the steps and hurried along the road to the hospital. She was determined to have Frank settled before her mother could change her mind. Above all, she wanted to avoid the possibility of him being posted to another unit outside the city if no local accommodation could be found. She arrived at the hospital just as the patients were finishing their evening meal. As usual, Frank was helping an injured soldier, sitting next to him, talking quietly, and encouraging him to eat his food. Angela did not interrupt but waited until he was finished before telling him the news.

Angela and Frank arrived at the house as the evening light was beginning to fade. Angela took him up to his new bedroom and helped him unpack his spare clothes. She showed him where to get water for the wash basin and oil for the lamp, where the shoe-cleaning material was kept, and where the privy was in the backyard. They then returned to the bedroom for him to make himself presentable before she took him to be introduced to her mother.

"I'm so indebted to you, Angela," Frank said. "I don't know what I would have done without you. If only I could get my memory back and remember who I am, I wouldn't be such a burden."

"Frank, you're not a burden at all," replied Angela. "You're the only good thing to come out of this war so far, and probably the last, the way it's going. I must go downstairs now. Come down when you're ready to meet my mother."

As she passed Frank on her way to the door, she brushed against him. He took her hand and held it in both of his. "Truly, Angela, I am so grateful. You've been my saviour."

"I thought I could hear a man's voice," boomed Mrs Cooling from the doorway. "What in the Lord's name is going on here, Angela?"

"Mamma, this is our new lodger, Frank English. Frank, my mother," she said to introduce them.

Frank looked at Mrs Cooling as she filled the doorway, and he swallowed nervously.

"Mrs Cooling, I was just thanking your daughter for being so kind to me. She nursed me back to health, got me a job at the hospital, and now she's found me some accommodation. I owe Angela a great deal, and I was just showing my gratitude. I hope you understand," Frank said.

Angela hoped this fulsome praise would please her mother and allay any suspicions that might have sprung to mind.

"She didn't tell me she was bringing a man home. I'm not sure it's a good idea having you here."

Angela knew Frank was going to have to make a big effort to satisfy her redoubtable mother.

"Angela, come with me," she commanded her daughter.

They left Frank alone in the room, but he could still hear what was being said just outside the door.

"You didn't tell me it was a man you were bringing here!" Mrs Cooling said in a too-loud whisper.

"I'm sorry, Mamma. I knew you'd say no if I told you. I just thought if you were to meet him first, you'd allow him to stay. He's lost his memory and has nowhere to go. Please let him stay," Angela pleaded.

There was a silence as Mrs Cooling considered the ramifications.

"He's English, huh?"

"We think so, but no one knows anything, really."

"All right. He can stay, but he's on probation. I don't want no shenanigans in this house. You hear me?"

"Thank you, Mamma. I'm sure he won't let you down."

Chapter 18

Despite Frank's bad start, Mrs Cooling soon came around, and she let him stay at her house. By the end of August, he was well settled in, and Mrs Cooling had decided he was a nice boy after all. Angela was forgiven, and he was explained away to her friends and neighbours as a convalescent who'd been injured and lost his memory at the Battle of Bull Run. This was pretty much the truth, as far as it was known.

Nevertheless, no one in the neighbourhood could resist speculating on how he'd come to be there, especially once it was discovered that he was English. Frank's consistent good manners, however, convinced everyone that all was well. He soon felt at home in the community, and he found his work at the hospital interesting and satisfying. His good fortune meant he now slept soundly every night.

As their wounds healed, the soldiers began to talk to him about the first great battle of the war. It had been their baptism of fire, and all of them had been amazed at the savagery of the battle. The noise of the guns, their acutely heightened senses, and the huge charge of adrenaline had made the time pass in what seemed like a fleeting moment, all the images and memories jumbled together. No sense could be made of anything until much later, and there came an overwhelming fatigue when it was all over. Even though they had routed the Yankees, they had little energy to pursue them.

Many observers thought this was a lost opportunity that the Confederates would regret in the future, but they weren't doing the fighting. They were all anxious to draw the war to a close, and the more far-sighted of them realised that the South would find a long war more difficult to sustain.

Frank found that, almost to a man, the soldiers believed their officers were incompetent. The more thoughtful among them excused their leaders on the grounds of inexperience. Most of the officers had been to military school, but they had been taught only fifty-year-old theories from the Napoleonic wars. A few of the men also noticed that the Northern officers who had, in the main, been trained in the same military academies were equally out of date.

Some of the soldiers thought they could have won a crushing victory if only they had been better disciplined. One even said that some in his unit had gone off to pick blackberries in the middle of a charge, and the lieutenant in command had been unable to make them obey orders.

One veteran of the war against Mexico said, "None of the men, even the officers, had the right frame of mind for a war. They thought it was all exciting and glorious, whereas, like all wars, it was uncomfortable most of the time, and the action was dangerous and bloody."

A youngster of only seventeen years explained to Frank that everyone found the heat, the heavy uniforms, and the lack of water intolerable, and many fainted. He added with a smile, "It affected the Yankees more than us, as their equipment was heavier and they came from colder climates.

It was nice to know that God was not only on our side, but he had even arranged the weather to help us!"

Frank found that there was a strong belief among the soldiers that God would make sure they won. He listened to their stories about their agony and the lack of help when they lay wounded on the battlefield.

One sergeant told him, "We tried to help one another as best we could, but we had nothing. Some men tore their uniforms to strips for bandages, but that was all. The men who weren't hit carried on with their advance, and the wounded were left on their own. We couldn't do nothin' for the really badly injured. I saw more than one man kill himself because he couldn't take the pain no more. They're gonna have to do something about the medical backup in future. You can't just leave half the army layin' around bleedin' to death. Apart from anythin' else, we're gonna need those men."

Frank made notes of all these remarks. He had an overwhelming urge to commit to paper everything of interest he was told, but he had no idea why. He sometimes felt this was something left over from his previous life, but still no memories came.

When Angela saw some of his writing, she was interested but pointed out that some of the spellings were incorrect. Where he wrote *labour,* for instance, she corrected it to *labor.*

He was sure he was right. "That's how we do it in England," he told her, without even thinking.

As she got to know him better, she found that he used many words, and some phrases, that would never have been used in America, especially the South.

It all emphasised to Frank that he really didn't belong here, but he still didn't know how to go about recovering his memory.

One day, Frank was taking notes while talking to the soldiers when the ward surgeon, Thomas Buston, noticed him.

"What are you writing?" Buston asked. "You seem to be taking a lot of notes there."

"I like to keep a record of what they tell me, sir," replied Frank. "I find what they tell me very interesting, and I'd like to keep notes so I can remind myself of their stories. It's history, sir."

"History, is it? Are you a writer then? A historian?" asked Buston with a hint of sarcasm. "Unusual to find an educated man in *your* position. Most of you can't even write your own name. What are you really, English?"

"I'm just a medical orderly, sir. This is something I do purely for my own interest."

"Maybe you were a journalist, eh? Mind you, I'm not keen on them, even in peacetime. In a war they can be downright dangerous."

Buston let him continue to take down the soldiers' stories but had started to ask others on the staff about Frank. Buston didn't like Frank's "fancy" accent, and he seemed to be growing suspicious of Frank's motives. The atmosphere had been soured, and there soon grew a mutual dislike between the two men.

"Why's he in our army? Have you met anyone who knows him? Anyone from his regiment? What's the real story here?" Buston would ask anyone he thought might be able to provide an answer, but no answers were forthcoming.

He couldn't help thinking that this memory-loss business was a little too convenient, and he was determined to uncover the truth.

Frank was becoming uneasy with the questioning, especially as he couldn't provide any answers. He had the feeling that this man was going to cause him trouble. If only something, anything, would come back to him! If it were not for Angela, these problems would have weighed heavily on his mind, but she made him forget all his troubles. Her laughter, her sweet nature, and the way she held his hand when no one was looking made him happy and content with life, and he took every opportunity to be in her company.

August was a wonderful month for Frank and Angela. The weather was sunny and warm, and the countryside around Richmond was beautiful. After hearing the soldiers' stories, Frank couldn't help feeling it was the calm before the storm, and so he made the most of his good fortune while he could. He had made friends with Mrs Cooling; but, at the same time, he had to make sure he did nothing to upset her, lest she unleash her temper on him. Now, though, she made up hampers for them to take on picnics in the surrounding area. At first, she came with them. But, as time went by, Angela and Frank started going off by themselves. It was a measure of her trust that she allowed it.

On these idyllic days, they went on long walks, held hands, chased each other round trees, and lay in the grass discussing every subject imaginable. As the days spent together became weeks, they became closer, and they eventually kissed. Frank was pleased, but not surprised, when Angela enthusiastically responded. Now, as he lay in bed at night, he could think of nothing else but her. Even his nagging worries about his past were disregarded as thoughts of Angela and what the future might hold took over.

One day, Mrs Cooling had gone to the Ladies of the Confederacy Sewing Circle to help make garments for the troops, leaving Frank and Angela alone in the house together.

"It's amazing how much life has changed, Frank, and the war has hardly started," said Angela. "All these troops everywhere. I don't know. Somehow, the old barriers of society seem to be disappearing."

"Surely that's a good thing, no?"

"I guess." She paused for a moment, a thoughtful look on her pretty face. "In her sewing group, Mamma has some very high-class ladies who would never normally speak to her. There are some others she would consider beneath her. And yet, they're all working together."

"For the common good," Frank put in.

"Sure. We're all in it together, but I wonder what'll happen after the war. I mean, look at us: Mamma would never have left me alone with a man before. Now I spend my whole working day with strange men and my time off with you! Time seems to be passing quicker, and the slow old South is changing," she said wistfully.

"Well, I suppose so, but as I said, surely it's all for the good. Everyone's pulling together. I can't remember what it was like before, so all this is perfectly normal for me."

"Do you love me, Frank?" Angela asked.

It came out unexpectedly, and he was taken completely by surprise. Like most men when asked this question so directly, he was a little reluctant to commit himself.

"Um, I suppose I do, yes," he answered, after a short pause.

"That's not very flattering," she said crossly, and she got up to leave the room.

"Angela, wait. I do love you. Really I do. You just took me by surprise."

She sat back down. "Are you sure?" she asked.

"I dared not tell you before. I thought you'd think I was too forward. I think you are wonderful, marvellous. I think of you all the time. I can't get you out of my mind."

"Well, that's all right then. I needed to know, Frank."

She didn't sound convinced, and Frank thought he'd better act fast to allay any doubts she might have. Angela had brought up the subject, after all. She was looking at him expectantly, so Frank took her hand and drew her towards him. He stroked her cheek, and to his delight, she leant forward so he kissed her full on the lips. They continued for what seemed like hours, their bodies becoming more entwined, the kiss more passionate.

"A-a-ah!!!" There was a scream from the doorway, and they broke their kiss immediately, but it was too late. Mrs Cooling had seen far more than she wanted to.

"How dare you! Out! This time you'll have to go! Angela, how could you?"

"I'm sorry, ma'am," Frank spluttered.

"You're goddamn right you're sorry!" she shouted, her language coarsening in her outrage. "You've taken advantage of me. You've taken advantage of my daughter. You've taken my hospitality, and this is how you repay me! How dare you!" she exclaimed again.

"It's not his fault, Mamma. It was me," interrupted Angela. "It really was me, not Frank."

"I can't believe that! Why would you …?"

"I love him, Mamma. He loves me."

"You're just a child, Angela. You don't know what love is. He's taken advantage of you, and he'll have to go. I will not have a man in my house who can't be trusted with my daughter. I should never have agreed to put you up in the first place," she said, turning to Frank. "You've let me down, young man." She pointed to the door. "Go upstairs and pack your bags. I want you of out here—now!"

"Mamma, please. Let him stay until tomorrow at least. It's late, and he'll have nowhere to stay."

"Perhaps he should have thought of that before behaving so badly! He's let me down, and I want him to go."

"If you throw him out, I'm going with him," cried Angela impetuously.

Mrs Cooling took a sharp intake of breath, her hand coming to her mouth. "Don't be stupid, child. Where will you go? You've never had to look after yourself. You don't know what you're saying."

"I look after injured and dying men every day! I think I can look after myself now." She ran from the room, crying, leaving Frank and Mrs Cooling glaring at each other.

They heard Angela's bedroom door slam shut.

"I know it looks bad, ma'am, but I wouldn't do anything to hurt Angela. If I go tonight, I think she may do something rash. If I could just stay for tonight, I'll look for new lodgings tomorrow."

Mrs Cooling glared at him with a mixture of anger and fear.

Frank realised that she was terrified of losing her daughter. Perhaps there was a way out after all.

Frank went up to his room and quietly closed the door. He lay on the bed, hands behind his head, just staring at the ceiling. The future was suddenly looking a lot less certain. He heard Mrs Cooling close the door to her room a little later, and soon he could hear her snoring contentedly. Still wide awake, he was going over the events of the day in his mind when he heard his door open. Angela crept over to his bed and lay down beside him.

"What will happen to you, Frank?" she whispered. "I want you to take me with you. I love you so much." She put her face against his cheek and whispered into his ear, "I won't let you go by yourself. I would feel so alone."

She leant in further, and Frank drew her to him, then stopped.

"Angela, we mustn't!" Frank had taken Mrs Cooling's anger seriously, and it wouldn't do to upset her further.

"If I didn't know better, I'd think you didn't love me. Show me you love me, Frank." She reached for him in the dark and started unbuttoning his shirt.

Frank found himself becoming aroused. He stood, removed his clothing, and slipped under the covers.

Angela, in complete silence, got there before him.

Again, they kissed, and her hands started exploring his naked body. He ran his hands under her nightdress, tracing the outline of her curves.

"Take this thing off," he commanded hoarsely.

She was giggling quietly but did as he said.

Frank, somewhat to his surprise, found that he knew exactly what he was doing. Another little reminder from his past life, perhaps? His hands roamed freely over her body, and they were both having difficulty keeping the noise down. Angela took him in her hand and guided him into her. Frank's instinct was to throw caution to the winds and hammer away as fast as he could, but a small part of his brain urged restraint, and so he slowed things down, enjoying the sensations, Angela's breath soft on his face. Soon he could hold back no longer, and he came forcefully, trying not to make a sound.

After making love, they were happy to lie in each other's arms, and neither of them slept that night.

As the sun rose, Angela slipped out from under the covers and put her nightdress back on. She kissed him softly and then whispered, "Now you *have* to take me with you, even if Mamma does throw you out of the house."

Chapter 19

Mrs Cooling sat alone in the kitchen. She was nursing her morning cup of coffee, reflecting on the unseemly events of the evening before. She knew, above all, that she didn't want to lose her daughter. Apart from anything else, she needed Angela's wages to help pay the bills—even more so now with prices rising so fast. She also needed the rent money from a lodger. She had surprised herself by becoming very fond of Frank in the past month. Barring yesterday's unfortunate incident, he'd been a model tenant. She told herself that Angela and Frank were simply engaged in a minor flirtation, and that she should give him a chance to redeem himself.

Frank came down for breakfast, followed closely by Angela. They both hesitated at the doorway.

"Good morning, Mrs Cooling," Frank said. He was about to add an apology for the day before, when she interrupted him.

"Come in, come in. You too, Angela. I feel I was perhaps a little hasty last night, Mr English." She still would not call him Frank, even though both he and Angela had pressed her to do so on a number of occasions. "In fact, I was too harsh with both of you. I quite understand you are fond of each other. I also understand that it must sometimes be difficult to control yourselves, especially when you find yourselves alone together. I, too, was young once, you know. That said, I simply will not have that sort of behaviour in my house. Do you understand?"

"I do, Mrs Cooling, and I apologise," Frank said contritely.

"Angela?"

"Yes, Mamma. I'm sorry."

"Good. I accept your apologies. We'll say no more about the matter. Sit down and have some breakfast, both of you."

Frank and Angela looked quickly at each other, glad that things seemed to have been resolved.

"What are you doing today? I suppose you're both off to the hospital?" Mrs Cooling said, answering her own question. "I sure do hope this war ends soon and the Yankees go home, then we can all get back to leading normal lives."

"I hope I can go on working at the hospital, even after the war. It seems strange, but I really enjoy the work," Frank said, half to himself.

"I'm sure you'll be able to," said Angela. "They'll still need nurses in peacetime."

"Yes, but a *male* nurse?" he asked. "Aren't nurses normally all female?"

"Well, yes, but why not a male nurse? You're good at your job, and as I've said before, there are some things a woman just can't do. Anyhow, I think that's all way off in the future. This war's got some time to go before there's any end in sight. After so many were killed and injured at Bull Run, the Yankees aren't just going to disappear."

"Sometimes, Angela," Mrs Cooling mused, "I wonder if I should ever have let you start working at that hospital.

You're picking up all sorts of gossip, more than I think is good for you. I'm going out into the yard to see if the girl's come to do the washing."

After Mrs Cooling had left, Angela turned to Frank and gave him a peck on the cheek.

"I wonder what Mamma would say if she knew what you did last night," she said, her eyes sparkling.

"What *I* did? I seem to remember that it was *you* who came to *my* room. I was all ready to go to sleep."

"Ha! Didn't you enjoy yourself, then?"

"Angela, please. Just behave for a moment. You heard what your mother just said, and you're already kissing me. What if she walked in right this second? Look," he said, clasping her hands in his, "you know I have trouble controlling myself when I'm with you, but I have to. And so do you. We'll find time to be alone, but we can't do anything in the house. We mustn't."

"You're very hesitant all of a sudden. Lost interest now that you've had your way with me, is that it?"

"Of course not. I love you. But I—we—also need somewhere to live."

"I'm disappointed in you, Frank English. If I hadn't made all the running, you'd still be looking at me with adoring eyes and doing nothing about it."

"I told you I love you, and to show you just how much— excuse me a moment," he said, and he rose from his chair. Still holding Angela's hand, he knelt before her. "Angela Cooling, will you do me the great honour of becoming my wife? Um, please?"

Angela's hands flew to her mouth.

"Frank! Oh, Frank, my darling, of course I will!" she said, her heart thumping in her chest. "Wait! I must tell Mamma."

"Later. We've got to go right now, or we'll be late. Tell her this evening when we've got more time."

They set off for work, chattering away, ten to the dozen. They always seemed to have a lot to talk about, but now there was even more. If they were not discussing the details of their life at home, then they were talking about their work or their plans for the future. When they arrived at the hospital, they parted with a quick kiss and went to their own wards.

Frank wasn't used to acting on impulse, and he wondered if he'd done the right thing.

Chapter 20

As August passed into September, the nights grew longer. The number of patients at the hospital had decreased as the minor casualties recovered, then either returned to their units or went home to harvest the crops. Only the seriously wounded were left, many of them dying from gangrene or septic sores. Frank did his best for them, but he could do little more than comfort them and listen to their stories. For the doctors, the only option was to amputate the affected limb before the poison reached the rest of the body.

Some of the remaining casualties who had lost limbs became bitter and very critical of the way they had been led at the Battle of Bull Run. Their commander had been General Beauregard, a veteran of the Mexican war and, for a short time in early 1861, the Superintendent of the United States Military Academy. He was dismissed when he joined the Confederacy and was then immediately made a general by the Southern command. He was put in charge of their forces for the very first engagement at Fort Sumter. Many of the men were prejudiced against him, as he was a French Creole from Louisiana and not a member of the Southern aristocracy.

"Why put in a man who ain't a gentleman? All our other officers are from Virginia or the Carolinas. We would have done better at Bull Run if General Lee was in charge," complained one man to Frank, while he was changing the dressing on the man's amputated leg.

"You can't think like that, soldier. If we're going to win this war, everyone has to pull together. As long as he can do his job, who cares where he comes from?" Frank told him.

"I don't think he can do his job. That's what I'm sayin'. We need proper gentleman officers."

"Well, perhaps he'll get himself killed soon, then they'll put a 'proper' officer in command."

The soldier did not approve of these sentiments, and later, Frank saw him talking to Surgeon Buston. Buston glanced his way while talking to the man, making Frank feel very uneasy.

"Angela," Frank said, during their walk home, "that surgeon keeps giving me odd looks. I'm sure he's discovered something about me. What do you think I should do?"

"Don't worry. I'm sure if it's anything important, he'll come and talk to you about it. Think about something else. Now that we're engaged, what about fixing a date for our wedding?"

"I hadn't really thought about it. Have you got any ideas?"

"Honestly! Do I have to do everything?"

"Well, I'd like it to be soon, but what about your mother?"

"There you go. There's a war on, so everything has to be done in a hurry," Angela teased him. "Don't worry; I'll fix my mother. I'll be able to talk her around."

"Ha! Now who's in a rush?"

They reached their home, and Angela ran up the steps before Frank could stop her. He realised, to his horror, that she intended to ask her mother to arrange the wedding right away! He climbed the steps and rushed into the room after her. Mrs Cooling, who was knitting, looked up in surprise as they both stood before her.

"Goodness me," she said as she put down her work. "You two look like you've run all the way home. What's so important that you had to get back so quickly?" she asked them. "Are you so hungry after a hard day at the hospital, or are you going out this evening? They want you back for another shift? Surely all those brave men must be healed by now. I sometimes wonder if those still there ain't malingerers."

"Mother, please! I want to ask you something. Something important." Angela panted, slowly regaining her breath.

"Whatever it is, compose yourself first, Angela. I'm afraid your manners are not what they once were. Especially since you started at that dreadful hospital," Mrs Cooling told her. "Just because we're at war don't mean everyone has to behave badly, especially a well-brought-up lady like you."

Angela could hardly contain herself. "Mamma! Please listen! This is important," she pleaded.

"Ain't nothing as important as good manners."

"Well, this is, Mamma. We would like to get married!" Angela told her mother.

Suddenly there was a deathly hush in the room. Mrs Cooling's mouth fell open and it seemed like an eternity before she made any sound.

"I can't believe you! What are you saying? Of course you can't marry him! You only met a month ago! And, in case you've forgotten, young lady, you don't know a thing about him. None of us do. He doesn't even know who his mother and father are. This is preposterous!" she remonstrated, her voice growing louder with each word.

"But, Mamma, we love each other!"

"No, no, *no!*" yelled Mrs Cooling. "I won't have it!"

Bringing her voice down to a more normal level, she turned towards Frank. "This is the end, young man. You have pushed me too far! Pack your bags, and leave this house immediately!"

Frank looked at Angela and shrugged in a gesture of resignation. He turned towards the door, but Angela spoke suddenly, astonishing both Mrs Cooling and Frank.

"Mamma, listen! I'm going to have a baby!" she exclaimed.

Mrs Cooling said nothing, just stared at her daughter, her mouth hanging open.

Angela continued in a quieter voice. "Surely you wouldn't want your first grandchild to be born on the street! If I don't marry soon, people will talk; if you throw Frank out, the baby will be illegitimate. Is that what you want, Mamma? A bastard grandchild?"

Mrs Cooling gasped, and the room grew even quieter than before. A tear ran down her cheek.

"Go," she said. "Leave me alone. I want to think."

Once they had left the room, Frank drew Angela to one side.

"Come on, let's go for a walk. We need to talk," he said.

Once they were alone, he asked her, "Expecting? How do you know so soon? And why didn't you tell me first?"

"I'm sorry, Frank, it just came out. I had to say something. I don't know if I'm pregnant or not. It's too soon to tell."

"You mean—" Frank was at a loss for words for a moment. "Angela, your mother's going to know that as well. She's not stupid. As she pointed out, we've only known each other for a few weeks."

"Well, what was I supposed to say? Don't you want to get married?"

"You know I do. I just wish you'd think a bit, instead of just blurting things out."

"Oh, that's good, Mr Smarty-Pants. And what would *you* have said?"

"That's just it, Angela. Don't you see? I can't just think of something straight off. I need to think about it. But, honestly, saying you were expecting—well, it was stupid."

"Stupid? How dare you! Girls get a feeling, you know."

"A feeling? What kind of feeling?"

"Just a feeling. A feeling that I'm expecting. I feel different. I really don't know how to explain it."

"Have you seen a doctor?" he asked, concerned now.

"Not yet, but I will. I promise. I'm past my date ... you know."

"What date?"

"My period, silly. I've never been late before."

"And that means you're expecting, does it?"

"I don't know, Frank. I'll go and see a doctor out of town, where we're not known. He'll be able to tell me. I'm not going to our family doctor. Do you know he damned a girl to hellfire when he found out she was pregnant out of wedlock? It's a bad-enough situation to be in without having some self-righteous man preaching at you."

"Well, it's early days yet. Will he be able to tell you for certain?"

"I don't know. I guess we'll find out, won't we?"

They were silent for the rest of the walk. For once, neither of them could think of anything to say, lost as they were in their own thoughts.

For his part, Frank didn't know whether to sympathise or to congratulate her.

Chapter 21

As the year wore on, supplies of most of life's necessities grew short, and prices rose sharply. The hospital, in particular, was badly affected by the lack of medicines and drugs. A few patients in the fever ward had malaria, which was usually treated quite effectively with five grains of quinine every two hours, for six hours. It was one of the medicines affected by the supply problems, so the doctor in charge of the ward instead prescribed whiskey with ground-down bark of the poplar, dogwood, and willow trees. The patients would only accept this unpleasant concoction as long as Frank added rather more whiskey than the doctor prescribed.

Diarrhoea was also becoming prevalent at the hospital. It was nicknamed the "Virginia Quickstep" or the "Richmond Quickstep" by the patients. The medicine used to treat it, called "Blue Mass" by the soldiers, and "Blue Chalk" by most of the medical staff, was a mixture of mercury and chalk. By the end of September, almost half the patients in the hospital were suffering from the condition, and a few, who were already weak from their wounds, died.

Frank noticed that the cleanest and most disciplined wards had less trouble with the outbreak. He also wrote in his notebook that the greater and longer the dose of the medicine, the more the soldier seemed to suffer. He added in brackets, "I think the medicine sometimes causes more harm than good."

After their day's work, Frank and Angela walked home together, as usual. The autumn weather was beginning to cool—a sure sign that winter was not far away. For a few minutes, they walked without speaking. Frank broke the uncomfortable silence.

"I'm sorry I spoke to you so sharply this morning," he said quietly.

"I'm sorry too, my love. But I'm so confused. I've been thinking about it, and I really don't know if I can be expecting. All the girls at school said you didn't fall until you've done it at least five times. So we should be all right, shouldn't we?"

"I don't know, Angela. That sounds like wishful thinking to me. I thought you were going to see the doctor about it anyway."

"Oh, I am. I have to know. I was just trying to make Mamma agree to a quick wedding, without a lot of fuss. Now I've made things worse! I know Mamma likes you—or, should I say, *liked* you—but I'm sure she doesn't think you're good enough for me. She thinks you may be from a poor background, or even a criminal family! I told her that was highly unlikely, as you speak so well and can write quickly and fluently."

"I hope you're right. I've got a lot of work to do to get back in her good books—and so have you! What do you think she'll say this evening?"

"I don't know. She might let you stay, and she might even insist we get married now. She knows I won't leave you."

"Please, Angela, don't provoke her. Let's just listen to what she has to say first. Don't just jump in; think about what you're going to say first."

"I will. I promise."

Frank noticed that they had taken a wrong turn somewhere.

"Where are we? We've gone the wrong way."

"We're just taking the long way round. I need to talk to you," said Angela.

"What is it?"

"I know it's early, but what if I'm not expecting? Would you still want to marry me?"

"Of course I would! I love you so much, I could forgive you anything. And, once married, always married. No one will be able to separate us."

"Oh, Frank, you're so kind and thoughtful," Angela said affectionately, taking his arm. "You know, I wasn't trying to deceive you before; it just came out in the heat of the moment." She paused a moment. "Jan Pickering fell for a baby before she was wed, and her man blamed her. He beat her wickedly, as though it was all her fault! They married, but it turned out bad for her. He was a real pig, Frank. God forgive me, but it might be for the best if the Yankees got him. She'd be a widow, and then she could marry again."

"Angela, how could you?" gasped Frank. "You're such a sweet girl, but sometimes you say the most wicked things! I think your mother is right about you knowing too much."

"Perhaps I do, but you're such a dreamer, always wondering about your past. It's just as well one of us is a bit tougher and more cunning," she added thoughtfully.

"It's strange, the way you say 'Mother' instead of 'Mamma'. Is that how they speak in jolly old England?" She laughed.

"Angela, please don't make light of it. It frightens me sometimes. Where do I come from? Who am I? I sometimes get the feeling I don't belong here, although I always feel good when I'm with you."

"I've never met anyone who's lost their memory before. I really don't know anything about it. Do you suppose it'll come back one day?"

"I'm in the dark as much as you. I want it to return, but who knows what it'll reveal when it does?"

"Well, we'll be married then, have our own little family. We'll cope with it together. Maybe with our own child too."

"We've still got to win your mother over, don't forget. I hope she lets us marry. I only feel safe when I'm with you. Sometimes I feel so apprehensive and nervous."

"I'm gonna look after you, Frank English. We're gonna be good together."

On arriving home, they nervously entered the kitchen.

Mrs Cooling looked up at them, a grim look on her face.

"Sit down, the pair of you," she told them.

"Mrs Cooling—"

She slapped her hand down on the table, interrupting him. "Quiet now! I've had plenty of time to think this thing through, and you're gonna listen to what I have to say."

Frank did as he was told, and then he reached under the table to hold Angela's hand.

"I'm not blind, and I can see you care very much for each other. Maybe you *are* in love; I don't know. What I do know is that it's too soon for you to know if you're expecting, Angela. I'm disgusted to think that you have had … um …

relations before getting married. Besides, you've only known each other for such a short time! When did this happen?"

"Mamma!" Angela protested, blushing profusely.

"A week ago? Two weeks? The day you met?" she yelled.

Angela wouldn't meet her mother's eyes and said nothing.

"It was about two weeks ago, ma'am," Frank said quietly.

"You may not like me asking you these questions, girl, but I'm trying to do the best for you here. I have to know."

"Yes, Mamma. It was like Frank said."

"Two weeks ago," continued Mrs Cooling. "Far too soon to know. Even the doctor won't be able to tell you for a good while yet. Nevertheless, there is a possibility that you are expecting, and I will not have you for an unmarried mother."

Angela wiped her eyes, looking at her mother hopefully.

"There really is no other course. You will have to get married as quickly as we can arrange things."

"Thank you, Mrs Cooling."

"Thank you, Mamma."

"Don't thank me. None of this changes my feelings about your behaviour. I am truly upset and disgusted with both of you. And one last thing. I *insist* that you behave yourselves from now on. I understand that you're courting, and you may hold hands or some such. That's all—no kissing or anything else until you're married. Do we understand each other?" she asked, staring hard at Frank.

"We do, ma'am. Thank you."

Chapter 22

News came into the hospital of a battle at Carnifex Ferry. It had taken place on 10 September, in south-western Virginia, where there were pockets of settlers who supported the Confederacy, while other areas were pro-Union.

"I hear that our troops were beaten at Carnifex Ferry. They had to withdraw across the Shenandoah River. The area's in the hands of the Yankees now," Frank said to Angela. "This must be bad news for the government. They would have wanted western Virginia to support them."

"You're always so pessimistic, Frank!" Angela scolded him. "I hear our troops fought ever so bravely, even though they were outnumbered. Some people say we really won the battle, as we gave them a pretty good hiding. They took lots of casualties. In any case, they say we're still ambushing them. Shooting them at the front is too good for them," she said with feeling.

A few days later, news came that General Lee had been beaten at Cheat Mountain. When Frank mentioned it, Angela turned on him.

"There you go again, always putting our side down! General Lee is a fine man and a good leader. His men let him down, and the Yankees took advantage. Sometimes I wonder just whose side you're on, Frank English."

Frank wisely decided to keep his thoughts to himself. Angela was very biased in favour of the Southern troops and hated to admit they could be beaten. Many Virginians were like her, and Frank didn't think it would do him any good to contradict her, especially in public. Anyway, what was the point of annoying the girl he loved? There were plenty of other more desirable topics of conversation, and certainly nicer thoughts.

It had been decided that the wedding should take place at the beginning of October, and Mrs Cooling had already started making arrangements. Frank and Angela thought they ought to see the doctor before then, so they set out early one Saturday on horses hired from the local blacksmith. They arrived just before noon at a village with only a small cluster of houses and a tiny church. The surgery was at the far end of the main street, and it was one of the more substantial buildings.

"What if the doctor says you're not expecting? Your mother may call off the wedding."

"Let's find out first, then we can decide what to do," Angela replied. "And try not to look so worried! We'll work it out. You'll see."

"What excuse will you give the doctor for arriving out of the blue?" Frank asked.

"Honestly, Frank! You *do* go on! I shall think of something if he asks," Angela told him. "I hope you remembered to bring the money. This doctor has quite a reputation for charging strangers as much as he thinks their pockets can stand. On the other hand, he's supposed to be very discreet, and they say he doesn't give moral lectures, like so many of them do. Now be quiet, and leave the talking to me."

Angela walked up the path to the large, white, wooden front door, followed by Frank. He noticed that not only were the walls of this building made of brick, unlike the rest of the houses in the village, but also that the door was of very heavy construction. There was a brass plaque to the side of it, inscribed with the words "Benjamin Jeffries, MD."

A hatchet-faced woman in her forties with a guttural German accent opened the door at Angela's knock. There wasn't even a hint of a smile of welcome. She looked both of them up and down and invited Angela inside.

"Your man cannot enter. If he is paying, get ze money off him now," she growled.

There was no doubt that it was a command, but Angela didn't ask Frank for any money.

"Won't be long," she said as she disappeared into the house.

"Ve are running a little late. Sit zere," the woman pointed to a bench. "Ze doctor vill call you ven he is ready."

She turned round sharply and marched down a short passage to a room at the back of the house. Angela watched her go, struck by her appearance. She had on a dark-blue dress, with a soiled white pinafore pinned high up over her chest. Round her thick waist was a well-worn leather belt and, hanging from the side, a large bunch of keys. Although she looked a little like the nurses at the Richmond hospital, she did not look or smell at all clean. She had the grainy look of neglected old furniture, and there was an unpleasant musty smell about her.

Suddenly, there was a scream from the room down the hall, and a girl's voice cried out. "Oh no! A-a-agh! The pain! Stop the pain!"

The German woman appeared again and went into what was obviously the surgery. Angela could hear a muffled conversation, and then the woman emerged with a tall, heavily-built man whom Angela assumed was Dr Jeffries. Between them was a very distressed girl of similar age to herself, whom they were helping out of the room. Once she was out, the doctor returned to his surgery, while the woman dragged the sobbing girl down the passageway to the rear of the building. The woman returned shortly with a long-handled mop and wiped away the trail of blood the poor girl had left in her wake.

After this little episode, Angela was tempted to run off without seeing the doctor, but just as she hesitated, he appeared, his hands dripping with water. He had just washed them but had not bothered to dry them.

"Come into the surgery, and we'll have a look at you," he invited in a surprisingly soft voice. "Lie down on the bed, and we will get you sorted out."

The woman came back into the room, and she deftly removed Angela's underclothes. She lifted her legs and strapped them up, wide apart, a procedure that was not performed with any gentleness. She pulled the straps down as tight as they would go, and the doctor turned towards a tray of gleaming metal instruments.

"I didn't think that all this was necessary, just to see if a girl was carrying a child," Angela whispered fearfully.

"Don't be silly, girl! You have come here to have it removed, have you not?" asked the woman brusquely. "You girls are happy to misbehave and have your fun, and ven you vant ze doctor to help you, you do nassing but vhine."

"Stop!" Angela yelled. "I don't want it taken away. I just want to know if I'm expecting. I want to keep the baby. Oh God. *Stop,* please!"

"What's going on here? You are Betty Rumbold, are you not?" asked Jeffries.

Despite her predicament, Angela was shocked to hear the doctor mention her well-to-do neighbor.

"No, I'm not. I didn't make an appointment. I only came here so that you could confirm whether I'm having a baby."

"Didn't you ask her name?" the doctor asked, turning to the nurse. "For God's sake, Helga! I've always told you to make sure you know who the patient is! How many times do I have to tell you?"

Angela thought he was about to poke the nurse in the stomach with his operating probe when there was a sudden knock on the front door.

"I wonder if *that's* Betty Rumbold. Well, go and answer it, you stupid woman!"

He turned back to Angela. "I am so sorry, my dear. This is no way to treat a lady." With a deft flick of his hands, he released each strap and lowered her legs to the bed.

Angela was shaking and had gone pale, in shock at what had nearly happened. The doctor brought her a glass of water. Angela was grateful for the gesture but just wanted to get out of the place as soon as possible.

"Are you all right, my dear?" he asked.

"Quite all right, Doctor, thank you."

"Now let's see. It won't take a moment," he said, running his hands over her belly. "As you had no appointment, I guess you haven't paid."

"That's right, Doctor."

"Usually I ask for payment in advance. Five dollars."

Angela looked at him in surprise.

The doctor thought for a moment.

"Owing to our little misunderstanding, we will lower the charge to two dollars. That's on the condition that you don't mention what has happened here to anyone."

"Of course, Doctor. It was just a mistake, and I won't say a word. My husband is outside. He'll give the money to your nurse."

"Good. By the way, you are pregnant," he added, almost as an afterthought.

The nurse came back into the room. She even made an attempt to smile as she showed Angela out of the surgery and then to the front door.

A young girl was sitting on the bench, and she blushed as Angela passed. It was Betty Rumbold, she realised with a start. She lived opposite Angela and her mother, and came from a wealthy family well known in Richmond society.

"Hello," Angela said with a smirk. "Fancy seeing you here, Miss Rumbold. I always thought that man of yours, the one you meet behind your garden hedge, would get you into trouble one day."

"How do you know about that? You won't tell my mamma, or especially papa, will you, Angela? They would throw me out of the house if they knew!" she pleaded.

"Your secret is safe with me, Betty, now that we know each other so well."

"Oh, thank you, Angela. It would be awful if they found out. By the way, why are *you* here?" she asked, suddenly suspicious.

"Frank and I were just spending a day riding in the country, and some thorns tore my skin. The doctor gave me a dressing. I'm certainly not here for the same reason as you!"

Betty blushed again and looked down at her hands.

"Goodbye, Betty," Angela said, a hint of sadness in her voice. She would never before have dared to call a high-society girl by her Christian name. In future, however, Miss Rumbold would be Betty to her.

As Angela walked back to Frank, she thought to herself that the day certainly had not been wasted. You never knew when it would be useful to have some secret information.

CHAPTER 23

Angela told her mother that the doctor had confirmed she was expecting a child, and so a definite date was set for the wedding. Mrs Cooling hid her anger and frustration by throwing herself into the preparations. She began by making a dress for her daughter, as well as dresses for each of the bridesmaids, her nieces Rosemary and Celia.

Angela decided to ask Betty Rumbold to attend her wedding. Before their meeting at the doctor's surgery, she would never have been so presumptuous.

One evening, as it was getting dark, Angela saw Betty in her summer house with her young man. Since he was only a horse-trader, he was not welcome in the Rumbold house, but Angela had to admit he was very handsome. She watched them from her garden, and as soon as he left, hugging the shadows as he went, Angela crossed the road and called through the bushes, "Betty! Betty!"

"Oh, my good Lord! You frightened me, Angela!" squealed Betty. "What are you doing?"

"I'm getting married soon. If I give your butler an invitation to the wedding, will you come?"

"You want me to come to your wedding? We hardly know each other, Angela, and we certainly don't move in the same circles," she said haughtily.

Angela decided that she needed to refresh Betty's memory about their last meeting. The girl was starting to behave in her superior manner again.

"Don't you remember our meeting at the doctor's, Betty? I'm just asking you to do me a little favour. After all, I *am* keeping a secret for you."

"Angela! Ssh! Keep your voice down."

"If you carry on with that fellow in such a passionate manner, you'll soon be needing another visit to the doctor," she told Betty. "Not only is it costly, but you know you'll eventually be found out."

"You promised not to say anything."

"And I'll keep my promise. Don't worry. I'm just saying that these things have a way of coming out. That doctor's none too gentle either. And, as for that nurse of his! I'm sure she's rough on purpose!"

"She sure is rough. I never want to go there again!"

"Well, let your man know when to stop. You have to, or you'll go too far, and you know what'll happen then. He's very free with his hands, isn't he?"

"You saw me with Ambrose? Were you spying on me?"

"Of course not. I heard some noise, and I just came over to see what it was. If I can discover you so easily, so can anyone else."

"Oh, Angela. He's so wonderful. I can't resist him when he puts his arms around me. I don't know what to do. I just can't stop seeing him, and I feel completely unable to resist him," Betty told her. "I just meekly give way. Angela, you're a nurse. Isn't there some way of stopping a baby?" Betty had become so emotional that tears welled up in her eyes.

"There is a girl at the hospital—a country girl. I've heard that she sells a potion. You're supposed to take it immediately after leaving your man, and again at the time of your monthly bleeding," said Angela. "I don't know if it works or what it costs."

"Oh, please try to get me some. I'm desperate, Angela. It doesn't matter what it costs."

"You will come to the wedding?"

"Yes, of course I'll come. You'll get the potion?" Betty pleaded.

Angela nodded. She was delighted. As soon as she had the potion, Betty would be dependent on her, and she would be a trustworthy ally—she couldn't afford to be anything else.

The date for the wedding was fast approaching. However, with Angela already nearly a month into her term, the child would be born, at most, only eight months after the marriage. This was bound to set tongues wagging, but they would deal with it when the time came.

Frank had no relatives that he knew of, and no close friends, so he asked some of the staff at the hospital to attend the wedding as his guests. He included Surgeon Buston on the list, in the hope that the surgeon would look on him more favourably now that he was to be married.

Among Angela's relatives, an aunt from South Carolina and a cousin from North Carolina were both coming. Mrs Cooling hoped that one of them would recognise Frank or be able to help with information about his background. Families were spread far and wide in the South, and gossip tended to do the same. Surely an Englishman would have attracted a lot of attention in such a close-knit community.

"I wonder whether Aunt Lillie or Cousin Gwendoline will know Frank," Mrs Cooling said to her daughter. "It would be nice to know who he really is before the wedding. He might be some farmer form the hills; you never know. Some real bad white trash," she speculated, only half joking.

"Mamma! It's a bit late now," Angela said, laughing. Then, she continued in a more serious tone. "He's not anything like that. Look how kind he is, what good manners he has, and how he eats his food. And that accent! I bet he's from a real good family who are missing him terribly. Really, Mamma, you do worry so much about where people come from. In any case, what would happen to me without him? And the baby without a father?"

"Perhaps I should have said this before. You *do* know there are ways of getting rid of unwanted babies, don't you? You're not too far gone."

"Mamma!" Angela said with a gasp. She had no idea that her mother knew of such matters. "How could you suggest such a thing?"

"Anything is better than marrying the wrong man," Mrs Cooling said. "Remember, you'll have to live with him for the rest of your life. I want you to be happy, Angela. We don't want a ne'er-do-well in this family. We can't afford it, for one thing. Look at what happened to the Whistlers. Their daughter, Emily, married that gambler, didn't she? He nearly bankrupted that family."

"I *am* happy, Mamma. Truly I am. I love Frank, and I can't imagine life without him. Please, try not to worry. I'm sure he's a good man."

The day of the wedding arrived, and the church was full of Angela's friends and relatives. Frank had asked a young doctor from the hospital, Samuel Thomson, to act as his best man. The wedding music started, and Frank looked round to see Angela coming up the aisle, looking beautiful in her special dress. Suddenly, he was seized by the feeling that he had been in a very similar situation only a short while before. Sweat began to run down his face, and he felt faint. He was swaying as if he were about to collapse when Samuel took his arm to steady him.

"Take it easy, fella. It's only your wedding, not a law court. You ain't on your way to the firing squad." Samuel smiled encouragingly.

Frank's giddy moment passed, but he was still in a state of panic and was now gripped by the urge to run. But then, when he looked at Angela, he wondered how he could think of doing any such thing. To the congregation, he seemed like the perfect bridegroom, and the whole episode passed as if he were in a dream. As he walked down the aisle, arm in arm with Angela, he felt like he was floating. Then, when they left the church and stepped into the road, reality suddenly returned. He looked around in bewilderment for a moment. When Angela squeezed his arm, he realised where he was and what he was doing. He found that he couldn't remember a thing about the service, but his feelings of uneasiness were replaced by a wonderful sense of pride and security as he realised he was at last married to this lovely girl who was carrying his child. Angela was the love of his life, the centre of his universe, and unlike most husbands, he also felt she was the rock on which his entire life depended. He looked into her eyes, smiled, then helped her into the carriage.

The wedding breakfast was held in the local hall, a white wooden-clapboard building that had been specially decorated for the occasion. While they were having drinks and chatting to the guests, Frank noticed Buston was among the guests. He nudged Angela and pulled her towards him.

"I was hoping Buston wasn't going to turn up. Did you hear that he had accepted? Or had your mother?" he asked.

"I have had no reply from him, Frank, and Mamma wouldn't have. She certainly wouldn't approve," she whispered.

"Shall I tell him to leave?" asked Frank.

"No, leave him. It would only cause a commotion," she responded.

At that moment, Ambrose approached Buston, and they were soon leaning in to each other in whispered conversation. Frank saw that he was the subject of their discussion when they both slyly looked over at him.

"Look at those two getting together. How do they know each other? I don't like it, Angela. They're up to something for sure," he said.

"Stop worrying, Frank. This is our wedding day, and there are lots of people who want to meet you. This is Aunt Lillie, who comes from North Carolina. She has lived in both the North and the South."

A small, plump lady, smelling strongly of perfume and with cheeks far rosier than nature intended, gave Angela an effusive embrace and kissed Frank rather sloppily on his cheek.

"So, this is the young man about whom your mother has written in such detail," gushed Aunt Lillie, adding coquettishly, "I must say, Angela, he's very handsome."

"And I'm very pleased to meet you, madam," Frank said with a small bow of the head.

"Please, call me Lillie, Frank. We're all family now! Gosh, that sure is some accent you got there. I'm afraid I don't recognise you though. I'd sure remember you! I'll have to make enquiries when I get home. Don't worry. I'll find out who you are—I'm a very persistent person!"

A tall, angular woman then approached, wearing a long string of pearls and a shiny silk dress that seemed to hang straight down from her shoulders.

"This is Cousin Gwendoline, also from Carolina."

"South Carolina, Angela," she corrected in a flat, unemotional voice. She turned to Frank and held out her hand. "Mr English," she said.

"Ma'am, call me Frank, please," he said, lightly shaking her hand.

"It's nice to meet you, Frank. Angela's mother has told me about your memory problems. I'm afraid I've never met you before, but I know lots of people in the area. I was a schoolteacher you know, and now I'm a school inspector. I'll make some enquiries, and I'm sure Aunt Lillie or I will be able to trace your family. It would be wonderful to be able to reunite you with them. I expect your mother and father are grieving for you."

Frank was starting to feel uneasy again, but he couldn't figure out why. What was going on? Had he committed a crime before losing his memory? He couldn't really imagine that he had; he didn't think he had it in him to break the law. How could his entire character have changed to the mild-mannered individual he was now if he had been a violent criminal? But, every time someone talked about looking into his past, this feeling of dread came over him, making him constantly on edge.

"Frank, you're dreaming again," Angela said, interrupting his thoughts. "You don't seem very happy. What is it? What are you worried about? It's not very flattering you know. We've only been married for five minutes!"

"I'm sorry, Angela. I just can't get it out of my head, especially with everyone wondering the same thing. Who the hell am I?"

At that moment, he saw Ambrose leaving the hall with Buston. They were an odd pair to join forces, a professional gentleman and a horse-trader.

"Excuse me, Angela. I won't be a moment."

"Frank? Frank! Where are you going?" Angela called, but he had already moved out of earshot.

Frank hurried through the doorway and down into the road. In the distance, he saw the two men enter a building used by the army police.

Chapter 24

The newlyweds had no time for a honeymoon. The only real difference to their lives after the marriage ceremony was that they were allowed to sleep in the same bedroom. Now that Mrs Cooling was satisfied that all was respectable—something very important to her—she would at last call Frank by the name Angela had given him. To him, however, she was still, and always would be, Mrs Cooling.

Frank was reading news of the war at sea while lying in bed, waiting for Angela to finish washing.

"It says here that the Union navy has captured Fort Walker and Fort Beauregard, and that means they now command Fort Royal Sound. It's not going well at the moment, I'm afraid."

"Oh, Frank, can't you find any good news?"

"I'm just telling you what it says here. I can't find much good news," Frank replied. "They do say that Santa Rosa Island, down in Florida, is held by a mere lieutenant. How about that? Most of the Union armies have given way to our forces, but the few that haven't will have to be captured soon; otherwise, they'll cause havoc behind our lines."

"Stop it, Frank! Let the soldiers do the fighting. Your job is to work at the hospital and to make me happy."

They agreed about almost everything except the war. Frank tried to look at it logically, while Angela was hopeful and romantic. She was also convinced that the Southerners were superior to the Yankees in every way.

Angela and Frank went back to work on the Monday after the wedding. Buston, the surgeon, sent for Frank and requested that he come to his office next to his consulting room. On entering, Frank found two uniformed military policemen waiting for him, one sitting either side of Buston. The office was bare but for a small square table and four chairs. A picture of Charleston hung on the wall, slightly relieving the room's sparseness.

"Sit down, English," commanded the surgeon. "This is Lieutenant Devereaux and Sergeant Corey. We have reason to believe you are a spy in our camp. You have some questions to answer."

"A spy?!" Frank exclaimed. He had been terrified until this moment, but such a ridiculous accusation made him want to laugh out loud. The trouble was, they obviously believed it, and that meant they were deadly serious. It was worse than anything he had imagined. What would they do now? Were they going to shoot him, without even having a trial?

"Excuse me, sir," said Devereaux. A young lieutenant, he was deferential to the surgeon. Addressing Frank, he continued, "Surgeon Buston has denounced you as a Union spy. What do you have to say for yourself?"

"The very idea is preposterous! I was brought here unconscious from a head wound at the Battle of Bull Run. I lost my memory, and it still hasn't returned. Believe me, I truly wish to know who I am and where I'm from, but I simply don't know. I don't know what's given him the idea that I'm a spy, but I can tell you I've done nothing wrong. I spend all my time here trying to help these men."

"Firstly, you speak with an English accent. How do you explain that?"

"I can't explain it," protested Frank. "I just told you that I've lost my memory!"

"Secondly," he continued, as if Frank had said nothing, "how do you account for the fact that you have been seen writing in a notebook on a number of occasions? I've heard of ladies keeping a diary, but they usually do their writing in private. It's very unusual behaviour for a man, especially an enlisted soldier."

"I told Surgeon Buston that I have this need—call it an urge, or a desire, if you will—to write down the soldier's stories. Maybe it's something carried over from my past; I don't know, as I can't remember. But I find all the stories interesting, and in a way, I'm recording history. I would like to write a history of the war after we've won."

"Pah!" Buston guffawed. "This is stupid talk. The man is clearly a spy!"

Frank looked at the three men. He could see no pity in the eyes of Buston or Sergeant Corey. However, Devereaux appeared to have some doubts.

"There is a case to answer here," the lieutenant said. "You will appear at a court martial which will get to the bottom of things. This case is too complex for me to make a quick judgement. I'll have to pass it on to higher authority.

"Corporal English," he added formally, "I will report this hearing to my colonel. You may not leave Richmond, and you will appear at any future hearing on the date specified. Do you understand?"

"Yes, sir," Frank said quietly.

"I know Mrs Cooling," the lieutenant continued. "She and her daughter are well known as strong supporters of the Confederacy. As you and Angela are now married, you may stay at their house. I know I can trust them with the responsibility. You are to go nowhere else, clear?"

"Yes, sir," Frank said again. "Just one thing, sir."

"Go on."

"May I continue to work at the hospital until the court meets?" Frank asked, not only because he needed to work but also because he felt it would count in his favour. "I don't want to waste my time doing nothing when I could be of use."

"I can see no reason why not," replied Devereaux. "In fact, I think we should ask Surgeon Buston to require you to come to work each day. Surgeon?"

"Yes, that'll be fine. I'll keep an eye on him, for sure," said Buston with menace in his voice. Turning to Frank, a smile playing at the corners of his mouth, he said, "You will report to me every morning at seven o'clock, every day at noon, and every evening at five o'clock. Make sure that you do so and that you are on time. Miss any of your appointments, or come in late, and I shall immediately report you as a renegade. I will issue orders that you are to be shot on sight!"

"I think that's a little harsh, Surgeon," said Devereaux. "After all, he hasn't been charged with anything yet."

"Lieutenant, you have left me in charge of this man while he is at the hospital," Buston said harshly. "I'll do as

I think fit to make sure he doesn't abscond. Some of you young officers do not seem to realise that we are in the middle of a war! Our way of life, our very existence, is in jeopardy!"

Turning to Frank, Buston said, "You are dismissed, Corporal."

Frank saluted, turned, and left the room. He had managed to get through the interview, and he was still, technically, a free man. He had no idea why Buston despised him so, and now he'd have to watch his every move. Buston had left Frank in no doubt that, given any excuse, he would delight in having him shot.

Frank left the office and hurried to Angela's ward to tell her what had happened. As usual, she gave him good advice and suggested he tell no one until they could discuss the matter on the way home.

Frank could hardly wait until five o'clock when he could finally go off duty. After reporting to Buston as instructed, he waited at the hospital entrance for Angela. It had been difficult for him to keep quiet about what had happened at the hearing. He'd wanted to tell his patients, especially his favourites, some of whom he now regarded as friends. He was keen to know what Angela would suggest for his defence, including who could act as a witness for him. In Richmond society, Mrs Cooling was the only person he knew, and she wasn't really high society. What he needed was someone from one of the most important families in the town to vouch for him.

At last, the time came to go home, and Angela met him at the hospital gates. She looked lovely in her uniform, and he realised how lucky he was to have such a beautiful, intelligent wife. He thought that she was gradually mellowing and becoming wiser as the war progressed. He also noticed that the belt round her waist was slightly tighter than usual, but the baby surely could not be beginning to show yet. She wasn't even two months along.

He hurried over to her. "I've been itching to talk to you all day," he said. "What do you think I should say at the court martial?"

"It'll be fine, Frank. Don't get too excited. Just act naturally. You've got nothing to fear, have you? I really do hate that Buston fellow," she exclaimed, in a sudden show of temper. "I'll make him regret the day he dared to get you into trouble."

"Don't get upset, Angela, it's not good for you while you're expecting. What we need is someone who will vouch for my good behaviour and loyalty. Someone of good standing in Richmond."

"I know just the person." Angela said with a sly smile. "Miss Betty Rumbold will, I'm sure, be pleased to help."

"Betty Rumbold?" asked Frank, puzzled. "Why should she?"

"Don't worry about why. Let's just say she owes me a favour. She may take a little persuading, but she'll do it," Angela said with determination.

Somehow, Frank always felt much better after sharing his problems with Angela. He now felt sure that the accusation of spying would be shown to be the farce it was. Now, if he could just recall something of his past, he could clear up any other concerns anyone might have.

On arriving home, they sat down and had their dinner. They had agreed not to tell Mrs Cooling too much, but they had to let her know that an army officer would be coming to see her and that Frank must not leave the house except to go to work.

"Why ever not?" she asked grimly. "I knew there was something wrong about you, my lad! Didn't I tell you he was a bad lot, Angela? But, no, you wouldn't hear a word against him. Now the army have him under house arrest! What are the neighbours gonna think?"

Once again, Angela had it all worked out and came to his rescue.

"Don't worry, Mamma. It's nothing serious. You must realise that they have to be careful now that there's a war on. Frank's lost his memory, so of course they want to know who he really is."

Mrs Cooling was only slightly mollified. "Well, at least it ain't a criminal matter!" she muttered.

Chapter 25

It had become quite the fashion in Richmond to throw parties in aid of the troops; as a result, some of the entrenched social barriers were breaking down. Old society families found it difficult to refuse invitations from tradesmen and others who had wealth but were of a lower standing. To refuse to go to a gathering in aid of the army would look rude and unsympathetic.

Angela thought she should ask her mother to have a small party in aid of the troops, comfort for the soldiers. She primed Frank so that he could sound very keen and offer to help prepare for such an event. If Frank could help her mother with the work, the prospect would surely be more appealing.

"Mamma, what do you think of holding a small party for our gallant troops? Mrs Fitzpatrick down the road has had one, and she's even less well off than we are. Remember, her husband's been dead these past five years, and now her son's been killed at Bull Run," Angela gushed, giving her mother no time to reply.

Frank took over. "I think that's an excellent idea, Mrs Cooling," he said. "I would be pleased to do anything I can to help. I can also help out a little with the expenses, as there's some left out of my last month's pay, even after paying for my rent and everything else," he said, reminding her that he was an important contributor to the household budget.

Mrs Cooling seemed taken by surprise by this two-pronged attack, but she quickly regained her composure. Angela thought her first reaction would be to refuse the notion of a party. She was surprised when, after a moment's reflection, her mother decided it might be a good idea after all. Angela knew Frank would contribute a large chunk towards the expenses, she would do most of the work, and her mother would gain a better reputation in the local community, something that would appeal to her immensely. Angela thought of Frank's offer of help. To her mother, he must seem like two people in one body. First, he'd do something to offend her, and then he'd make a gesture like this. One minute, she seemed to dislike and distrust him; the next, she'd praise him as the perfect son-in-law.

"Very well, but I shall hold you two to your promises. I'm not doing all the work myself. First, we must make a list of the people to invite," Mrs Cooling said. She then reeled off the names of every friend she could think of.

"We mustn't only have friends, Mamma," said Angela. "It's usual to invite a few wealthier people, businessmen, and some of the older families. What about Mr Rowlinson?"

Angela knew her mother had a soft spot for Mr Rowlinson, a local business owner, despite the fact that he was a married man. She had seen them talking and laughing in his shop when there was no-one else there and his wife was out the back. It was unusual to see her mother laughing at any time, but she'd even seen them touching hands while he helped her get something down from a shelf. Even if her mother snootily regarded him as "trade", she would still want him to come.

"I suppose that would be the right thing now that we are at war," said Mrs Cooling, blushing slightly. "Angela, make a note. We will head the invitation 'A Party in Support of Our Gallant Soldiers'. I think that will make it clear that not everyone present is an intimate friend."

"I think we should also invite the Rumbold family," said Angela. "I know Betty quite well. Her family would add a touch of class to the party, and they'll have to donate more than everyone else because of their standing."

"I really don't know, Angela. I've never known you call on them. They didn't even speak to me at your wedding. Do you really think we should invite them?"

"I often speak to Betty, Mamma. I call her Betty, and she calls me Angela. We're quite old friends now."

"You *do* surprise me, Angela. Again, you seem like such a sweet girl most of the time, and then, all of a sudden, you behave in the most unconventional way. You must get it from your father. He could be quite the maverick at times," Mrs Cooling said wistfully. A tear welled up in her eye as memories of the past came back. She quickly wiped it away before it rolled down her cheek. Her ample bosom rose and fell as she gave a large sigh.

Angela crossed the road as the sun went down that evening, and she saw Betty in the Rumbolds' summer house, waiting for her lover. Angela called out, and Betty turned round, clearly startled.

"Angela! You frightened me. I thought for a moment you were my mamma," said Betty in a hoarse whisper. "What do you want?"

"We're having a party in aid of the troops, and we would like your family to come. I want to make sure your father and mother accept the invitation. You owe me a favour, after all."

"If I persuade Papa to come, then I want you to forget where we met, Angela."

"I don't think you're in any position to make demands of me, Betty, do you? Anyway, don't you want the medicine we spoke about?"

"Of course I do! When can you get it?"

"I'll get it as soon as I can. What's the urgency? You're not expecting again, are you?"

"No, of course I'm not!" Betty said crossly.

"I'm only asking. I can see you in the bushes most nights, cuddling your man. It would hardly be surprising."

"Cuddling is all we do now."

Angela raised a sceptical eyebrow. She said in a loud whisper, "He won't be satisfied with that for long, I bet. But your secret is safe with me. See you at our party."

CHAPTER 26

The day of the party arrived, and all of the guests that had been invited came, including, to Frank's surprise, Surgeon Buston.

"What's he doing here? He's the last man I wanted to see," hissed Frank angrily into Angela's ear.

"It's all right, Frank. I invited him."

"But why?"

"You ought to know by now that there's always a reason for everything I do. Just be patient, and you'll see. What I'm doing is going to help you."

"Help me how?"

"Patience, Frank, please! Sometimes you just seem too naive; you don't seem to understand the ways of the world at all. Let's just say that, occasionally, for the sake of self-preservation, we have to do things that are not very nice," she said mysteriously.

"Angela, I haven't a clue what you're up to, but you know I trust you. I'm sure you're acting in my best interest. I'm a lucky man to have you to protect me. I don't know where I'd be without you." He sighed. "Just please don't do anything stupid."

Angela smiled at him and squeezed his hand before moving off to resume her duties as hostess, greeting new arrivals and handing out the treats she and her mother had made. Mr Rowlinson arrived alone, and Angela saw her mother go directly to him. She was obviously pleased to see him but treated him no differently from any of her other friends. Angela was impressed with her acting abilities, given what she knew of their relationship.

At last, Angela sought out Mr Rumbold and managed to speak to him as he was moving from one group to another.

"Mr Rumbold, I would like to ask for your help and advice on a small matter. May I come and see you some time?"

"Certainly, my dear. Let me see, I have a little time to spare tomorrow afternoon. Shall we say about four o'clock?"

"Four o'clock. Thank you, sir."

"It's nothing serious, I hope."

At that moment, a neighbour came bustling up and said gushingly, "Oh, Mr Rumbold, it's wonderful to see you at the parties supporting our troops, you being such a pillar of the community an' all."

"I wouldn't miss it for the world, ma'am."

Angela left them to it and continued round the room, offering her guests canapés. She had found Mr Rumbold far more approachable than she had expected. His cultured manner and deep voice, with just a trace of a Southern accent, were most appealing. As she made her way back down to the kitchen to replenish the plates, Mr Rumbold called to her from a side room.

"Don't worry, dear. I know you wanted to speak to me, and it's difficult to find somewhere quiet at these parties. What can I do for you?"

Angela had been startled when he called out, but his pleasant voice calmed her nerves. She entered the room and closed the door behind her.

"It's about my husband, Frank," she began. "He's been accused of spying, and he has to appear at a court martial. The whole thing's ridiculous, of course, made up by a nasty, vindictive man with nothing better to do. I hoped you could give me some advice about what to do."

"Advice, huh? And if I advise you, what will you do for me?" he asked, running his finger down her arm.

"Whatever do you mean, sir?"

"I mean, one good turn deserves one in return, does it not?"

Angela noticed his hands were much larger and stronger than Frank's. She knew she should put a stop to whatever he had in mind, right now. Instead, she heard herself say, "I'll certainly help you if I can, Mr Rumbold."

"Excellent, Angela. May I call you Angela? I think I may be able to help you." He gently brushed her hair away from her face. "Yes, I believe we could cooperate. Yes, indeed."

Angela was starting to shake. Surely he didn't mean what she thought he meant. He was just being friendly, wasn't he?

"I'm on the committee that liaises with the army on these sorts of matters. I'm sure I'll be able to help," he said.

"Oh, thank you, sir. That would be so good of you."

She turned to go, but he gripped her arm and pulled her to him. He looked into her eyes and seemed to have a hypnotic effect on her. She didn't resist, although a part of her mind was telling her to get out of there right now. He ran his hand over her breasts and stomach while she stood as rigid as a statue. She knew she should stop him, but she stifled a scream and let him continue. He'd said he would help Frank, and that was all that mattered to her. If she offended him now, she knew he would be very unpleasant. Frank could go to jail or even be shot, and Rumbold would probably help him on his way.

"Don't forget, Angela. My house tomorrow afternoon at four. My wife and children will be visiting their aunt, and we won't be disturbed. My maid won't disturb our meeting. She owes me a few favours," he smiled slyly.

"I'm working at that time, sir."

"If you want my help, my dear, which, of course, I'll be delighted to give, I'm sure you'll find a way to be there."

His warm hand caressed her belly. "I think you are in the family way, are you not? How long have you been married? Three weeks, isn't it? I think you're a little further along than that."

"How do you know?"

"Well, I have had five children, you know. Five that I know of, anyway." He chuckled.

He finally let her go, and Angela returned to the party. Frank saw her enter the room, looking pale and shaken.

"Whatever's the matter, darling? You look like you're ill."

"I think I am, Frank. I need to lie down. You stay here; I'll be all right. Just tell Mamma where I am if she asks."

"I'd like to come with you. You might need some help."

"Really, Frank. Please stay here. I want to be on my own."

By the time the party had ended and Frank went to bed, Angela was already fast asleep.

The next morning, she seemed her usual self, and they went to work as normal. When Frank asked her about the previous evening, she passed it off as "morning sickness", something Frank had never heard of, but evidently was quite common during pregnancy.

"Morning sickness? It was seven o'clock in the evening," he protested.

"Frank, please. So many questions. That's just what it's called. It can strike at any time, Mamma says."

From the tone of Angela's voice, Frank thought it best not to pursue the matter any further.

Later in the afternoon, Angela went to see Dr Robinson, her boss, feigning illness. When he asked her for more details, Angela only had to mention "women's problems" for him to dismiss her early.

She left the hospital without seeing Frank, and went directly to the Rumbolds' house. She knocked on the door at four o'clock exactly, her heart thumping and her hands sweating. For a moment, she thought she would faint, and then the door opened.

"Yes, miss?" the servant girl greeted her.

Angela put an arm up to the wall of the house to steady herself.

"Are you all right, miss?" the girl asked.

"Just a dizzy moment, that's all. I'm here to see Mr Rumbold. I have an appointment for four o'clock. My name is Angela English."

"This way please, miss," the girl said, inviting Angela into the house.

Leading Angela across the imposing hall to a door on the right of the stairway, the girl knocked and entered the room.

"Mrs English, sir," she announced.

"Come in, Angela. That will be all," he said, dismissing the maid.

"A drink?" he offered, walking over to the drinks cabinet.

"No, thank you."

"Please, have a drink, my dear. It will relax you. You look very tense."

"I don't want to be relaxed, Mr Rumbold."

"You can call me Henry now that we're such good friends, Angela."

"We are not, and never will be, friends, Mr Rumbold."

"Oh?"

"Whatever you think is going to happen here today, isn't going to happen, I'm afraid," she said, looking him directly in the eye.

"We had an agreement, Angela. Don't you want my help?"

"Yes, sir, I do. I have a proposal for you."

"A proposal?" he asked, raising his eyebrows. "Go on."

Angela took a deep breath. "I will give you what you want, Mr Rumbold; but, first, you must speak up for Frank. Get them to drop this silly charge."

"That's not how it works, Angela," Rumbold said, mildly annoyed.

"If I submit to your demands now, what guarantee do I have that you'll help us?" she asked.

"You have my word, of course."

"I'm afraid that's not good enough, sir."

"How dare you! I am one of the most prominent and upstanding citizens in the whole of Richmond! And you, a little slut who gets herself knocked up before she's wed, *you* are making demands of *me!*" He moved towards her.

"One more step, and I shall scream loud enough for the whole town to hear. Stop right there, Mr Rumbold!"

He did as he was told, anger and confusion playing across his features. How could she have turned the tables like this?

"Now, then, I think we understand each other, don't we? Speak for Frank, and then you'll get your way."

"Get out of here, girl. I've heard enough from you. Out!"

Angela left as quickly as she could, lest he change his mind. She'd done all she could; now she'd just have to wait and see if Rumbold was greedy enough to take the bait.

CHAPTER 27

Frank was instructed to attend a pretrial hearing before a panel of three officers, one of whom was Surgeon Buston. News had come in some days before about the Battle of Ball's Bluff, which had taken place on 21 October. Colonel Edward Baker, once a senator for Oregon, and a friend of President Lincoln, had been badly defeated. Baker had led his troops into Virginia without orders to do so, and was completely overwhelmed by the Confederate forces. The colonel had been killed in the action.

Although, in actual military terms, Ball's Bluff was a small victory, the skirmish was blown out of all proportion by the Confederate authorities and the press. It was put about that it had been a major success, which caused jubilation among the populace. This should have had no effect on the hearing; however, there was no doubt that the three officers judging Frank were in a brighter mood than might otherwise have been the case.

While Frank and Angela were waiting outside the courtroom, they noticed Mr Rumbold enter the building. He seemed to catch Angela's eye and raised his hat to her. He knocked at the door of the courtroom and went inside.

"What's he here for?" asked Frank.

"Oh, I expect he's just interested, as we're neighbours. He probably heard all about it at the party we had," Angela said, turning away to hide her blushes.

"I know he's an important man in this town, and a rich one too, but there's something about him I don't like."

"Are you just a little envious, Frank? Men never like other men who are rich, charming, and successful," she teased. "Let's just hope he's on our side. That's one of the reasons I invited him to our party. I wanted him to get to know you a little better and for him to see just what kind of a weasel Buston is. Mr Rumbold has a lot of influence, you know."

"Maybe he does, but I still don't have to like him."

"Just be polite and make a good impression if he speaks to you," said Angela, exasperated by her husband's attitude. "You don't have to like him, Frank; just don't let him know that."

Frank was called into the small courtroom, and Angela went up into the gallery. As she sat down, Rumbold came over and sat next to her. She looked at him, and he smiled back. She felt his large hand encompass her much smaller one as he leant towards her and whispered in her ear.

"Your young husband will be acquitted, Angela. I shall look forward to collecting my reward sometime soon. I've done my part, and I expect you to do yours. If you do, I won't embarrass you in any way, especially where your husband and mother are concerned." He squeezed her hand firmly, then rose and disappeared quietly down the stairs, leaving just a whiff of cologne in his wake.

He was so different from Frank. Once again, she found that his power and charm fascinated her, despite her better judgement.

The hearing began, and Frank was asked why he took so many notes and why he had often wondered in public whether the Confederacy could win the war.

Before he could reply, and to everyone's amazement, Buston stood up and asked the court if he could make a statement.

"I know that I have been instrumental in bringing this young man before the court today. However, I have been watching him since I made my complaint, and I have changed my mind. I have decided that he is a loyal supporter of the Confederacy after all. I formally withdraw my accusation," he said. He then sat down, looking a little flustered.

Buston's statement caused some consternation in the courtroom, and a flurry of whispered conversation broke out. The other officers on the judging panel held their own discussion and seemed to come to a quick agreement. Banging his gavel on the bench, the senior colonel called for order in the court, and the loud buzz of chatter faded away.

After what seemed an eternity to Frank, he was asked to step forward to hear their judgement.

"Corporal English. We have decided not to refer you for trial, but to bind you over for good behaviour. You will continue under the supervision of Surgeon Buston. Furthermore, you will cease to write down your observations, and you will be sent to the front lines as a medical orderly as soon as possible.

"Yes, sir. Thank you, sir," Frank said with great relief. He certainly wasn't keen on the idea of going up to the front, but anything was better than an army prison. He had heard that the meanest soldiers in the army were in charge of such places, and very few men came out of one without some permanent damage.

Angela was overjoyed and flung her arms round him as he left the court. "Isn't it wonderful? Isn't it wonderful?" she repeated. "Now all we have to do is keep you away from the front line! We'll find some excuse. What about bad feet?" she added, laughing.

"What I can't understand is why Buston suddenly changed his mind about me. Why would he change his view like that? There must be a reason, mustn't there? Do you think Mr Rumbold had anything to do with it? He did go into the courtroom early. Maybe he said something to them."

"Stop questioning your good fortune, Frank. Just be glad it's all turned out so well," Angela said, dancing round and round.

"Angela, you're making a spectacle of yourself. For goodness sake, behave yourself! Sometimes you behave like one of those girls in the downtown dance halls!" Mrs Cooling's strident voice interrupted their celebrations.

Neither Frank nor Angela knew she had attended the hearing.

"Mrs Cooling," said Frank. "How good of you to come and support me."

"I came and sat up in the gallery, behind Angela. Congratulations, Frank, I'm very pleased for you." Mrs Cooling turned to her daughter. "I noticed Mr Rumbold come and sit beside you. He whispered something to you. What's going on Angela? What did he say, and why's he in court at all?"

"I was wondering the same thing," Frank said, "but I didn't see him talking to you. What's going on, Angela?"

Angela had stopped dancing, and Frank thought she was suddenly looking very uncomfortable.

"Nothing's going on. Whatever do you mean?" she asked indignantly. "He just said that Frank had impressed him at our party and that such a dedicated man, who spends such a lot of his time and effort tending our troops, couldn't possibly be a traitor." Angela paused for breath, amazed again at how easy she found it to distort the truth. Before anyone could speak, she continued, "He also said that he would give us any support we needed. I thought that was very nice of him."

"Oh, well that is good of him. We will have to invite him to another party before Christmas. I think we should have another one soon, as the first was so successful," Mrs Cooling said enthusiastically.

Frank wasn't so sure. He thought he knew Angela quite well by now, and he was certain she was keeping something from him.

The next morning, Frank was determined to find out what Angela was hiding but had to wait until they left for work before he could speak to her alone.

"I want you to tell me what's happening, Angela," he said.

"Happening? What do you mean?"

"Let's stop playing games. Something's going on with you and Rumbold. He wouldn't just get the charges dismissed out of the goodness of his heart. And then he comes and whispers things to you during the hearing. When he came into the courthouse, you looked flustered too. Tell me, please," he pleaded.

Angela didn't reply for a few seconds, trying to get her thoughts in order. She decided she had to tell Frank everything. After all, they were married now, and there should be no secrets between a man and his wife.

"I asked Rumbold for his help at the party, maybe to put in a good word for you. After all, he knows nearly everyone of any importance in this town. He lured me into one of the side rooms and told me that there's a price for everything. Oh, Frank, it was awful. He let his hands roam all over my body, and I was so frightened I couldn't even call out. I just stood there as rigid as a statue and took it," she confessed with tears in her eyes.

"That bastard!" Frank exclaimed. "The next time I see him, I'll teach him a lesson or two about how to treat women!"

"Frank, wait, I haven't finished," she said.

"There's more?" he asked, wide-eyed.

Angela told him of her visit to the Rumbolds' house and how she'd got the upper hand. "Temporarily, anyway," she added. "He's done his part in getting you freed, but now he expects to, as he put it, 'collect his reward'."

"Well, he can forget that. I know everything now. I wouldn't be surprised if he reached his position of power by using blackmail. You're probably the latest in a long line of people he's stepped on during his career. I know it's difficult for you, darling, but you've done the right thing by telling me."

Angela sighed with relief, and the tears came freely now that the burden had been lifted from her shoulders. Frank put his arms round her, and she soon felt much better. His comforting words had made her love him even more.

There was also good news from the war. An officer friend of Mrs Cooling had told her that he thought the war would lose momentum, or even cease altogether during the winter months. This would mean Frank wouldn't have to go to the front until the spring. It seemed as though fortune was on their side for now.

They were almost home when Betty called out from her garden.

"Angela! Angela! I need to speak to you," she said, then looked at Frank. "In private, if you could."

"Go on, Frank. I'll see you in a minute," Angela told him.

As he disappeared into the house, Betty asked Angela, with a note of urgency in her voice, "Did you get the medicine?"

"I didn't know it was so urgent. I'll get it tomorrow. Have you conceived again?"

"I don't know. Get it tomorrow, Angela, and don't forget—or I'll tell your mother that I saw you at the abortionist's office."

"If you do that, your family will know as well."

"I don't care," replied Betty. "I'm desperate. I can't steal any more from Mamma's purse to pay the doctor; she's bound to notice. I shall say you helped me."

Angela could see that the girl was very distraught and emotional. She was behaving illogically, but if she carried out her threat, it would be catastrophic for both families, leaving their reputations destroyed. If Angela mishandled the situation, her ally could become a dangerous enemy.

Chapter 28

Mrs Cooling's friend was proved correct. As the weather grew colder, the fighting virtually stopped in the east, with just the odd skirmish here and there. The hospital was emptying quickly, and only a few badly wounded men were left. The year ended with good news for the Confederacy from the western theatre of the war.

On 7 November, General Grant had attacked the small town of Belmont, Missouri. News of the battle filtered through to Richmond that three thousand Union men had charged straight into the Confederate lines. After two hours of fierce fighting, the rebels finally gave way. Unfortunately for Grant, his soldiers started looting the town, allowing the Confederate soldiers time to regroup, after which they returned and forced the Union troops back down to the river and into their boats. It was considered a Confederate victory in Richmond, although there were about six hundred casualties on each side. As so often in this war, both sides lost a similar number of men.

"How wonderful to end the year with a victory," said Mrs Cooling at breakfast.

"Yes," Frank agreed, having learnt to keep his real opinions to himself. He understood that all that had happened was that the Confederacy had held a minor town, but with a lot of men killed and wounded on both sides. The South had fewer men and could ill afford to lose soldiers, as the North had greater reserves, so what seemed a victory now was in the long term a defeat. He was sure the Union troops would learn from their mistakes and be better trained in the future.

"Don't you think it's good news, Angela?"

"Yes, Mamma, of course," she answered distractedly.

To Frank, her reply didn't feel convincing. In the last few days, he had noticed that Angela's optimism for a Confederate victory in the war had waned somewhat. She certainly seemed to be of the view that things would not be as easy as she had once thought. He would try asking her for her real thoughts when they were alone, perhaps after going to bed that night. He might get a more honest answer after he had comforted her with a cuddle.

They finished their breakfast, and Frank and Angela went to work, well wrapped up against the cold weather.

At last, Angela managed to see the nurse who had promised her the potion for Betty.

"Have you managed to get the medicine?" asked Angela.

"I've got it here. I've had it in my pocket for the last few days, but I couldn't get over to your side of the hospital," replied the nurse, a well-built girl with rosy cheeks and the healthy glow of someone who spent a lot of time outdoors. "That will be a dollar."

"That's a lot of money. I'll give you half a dollar, and that's being generous."

"If you want it, the price is a dollar."

"I don't need it *that* much," Angela told her. "I can get it somewhere else." She turned to walk away.

"Wait, wait a moment. Listen, it costs me half a dollar. I can't sell it for the same price. Eighty cents, and it's yours."

"Eighty. Here," said Angela, handing over the money. "What's in it, anyway?"

"It's ergot. That's a kinda hard red fungus. It grows in the ears of oats. It has to be ground up and then dissolved in water with some herbs. There's a thick sediment, so be sure to give it a good shake before you use it."

"How much should my friend take?"

"I don't really know. I'm not a doctor. Just tell her to take a large spoonful. More if it don't work."

"It all seems a little haphazard," noted Angela.

The nurse gave the matter a little thought and said, "Well, I guess it is. Girls get to know what to take by trial and error. It's the way of the world, ain't it, that us women have to suffer for men's pleasure. If she don't want babies all the time, a girl has to take a risk. Anyhow, I can't stand here all day; I've got to get back to my ward. I've got a pig of a ward sister in charge. If she finds me gossiping, she'll take it out on me for days."

Angela met with Betty again and told her that she had the medicine but that it would cost her two dollars.

"How will I get two dollars?" gasped Betty. "My father only gives me a small allowance."

"Well, you'll have to get it. That's what it cost me, and I went to great lengths to get it for you. What about Ambrose? Can't he help?"

"He never has much money, and what he does have, he needs for his business."

"Not much good having a man like that, even if he *is* handsome. Better to have a plain man who's rich," Angela told her. "Why don't you borrow it from your mamma's purse again?"

"She'll get my father to beat me if she finds out. Lord, sometimes I wish I were a man. Their lives are so much simpler."

"Oh, sure they are, then you can join the army and get your limbs blown off and spend your dying days in our hospital. You should thank God you're a woman and can't go to war. Why don't you become a nurse? Then, you'll see some real life!" Angela said with feeling. "And you'll earn some money. It's not much, but at least you'd be able to pay your debts."

"My father wouldn't allow me to work," said Betty, with a note of pride in her voice. "He would think it beneath his dignity for one of his daughters to take a job."

Angela rolled her eyes, thinking what strange morals people had, remembering Mr Rumbold's intentions where she was concerned. She'd had enough of this silly girl for one day. "I'll see you tomorrow with the medicine, and you can give me the money then."

The following evening, Angela went out to find Betty. Suddenly, she felt a large arm circle her waist. "Well, well, Angela, my dear. I didn't expect to see you out this late."

Angela was taken by surprise but quickly regained her composure. "I often take a walk in the evening to clear my thoughts, Mr Rumbold. It is hard, stressful work looking after our brave wounded soldiers at the hospital. We're going to need more young ladies to help with the nursing if the war goes on. Perhaps your daughter, Betty, might consider working for our cause. If we are to win this war, everyone needs to pull together. I'm sure a little guidance from you would help her make a decision in that direction. The men won't be so willing to fight if there's no support when they're injured."

Rumbold was taken aback by this long and intense diatribe. He had wanted some light, flirtatious banter, not a lecture on the conduct of the war, or how his daughter should be supporting it.

"You really surprise me, Angela. It's not really any of your business, but let me tell you I have absolutely no intention of allowing my daughter to work in any way except to give parties to raise funds for the war efforts," he said. "Now, then, you still owe me for getting Frank off those spying charges. You hadn't forgotten, had you? I want to arrange payment—and soon."

"Later, sir, I can't stop now." Angela told him, freeing herself from his grasp. She rushed off towards her house before he could say another word. She saw him watching her, so she made it look as if she were going into the house, until she saw him turn towards his own doorway. As he did so, the bushes at the end of their garden shook, and Betty emerged. She stood on the sidewalk, and Angela went over to her.

"I have your medicine, Betty. Have you got the money now?"

"What did my father want? He seldom goes anywhere at night except to his club. What did he say to you?"

"Nothing. He was just passing some remarks about what a lovely evening it is. Now, what about this medicine—do you want it or not?"

"Yes, of course I want it, but I could only get one dollar. Can I owe you the rest?"

Angela thought for a moment. She was going to double her money anyhow. If Betty owed her money, she'd still have a hold over her.

"That'll be fine, Betty. Here," she said, passing her the small jar. "You owe me a dollar."

"How much do I take?" Betty asked nervously.

"It's rather up to you, but don't take too much. Just a large spoonful should be enough, then give it some time to work. Don't be impatient; it's not going to work straight away. It's a good idea to take it at your time of the month, if that hasn't already passed."

Chapter 29

It was the day after Christmas, 1861, and Mrs Cooling, Angela, and Frank were relaxing at home when suddenly there was a loud, agitated knock on the door. When Frank opened it, he found the Rumbolds' black maid, standing on the doorstep, clearly distressed.

"Massa, could Miss Angela come, please?" she asked breathlessly.

"Calm down now," Frank said as he tried to soothe the girl. "Take a deep breath. Now, what's the problem?"

"It's Miss Betty, Massa. She very sick an' doubled up in pain. Mrs Rumbold cain't get the doctor; he away for Christmas. We all real worried. Can Miss Angela come, please, sir?"

"We'll come straight over and see if we can help," Frank told her. Seeing the look of surprise on the maid's face, he quickly added, "It's all right. I work at the hospital as well."

"Well, if you say so, sir. Thank you, sir. I gotta get back, but the butler'll be standin' at the front door to show y'all up to the bedroom."

Frank rushed through the house to the kitchen, where Angela and her mother were discussing the meals for the day.

"What is it Frank?" Angela asked him as he hurried into the room. "You look a little flustered all of a sudden."

"That was the Rumbolds' maid at the door. She's been sent over to ask you to come over and have a look at Betty. It seems she's been taken ill, and she's in a lot of pain. The doctor's away, so I've agreed that we'll both go over and see what we can do."

Frank could see Angela was worried. He wanted to go over to the house with her, but he didn't know about the medicine that Angela had sold her, and so she tried to put him off coming. He knew nothing of her and Betty's secrets.

"What's wrong, Angela? What are you waiting for? Come on, let's go."

"I'm coming, Frank. Don't rush me. I really don't know what they think I can do. I'm not a doctor—far from it."

"Don't look so worried. You can only do your best, and I'm sure it won't be as bad as some of the things you've seen at the hospital," Frank said, trying to reassure her.

"There's no need for you to come, Frank. I can manage by myself. If I need you, I'll send the butler over to get you."

"I'm coming with you, Angela. I'm not leaving you alone if there's any chance of Rumbold getting up to his tricks again."

"He wouldn't! Not while all his family are there!"

"I don't care. I'm not taking the chance and neither should you. Ready?"

"Yes, I'm ready," she said. Frank would not be deterred. She would just have to hope that Betty didn't mention the medicine. She suddenly realised that a far greater worry was if someone found the jar itself. If they tried to find out where it had come from, she could be implicated, and then she'd be in a world of trouble. She was very apprehensive as she rushed across the road with Frank.

They didn't need to knock at the door, as the butler was holding it open for them. He showed them up the large staircase to Betty's bedroom. It was much larger than their own bedroom, and very luxurious too. There was an ornate dressing table and a matching desk, a heavily padded armchair, and thick red curtains at the window.

Betty was lying on the bed, her head turned to one side. She was ashen, and her face was twisted in pain. Her mouth hung open, and in between retching, she emitted a long and agonising groan.

Angela had brought with her a small medicine bag. From it she brought out a potion that induced vomiting. She realised it was essential to remove what was left of the abortion powder from Betty's stomach as soon as possible. Whether it had any effect was of little concern. Keeping her alive was the important thing.

"Frank, hold her head up and keep her mouth open."

As he did so, Angela poured the medicine down Betty's throat. Although a lot of it ran down her chin, Betty swallowed enough to make her bring up the contents of her stomach. Angela could see signs of the ergot in the vomit, so she decided to get it removed as soon as possible—and certainly before any doctor could examine it.

"I'll clean up, Frank. You look after her."

Angela wiped up the mess from the bed and cleaned Betty's face round her mouth. She was very methodical about cleaning up and took a long time to do it. It was essential that no evidence should be left. She went downstairs with the china bowl containing the vomit, which the maid tried to take from her hands.

"Don't worry, I'll take care of it. It may be full of germs and could make you ill," Angela told the girl as she hurried by on the way to the washroom at the back of the house. She washed the sick down the large basin, which was connected to a soak-away in the garden. She poured some lamp oil on top of it and went back through the kitchen. She instructed the maid to pour lots of water down the sink so that all traces of Betty's vomit would disappear.

"Thank God you're back," said Frank. "Where have you been all this time?"

It was then that Angela noticed a red-faced and irate Mr Rumbold had followed her into the room, with his wife cowering behind him.

"What are you doing in my daughter's bedroom?" he asked Frank angrily. "How dare you come in here!"

"Look here, Mr Rumbold—" Frank began.

Angela interrupted before he could say anything further. "He works at the hospital, attending the wounded soldiers, and he's highly regarded by the doctors. He knows a lot about this kind of illness, and I need his help. Your daughter's very ill, Mr Rumbold."

"I don't like him being here."

"Do you want your daughter to die? Is that it?" Angela said, exasperated at his attitude. Her words caused Mrs Rumbold to burst into tears as she realised just how bad the situation was. "If we are to save her, I need Frank with me. He's the only trained person here until a doctor arrives. You have called a doctor, haven't you?"

"Of course I have. A fine family doctor by the name of Hancock. He's the doctor to most of the Richmond gentry; naturally, he has an excellent reputation."

Angela had heard some of the younger doctors at the hospital express rather different views about Hancock's abilities. One had said of him, "If his medical knowledge matched his fees, he'd be a genius. Unfortunately, the opposite is the case."

Without thinking, Angela said to Rumbold, "I would advise you to try to get Surgeon Forsyth from the hospital. He specialises in stomach illnesses. If I write you a note, that may persuade him to come down. You could send it with one of your servants, and tell him to run—it's a matter of life and death."

Rumbold flushed angrily, looking ready to explode. "How dare you question my choice of doctor? Who are you, anyway? Just a simple nurse from a poor family."

Angela had heard quite enough. She quietly closed her medical bag and got up. "Come along, Frank. We're obviously not needed here."

Rumbold looked aghast. "Where are you going? You can't just leave her."

"You've made your views quite clear, Mr Rumbold. You obviously don't want my advice, so I'm going. In any case, I can hear horses on the road outside. Your Dr Hancock is probably here, so I will no longer be needed."

Angela crossed to the window and looked down onto the road. "Yes, it's the doctor you've been waiting for. Come along, Frank, let's go home."

"You go ahead, Angela, I just want a quick word with Mr Rumbold."

Angela looked at Frank curiously but did as he said.

"What now?" asked Rumbold, still angry.

"Angela has told me everything, Rumbold," Frank said quietly. "Your attempts at blackmail won't work. She's saved Betty's life tonight. Consider *that* your reward for getting me freed. We're even."

Rumbold looked as if he couldn't believe what he was hearing. His mouth dropped open, but he said nothing.

Frank left before the man could reply.

Dr Hancock passed them on the stairs as they were leaving, but he didn't acknowledge them. He walked along the landing and went straight into Betty's bedroom, without knocking.

Angela and Frank were almost back at their house when the Rumbolds' maid ran across the road, calling to them. She was again very agitated and wanted them to return.

"The doctor wants to see you, missus. He say you gotta come back. He mighty annoyed that you left. Lordy, he angry."

"You tell him I'm not one of his servants. If he wants to know my views, he can call at my house. We're only too pleased to help if he wishes to talk to us in a civil manner. I'm not employed by him, nor is my husband. We're under no obligation to obey any of his demands."

Leaving the maid standing in the road, they continued back to their house, where Mrs Cooling had a hot meal ready for them. She wanted the details of everything that had happened and was taken aback when Frank told her the message that Angela had sent back to the doctor.

"I hope you haven't offended him, Angela. He's one of the richest and most respected doctors in town."

"Yes, so rich that he wouldn't come to treat the likes of us, no matter how sick we were," Angela said vehemently.

At that moment, there was a knock at the front door. Frank answered it and showed the caller into the small room they used for guests.

Angela could hear a man's voice and knew it was Dr Hancock. She reluctantly got up to go to the guest's room. It was not an interview to which she was looking forward.

"Angela," said Mrs Cooling. "Why don't you wait until Frank tells you who it is? It's not ladylike to rush to see people before you know their names."

"I know who it is, Mamma," said Angela, and she turned and walked into the room. "Welcome to our home, Dr Hancock. It's a pleasure to see you, of course, but what brings you here?"

"I'll come straight to the point, Mrs English. I was disappointed that you left my patient, Miss Betty Rumbold, before I arrived, and therefore could not give me any details as to her condition or your diagnosis, if you had one."

"Dr Hancock, perhaps you were not informed, but I was told to leave by Mr Rumbold. His wife was present and will be able to confirm what I say. Under the circumstances, how could I stay?" Angela was determined to stay calm, even though she was seething inside.

"You, of course, are much more knowledgeable than either my husband or I, since we are mere nurses. Perhaps you would do me the kindness of letting me know your views on her condition. I'm always eager to expand my medical knowledge."

The effect on Dr Hancock of being told that Frank and Angela had been ordered out of the house, combined with this fulsome and effusive praise, made him much more amenable. Her sarcastic tone passed by unnoticed.

Angela could see him relaxing and decided to make another gesture, to put him further at ease. "May I offer you a coffee, doctor?"

"No, thank you," he said with a smile. "I believe Miss Rumbold has eaten some rotten food. Perhaps one of the servants didn't clean the fruit properly. Maybe they didn't wash their hands before preparing a meal and have passed on some disease. We're having all the servants checked, of course. It was a pity you were so thorough in cleaning up, as the contents of her stomach might have told us more about her illness."

"I'm sorry about that, Doctor. It's the training I've had at the hospital. They'd soon get shot of me if I left things like that lying around," replied Angela, relieved that he hadn't found any vomit that she had missed.

Hancock suddenly seemed embarrassed. He was not used to dealing with these modern young nurses. "What was strange was that there was heavy bleeding from her, um, her, ah, down below."

"Oh, you mean from her anus?" asked Angela, knowing full well that was not what he meant. She wasn't going to help him out of his predicament.

"No, no. I don't mean *that* orifice. I wouldn't have been surprised if that had been the case. No, there was a considerable amount of bleeding from her, er—"

Although allegedly a doctor, he seemed remarkably reluctant to be specific. Angela wondered whether it was because he was talking to her, or if he was like this with everybody.

Finally, she'd had enough. "You mean from her vagina, Doctor?"

"Er, yes," he said and coughed into his hand.

So, the pregnancy had been aborted. Betty would be relieved on that account, at least. It was all that mattered to her. Angela heard herself say, "I expect it was just an excessively heavy monthly flow."

"Mm, yes," said Hancock. He seemed to have missed the fact that any illicit medicine had been taken. What they said about him at the hospital was true—he really didn't seem to know much. But, then, he surprised her.

"There's something unusual about this case. Something I can't quite put my finger on. I'm wondering what she's been up to, you know. Sometimes these young girls let their hearts rule their heads. I shall tell the parents to keep a strict eye on her, and I've told Mrs Rumbold to search the room."

He was not so naive after all.

They went back into the dining room after the doctor had left, and Angela told her mother that he had asked her to visit Betty immediately. She said that she wouldn't be long and there was no need for Frank to go. None of this was true, but it was essential that she found the remains of the medicine before Mrs Rumbold did.

"I told you before, Angela, I'm coming with you. Anyway, I have something to tell you," Frank said.

"What is it?" Angela asked as they crossed the road.

"I spoke to Mr Rumbold just before we left, and I told him that you saving Betty's life had settled any debts that you may owe him. That's the end of the matter. If he tries anything, just tell me, will you?"

"Frank, you truly are a gentleman. I was so worried about what you'd say. I thought you might hate me, but now I'm so glad I told you." She took his hand, and they continued to the Rumbolds' house.

Angela knocked on the door, and again the butler opened it.

"The doctor asked us to see Miss Rumbold again."

"I thought Mr Rumbold told you not to come."

"And now the doctor's asked us back. Are you going to let us pass, or shall we call Mr Rumbold?"

The butler hesitated for a moment. "Of course, miss, sir, please come in."

Angela brushed past him, bounded up the stairs, and marched into Betty's room. "Wait here," she told Frank. As she went into the room, the first thing she saw was Mrs Rumbold rummaging through the chest of drawers. She turned round and saw Angela.

"What are you doing here? Didn't my husband tell you to go?" she asked, still clearly upset.

"The doctor came to my house, and we discussed Betty's symptoms. I've agreed to come over and look after her, Mrs Rumbold. Your daughter is very ill, and I would never forgive myself if anything happened to her. I've also got to give her some medication. Could you leave us alone, please? Betty needs quiet and rest. You go too, Frank."

"The doctor asked me to look around her bedroom to see if Betty had taken anything that she shouldn't have," said Mrs Rumbold.

"Well, leave us for a little while I see to your daughter, and then you can continue. Whatever it is, it won't disappear."

Mrs Rumbold left the room and Frank closed the door, standing guard outside.

Angela turned to Betty and whispered in her ear, "Where's the powder I gave you? You must tell me, or we'll both be in trouble."

Betty just turned over and began to mumble.

Angela shook her, to no avail. She reached into her bag and pulled out the smelling salts that she always carried. She ran them under Betty's nose, and the girl immediately opened her eyes, trying to blink away the fumes. Again, Angela asked her where she had hidden the medicine.

This time, she got a mumbled but understandable reply: "Shoes." Then, after a pause, Betty added, "Bottom of the cupboard."

Angela rushed over to the cupboard and quickly started searching through the shoes. Suddenly, she heard footsteps on the landing. As she put her hand into one of the last shoes, she discovered the small jar of potion. She got up and turned to the door, just as it opened. Mrs Rumbold came into the room, and Angela said, as casually as she could, "I've finished for now, but I'll be coming back tomorrow, Mrs Rumbold. You may continue searching the room."

Over the following days, Angela continued to see Betty, who gradually recovered. They were now seeing so much of each other that they were becoming good friends. They began exchanging confidences and found that their differences receded as time went by.

CHAPTER 30

The start of the New Year was a jolly time for all, and for a short while, the war was forgotten. Angela continued to see Betty, and by the end of the first week of 1862, the girl had fully recovered. Mrs Rumbold was so grateful that she gave Angela a small silver pin box. Furthermore, it looked like Frank's chat with Mr Rumbold had the desired effect—there had been no more trouble from that direction.

The war in the western theatre picked up pace in January and February, with victories for the Union at Middle Creek, Mill Springs, and then against General Grant's forces at Fort Henry on 6 February.

It was all far away to the people of Richmond, and few of them realised the significance of losing ground in such a comparatively remote area.

Frank and Angela continued working at the hospital, but by now, only the worst of the wounded were left. Inevitably, they died one by one, leaving the staff saddened and the hospital empty.

The war in the east started in earnest again on 8 February, with the Confederates defeated five times in succession, at Roanoke Island, New Bern, Kernstone, Yorktown, and Williamsburg. But, in May, General Jackson won three battles in a row, at Fort Royal on the fourth, Newtown on the twenty-fifth, and Winchester on the twenty-sixth.

Angela's pessimistic view of the way the war was going started to change. Frank did his best to keep news of the Confederate defeat away from her, especially given her condition. It wasn't always easy, as the number of wounded at the hospital was increasing again, and they told the staff their stories of battle—whether they had won or lost, and the awful conditions for the army in the field. Frank decided that it was time that she gave up work and stayed at home to concentrate on getting clothes and the house ready for the baby, all of which would help him control the flow of news. He decided to speak about the subject at dinner that night.

"Angela, dear, don't you think it's time to stop working at the hospital and stay at home now?" asked Frank. He turned to Mrs Cooling, whom he knew would be on his side. "What do you think, Mamma? Don't you agree that she ought to stop working—it's very strenuous and quite emotional too."

"Yes, dear. Frank is quite right. You should stay at home with me until the baby is born."

"I want to go on working until nearer the time. Why can't I? The poorer women on the farms keeping going. A lot of them go on ploughing and harvesting right up to the last few days."

"I know that, dear, but you are not a poor farm girl. You are a lady and not as strong," said Mrs Cooling.

"Thank you, Mamma, that's made my mind up. I shall go on working until I am ready," said Angela stubbornly.

She stood up quickly, knocking her plate from the table and onto the floor as she did so. She hurried from the room, complaining that neither of them understood how she felt.

As she went to climb the stairs, she tripped over the bottom step in her haste. She stopped at the top and leant on the bannisters, looking down at Frank, who had left the table and was about to follow her up the stairs.

"Don't come any further, Frank! I don't want to see you. How could you say that in front of my mother? You knew she'd agree with you and turn on me!"

"Angela. Angela! I didn't mean to upset you! I did it for your own good," cried Frank. "Please come down and finish your meal, and we can talk about it. It's not good to get so worked up in your condition."

"Well, it's a bit late to think of that," she said angrily, then turned and went into their room, locking the door behind her.

Frank went back into the dining room and sat down next to Mrs Cooling. She hadn't moved, but her face was ashen. She had never seen her daughter so annoyed or adamant.

"You know, Frank, there are times when I just don't understand Angela. She's become so sure of herself and so stubborn. She was so sweet and kind before this war started. It seems to be changing us all. Goodness knows what it'll be like when it's all over!"

"Don't worry, Mamma. As soon as I've finished eating, I'll go up and see her. I expect she will have calmed down by then. She's bound to be quite up and down as her time gets near."

At that moment, there was a loud scream from upstairs. Frank jumped to his feet and bounded up the stairs two at a time. He turned the door handle, but Angela had locked it from the inside.

He picked up a heavy metal doorstop and began beating at the door. It was a sturdy structure, but it soon began to give way under Frank's onslaught. One of the thin panels in the wood gave way, and Frank reached through the hole. He felt for the key, and with a stretch, managed to turn it. The door opened. Angela was moaning and lying on her side, holding her stomach.

"Frank! Oh, thank God. It's coming!"

Fortunately, he had spent a short time in the maternity ward with one of the young doctors during a lull in the fighting at the beginning of the year. This training was going to stand him in good stead.

Frank gently laid Angela on her back and undressed her, leaving only the clothing on the top half of her body. He told her to lie on her back, then he covered her with a blanket.

"Bend your legs, and try to relax," he said.

"Thank goodness you're here, Frank."

"Ssh. Where else would I be? Now just keep quiet and concentrate on the baby."

"The pain's gone now."

"Good, that's good. I'll go and get the doctor soon."

"No! Don't leave me Frank," she pleaded.

"We need a doctor, Angela. I can't ask your mother to go."

"I'll ask her. I need you here. Where is she?"

Mrs Cooling, who had been waiting outside, came into the room, looking very worried. She had heard everything.

"Don't worry, Frank. You don't have to ask. I'll go and get him."

"Really, Mamma, it'll be better if I go. I'll be quicker, and I'm sure you can look after Angela for a few minutes."

Just then, Angela screamed again and doubled up in pain. The sweat broke out on her brow, and she gripped Frank's hand like a vice.

"What's happening?" Frank asked, getting more distressed by Angela's discomfort.

"These are contractions, Frank. They'll get more frequent as the baby gets closer to coming out, but it'll be a while yet. You go and get the doctor."

"If you're sure."

"Go. And be quick," Angela said as the pain once again subsided.

Frank kissed her and left. He ran down the stairs and out of the house. He knew where Dr Edmonds's house was on Nineteenth Street and ran all the way there, drawing curious looks from the few pedestrians who were out.

He knocked sharply at the doctor's door, which was opened by his nurse.

"I need the doctor urgently! My wife's pregnant, and she's going to have the baby at any moment! It's Angela English, on Twenty-Third Street," Frank told the girl as quickly as he could, then ran back home.

When he got back, he was out of breath and sweating more than Angela, but he was relieved to see that nothing had changed. It wasn't long before another contraction started, only to subside again. Soon after, Dr Edmonds arrived and let himself into the house—the girl's screams were loud enough to hear from the street. As he entered the room, all eyes turned to him as he took charge.

"Firstly, we need some clean towels and some boiled water. Would you arrange that please, Mrs Cooling? Mr English, you hold her hand and keep her calm. This can be an anxious time for first-time mothers, and she'll need your reassurance. Now, then, Angela, let me examine you."

The doctor was completely unflustered, and his calm manner settled Frank and Mrs Cooling, as he obviously knew what he was doing.

Frank did as he was told, and wiped the sweat from Angela's face with his free hand. As the night wore on, the contractions came and went, but nothing seemed to be happening, and Frank was getting worried.

"Is this normal?" he asked. "Surely the baby should be here by now!"

"Mr English, this is entirely normal. I've known labour to continue for two days for some women."

"Two days!" Frank and Angela exclaimed together.

"I can't do this for two days. I'm already exhausted."

"Keep drinking the water; that'll help," the doctor told her.

By midnight, Angela was spent, but every time she started to fall asleep, another bout of pain would wake her, and the intervals between each episode were getting shorter.

At around four in the morning, the doctor said he could see the head. Frank was still very worried by the pain his wife was having to endure, but fascinated by it at the same time. The doctor told her to push gently as each contraction came, and Angela did her best, even though doing so made the pain even worse. She was pouring with sweat, and her screams were louder than ever. The bedsheets were soaking wet, and Angela thought she couldn't take any more.

"This time, push as hard as you can," the doctor told her.

"No. No more. I'm tired. I want to go to—" With that, she screamed.

"Now! Push! Push hard," the doctor urged her.

"Come on, darling. One last push," Frank said.

Angela heaved as hard as she could, straining every fibre of her being. With this final push, Angela was able to deliver the baby. She collapsed on the bed, exhausted. The doctor cleared the mucus from the baby's mouth, and within a few seconds, the baby gave out a loud cry. The umbilical cord was then cut by the doctor. He cleaned the baby and examined it to make sure there were no abnormalities. As he handed the baby to Mrs Cooling to be wrapped in towels, he said "Congratulations! You have a healthy baby girl."

After Mrs Cooling had wrapped the baby girl, she handed her granddaughter over and placed her in Angela's waiting arms. From then on, Angela only had eyes for the baby. It was as if she were suddenly alone, and all the pain and anguish of the night was quickly forgotten.

Mrs Cooling stayed with her daughter and granddaughter, while Frank thanked the doctor and helped him with his things, then saw him out. Frank looked at the clock. It had already gone five o'clock in the morning, and he still had to go to work! He was about to go back upstairs when he noticed a letter had been pushed under the door. It was addressed to him. He tore it open and quickly scanned the writing, intending to read it properly later on. He was stunned by its contents and amazed that it should come at this time. It told him to report to a field medical unit under Surgeon John Walton in two days' time, for immediate duties at the front line.

Chapter 31

Frank had a busy two days before reporting for his new duties. He had been told to report to a unit at Mechanicsville, just to the north-east of the city, where General Lee had taken over from the wounded General Johnston. Prior to his departure, Frank wanted to spend as much time as possible with his wife and his new daughter, whom they had named Amelia. Angela was still very emotional and tired after her labours, and she was unhappy that he had to leave so soon after the birth.

"Someone's arranged this posting as a reprisal against us!" Angela cried when she heard the news. "I bet it's Buston! Whoever it is, I'll get even with him. I'll make him suffer for his spite!"

Frank always found it surprising how even the kindest, gentlest, and sweetest of women could behave like wild mountain lions when one of their own was treated in a way they didn't like. Whether the action was reasonable, or even necessary, made little difference; they behaved like cats defending their young against overwhelming odds. Frank suddenly stopped musing. It was strange that, even at such a time of upheaval, he could still query the workings of women's minds and marvel at how impossible they sometimes were for him to understand.

"Someone has to go," Frank told Angela. "It's probably just a coincidence that I was selected right after the baby was born. But just think how upset you'd have been if this had happened three or four days ago," he said, trying to make light of it, even though he secretly agreed with her.

"Sometimes you're so naive, Frank. It really makes me wonder who you were, what you did, and how you made your living before you lost your memory. It's obvious to me that someone has deliberately picked on you," Angela replied. "You know, they usually have two men in each company to act as stretcher bearers. They bring the wounded men to the unit where the surgeon attends to them. They don't use trained men like you to carry stretchers!"

"I heard they were changing their methods. Too many men are dying before they even reach the hospital. It's bad for morale if the soldiers think they won't be seen by an experienced medic quickly," Frank explained patiently. "They want a trained man or a pharmacist to travel with every ambulance unit. People like me, Angela. It's all quite innocent and just bad luck that it should be now."

Angela was too exhausted to continue arguing, and she soon fell into a light sleep. Frank took the opportunity to pack up his spare clothes and a few medicines. He also had to get a new army uniform. Up until now, he had been wearing a white coat over his own clothes while at work. His title was now Medical Steward, and Frank thought that this promotion would at least give him a definite position. It would also mean he wouldn't be called upon to go to the front line and get involved in the fighting.

When he returned to say goodbye to Angela, she became very weepy. She would normally have been impressed with his promotion and new uniform, but now she could only think about how much she would miss him.

Frank left the house, closed the front gate sadly, and walked up the road to the assembly point, ready for departure.

The area was crowded with fighting men, and Frank sought out the sergeant who appeared to be in charge.

"I'm Medical Steward English, Sergeant, reporting for duty."

"Well, now! Look what we got here. A *gen-yew-ine* Limey, for Chrissakes! I've been hearin' about you, English, an' I don't like all I hear."

"Just here to do my duty, Sergeant."

"We'll see 'bout that, mister. Go stand over there." The sergeant pointed to a group of about thirty other soldiers. "We're leaving in five minutes."

"How far is it to the lines, Sergeant?"

"Jeez, don't you know nothin'? I guess a medic cain't be 'spected to know much. Always safe and sound away from the action. It's about time you saw some fighting for yourselves," growled the sergeant. "Now fall in, soldier!"

Frank could tell that the front-line troops didn't have a lot of sympathy for the support units behind the lines. In the case of the medical units, he thought this feeling arose because many of the wounded had suffered at the hands of poorly trained and unfeeling doctors. Tales of brutal surgery and total incompetence were rife.

"How far is the front line?" he asked the soldier next to him.

"It's only about two miles out of town, thataways," the man said, pointing to the north-east.

"Really? I'm amazed! No one at home knew the Yankees were anywhere near that close!"

"I think they wanna keep it quiet, or the civilians could panic. Then, the roads would all get clogged up with refugees, and the army wouldn't be able to move. So, don't let on when you get home."

"I'll be careful," Frank said, but he wasn't satisfied with this explanation. He kept thinking of Angela and Amelia. "Do you think they'll attack the city?"

"Ha! Not a hope now that General Lee has arrived to take command. In any case, what's it to you? You're just a medic, ain't ya? And a goddamn Limey, to boot! You just concentrate on patching us up when we need it, fella, and leave the running of the war to the generals."

Some other soldiers had heard the exchange and were now laughing and jeering at the man's answer. The sergeant called them to attention, and they started to march off towards the front. They reached the outskirts of Richmond and made their way down country roads and past sleepy farms. It all seemed so normal; the war could have been a thousand miles away.

When they arrived, Frank left the main body of troops and reported to Surgeon John Walton, the doctor in charge of the medical unit.

"I would like to welcome you to my medical unit, English, but from what I hear, you may be more trouble than you're worth," Walton said.

Walton then gave Frank a distasteful glare. About fifty years old, Walton was from the deep south of Georgia. He had been a rural doctor before the war, and he was far more used to treating slaves and farmers with broken limbs or cuts and grazes than soldiers with horrific battle injuries. He was rather old for a field command, and set in his ways, but even so, he was more up to date and better informed than most of the medical officers of the time. He lived for his work, and he was strict but fair.

He advised the newcomer, "I hear that you are liable to question authority and that you have rather liberal views about obeying orders you don't like. You had better not take that attitude here."

"I shall obey your commands and do my duty, sir," replied Frank, but he felt the need to defend himself. "I don't know who's told you these things about me, sir, but I can assure you that they are not correct. I always do my duty to the very best of my abilities. I may sometimes suggest, and only suggest, that there are different treatments or that the way of doing the work in hand could be better. If my suggestion is rejected, I'll do as I've been ordered. I won't be insubordinate, sir, but I feel it is my duty to try to make things a little better for the injured men."

"That's a mighty long speech from a mere medical steward. I can see you're a smart fellow, English, but we don't want any barrack-room lawyers here, understood? Now, you've got ten minutes to settle in and prepare for the first casualties," Walton growled as he walked away.

Frank saluted and walked over to his quarters to unpack. He was pleased he had a tent to himself, something very unusual for a noncommissioned rank, but the casualties from the battles would be going right past it, carried by two men from each front-line unit. Frank had been told that this task was delegated to the strongest men in the regiment, as it was very heavy work. Sometimes they had to carry men on their backs or over one shoulder.

Frank arrived at his unit on 25 June, and the following seven days would live in his memory forever.

Frank was so busy he hardly slept during the entire week. The men were terrified that if they didn't succumb to their injuries, they would die at the hands of the surgeons. Frank did his best to calm them, and he assisted at countless operations. He kept asking himself whether all the slaughter was worth it, although he would never dare to say so out loud. He increasingly had the feeling that he was an outsider and this was not really his war.

After days of fierce fighting, the Union troops finally broke ranks. Rebel soldiers under the command of General Magruder advanced and took a large number of weapons, including cannons and much-needed ammunition. They also overran the Union hospital and captured 2,500 sick and wounded soldiers, something they could have done without. This new influx of men became a heavy burden on the Confederate medical services, which were unable to cope with even their own casualties.

Frank was tending to some of these Union troops when he was startled by a bellow from behind him. "Why in God's name are you treating these swine when our own men need attention?"

He looked around to see a large Confederate cavalry officer, red faced and apoplectic with rage. The man had just dismounted from his horse, and he raised his whip to strike Frank.

At that moment, Walton appeared from behind a tent on his dappled grey horse.

"What's going on here?" he demanded.

Frank's heart sank. He expected his commanding officer to take the same view of the situation as the irate cavalry officer.

"How dare you raise a whip to one of my soldiers, sir! This man is on my medical staff, and he's been taught, in the best tradition of our profession, to treat the injured wherever—and whomever—they may be."

The officer lowered his whip. "So, you agree that the enemy should be treated before our men, is that it?"

"No, sir. But I do agree with treating the wounded wherever we find them. Of course our troops are important, and we do our best for them with the limited resources we have. That does not mean we just leave Union troops to die."

For a moment, it looked as though the cavalryman would lose control, but Walton continued. "There are only Union troops in this tent. Do you think my medic should just stand by and do nothing? Well, sir?"

The cavalry officer continued to glare angrily at Frank but said nothing.

Walton hadn't finished. "Some of you men seem to have lost any civilised feelings you may have once had. I wonder how long it will be before you're behaving with as much compassion as the alligators from the Florida swamps! What if the situation were reversed? Would you expect a Union doctor to let our men die without any attempt to treat them? What do you say to that, sir?"

The cavalry officer got back on his horse, still glaring at Frank. "I think I owe you an apology, Surgeon. I have just lost more than half of the men in my command, men that I grew up with back in Georgia. My best friend had his stomach blown away as he was standing next to me. He died in agony, sir, lying in his own blood and whimpering like a beaten dog. Such experiences do not incline a man to behave rationally, fairly, or in the manner of a gentleman."

"I understand," said Walton in a gentler tone. "The strain of this war is sometimes too much for even the bravest of men." He saluted the officer. "Good day to you, sir."

Frank's fear and anger towards the officer turned to pity. How many more men were there who had also lost friends and relatives? The Confederates were more likely to suffer in this way, as their units were often made up of men who came from the same towns as each other. They would see their companions, whose mothers and fathers they knew, cut down before their eyes.

Walton interrupted his thoughts. "I saved you from that officer, English, but don't think I did it because I approve of your attitude. I hope you are not spending time attending these Union troops out of anything but duty."

"What do you mean, sir?"

"I know that you were once suspected of being a spy. If I find out that this is, after all, the case, I shall have no pity on you. A traitor at the front line can be shot by his superior officer, and I shall have no hesitation in doing so." Walter stared down at Frank, who understood that he meant exactly what he said. There was a steely hardness in his eyes that gave no room for misunderstanding. He was very good in his medical work and could be kind at times, but he held firm views about duty—his own and everybody else's.

Frank once again felt the need to defend himself. "I am not, and have never been, a spy, sir, and I resent your implication. I am here to do my work as a medical aide, and that's all. Do you think these injured men are going to suddenly jump up and run off back to their lines with information I've given them?" Frank stopped, realising he'd said enough, perhaps too much.

"Enough!" shouted Walton. "You're getting mighty close to finding yourself on a disciplinary charge, English! Don't say another word!"

Walton glared at him for a few seconds and then slowly rode off.

Frank continued attending to the wounded and dying until well after dark. When he got to his tent, he lay down. As usual, he immediately fell into a deep sleep. He was utterly exhausted, both physically and emotionally, but the horror went on until the Seven Days Battle, as it would be called, had ended. The aftermath of the fighting littered the battlefield: broken guns, dead bodies of men and horses, and the wounded who had not been brought back to the hospital. It was a pitiful sight.

Nightmares of carnage, gore, and the never-ending stream of injured men would wake him at night. Sometimes it was so bad that he would sob with pity and frustration. The period was called the "Seven Days Battle", during which General Lee forced back the Union army and their leader, General McClellan, from the borders of Richmond, saving the South from an early defeat. Many thought that if the Union had taken the capital that day, the war would have been over before it really began, a blessing for all concerned.

The Seven Days Battle ended with the Battle of Malvern Hill on 1 July, and casualties on both sides were high. The Confederates suffered a considerable blow, with 3,286 men killed, 15,909 wounded, and 946 captured or missing. The total losses to General Lee's army were perhaps 25 per cent higher than those of the Union forces. At Malvern Hill, the North's artillery was so accurate and devastating that more than five thousand wounded and dead were strewn about the battlefield when it was over. Some of the injured were able to move a little, and it was said that they gave the impression of the land heaving like a giant blanket in the wind.

There was one incident that Frank found particularly disturbing. When the Confederate forces overran the Union field hospital, one of their doctors stayed behind to attend the injured men. Unlike his fellow medical officers, he chose not to retreat. A detachment of Confederate soldiers had been detailed to search the battlefield for the wounded and to pick up any stragglers from the enemy forces. They called in at the hospital, and their officious young lieutenant, straight from the academy, had to be persuaded to leave the wounded Union soldiers under the care of the medical authorities. Then, discovering a Union doctor operating on a soldier's leg, he barked out a command to his men to immediately take him to a prisoner-of-war camp.

Frank protested loudly, but he was overruled.

"This man is from the Union army, the same army that has been killing our soldiers."

"But he's a doctor! He is performing an operation on one of our men right at this moment," Frank replied.

"Don't you question my orders, soldier. Any more interference from you, and you'll be locked away as well!"

Once again, Walton arrived in time to save the day. It was unusual for him to speak quietly, but on this occasion, he must have decided that it would have more effect.

"I shouldn't do that if I were you, Lieutenant. One day, you may need his help, and we have very few medical men available. Perhaps you didn't know, and I'll give you the benefit of the doubt, but this man has helped me operate on our troops too."

"Yes, sir." The sudden appearance of a senior officer, and the quiet but firm rebuke, made the young lieutenant hesitate.

The surgeon pushed home his advantage.

"I would like you to note that the doctor is operating on a soldier from South Carolina. I would guess from your accent that you're from around there too, correct?"

"If that's all, sir?" was all the lieutenant could find to say. He turned to his soldiers. "Come on men, fall in, and we'll take these prisoners to the camp." He was fuming at the rebuke he had received, but he didn't want to lose face in front of his men. In a low, flat voice he said, "I shall return for him when he has finished the operation."

"Didn't you hear me, Lieutenant?" shouted Walton. "We need every medical man we can get. He stays here until I say otherwise! Do you understand?"

"Yes, sir, I understand," said the lieutenant, red in the face at this humiliation. "By the left, quick march!"

As the soldiers and their prisoners marched away, Walton spoke to Frank in a low and menacing voice. "It seems you have a habit of getting into scrapes while protecting the enemy. I hope this is just a coincidence."

"I'm sure you would have stopped me if I was doing anything wrong, sir," Frank said, managing to stop himself from saying any more, but the sarcasm went unnoticed by Walton.

Frank worked at the hospital until all the wounded Southern troops had left to return to their units or were sent home. Those soldiers who were too badly injured to patch up were taken back to the hospital at Richmond.

The Union troops were dispatched to the rails heads and then taken down to the new prison camps in the Deep South, so far from their lines that there was little point in trying to escape. However, rumours were already beginning to circulate that these new prisoner-of-war camps were poorly run and very unpleasant places.

CHAPTER 32

Frank was sent back to the Richmond base hospital, along with the badly injured Confederate troops. His main task was to keep as many men as possible alive as they travelled over the bumpy roads. It was only a few miles, but despite his best efforts, some still died, mainly from haemorrhaging caused by the shaking of the carts. The bodies had to be thrown out onto the side of the road, and a special detachment of soldiers would follow to bury them. Letters and other personal possessions were removed from the corpses to send to their families.

When Frank returned to Richmond, he immediately applied for leave so that he could see his wife and child. He was relieved when it was granted, as he'd had a gruelling time and was exhausted. He was given a whole week away from his duties but was told to be prepared to be recalled at any time should the workload require it.

Angela, of course, didn't know he was coming, and she was delighted to see him.

"Frank!" she cried as he came through the door. She jumped up from her seat and rushed over to him, managing to avoid crushing Amelia between them as she hugged him.

He was so exhausted that he nearly fell to the floor at Angela's onslaught, but he stayed awake long enough to explain his presence.

Angela was very proud of him. Even Mrs Cooling seemed pleased to see him now that he was in his new uniform, though it was somewhat soiled. Frank finally felt that she was proud of him. She had a son-in-law she could boast about to her friends and neighbours—someone who had been with the famous General Lee, defending the capital! Angela was now a picture of health, as was their daughter. She was nursing Amelia, who looked very happy and had grown substantially in just the short time he'd been away. He spent his week getting to know his new child, being pampered by the two women, and sleeping off his exhaustion. Mrs Cooling cleaned and repaired his uniform, and all too soon, it was time to return to the hospital.

Casualties were coming in every day now but in no great numbers. There were, thankfully, only a few from the battles of Cedar Mountain and Catlett Station, both of which were Confederate victories.

Frank made a new friend, a soldier who lived on the southern outskirts of Richmond. Knowing the local area very well, he had acted as a scout, spying behind enemy lines and reporting on troop movements for the generals. The soldier, Richard Ballard, had a minor leg wound caused by a fall. The wound had turned septic. With considerable and meticulous care from Frank, it began to heal. In all too many cases like this, the surgeon would have had to amputate the limb.

"Frank, my friend," said Richard, "I really want to thank you. You've done me a real good turn in saving my leg. Without it, I'd have been useless in the war and no good at home. No one wants to employ a cripple."

"Richard, that's my job. Compared to some of my other work, this has been very satisfying. Anyway, you're welcome. I'm glad you're better."

"Well, I've got something for you in return."

"Really, Richard, there's no need. Just seeing you healed is enough for me."

"Lemme finish, Frank. I've discovered some secret information. There's gonna be a massive attack against us by a new force the Yankees are putting together. They're calling it the Army of Virginia, and it's commanded by John Pope. He's one of their best leaders, and he's done well in the west," said Richard, keeping his voice low, so no one else in the ward could hear. "So far, they've got about forty thousand men, and they'll completely swamp our boys! If they add in McClellan's troops, they'll have more than seventy thousand! I'm telling you this as a favour, so keep it quiet, but take my advice. If I were you, I'd try to keep well out of the way when the battle comes."

"Hmm, thanks Richard," replied Frank, looking thoughtful. "A few of the wounded men from Cedar Mountain said they thought something was building up."

Early in the morning of 26 August, Frank was told to report immediately to Surgeon Walton, who was at the base hospital, putting together a new unit to run a large field hospital.

"I'm happy that you know your job now, English, and I think I can trust you," he said, and then he waited for a reply.

Frank said nothing, wondering what was coming.

"I want you to take charge of the packing and transport arrangements for the medicines, bandaging, and surgical instruments. Can you do that?"

"Yes, sir. When are we leaving?"

"Tonight. We must have this new unit set up by tomorrow."

"Can I just take an hour to go home, sir? I need to tell my wife what's happening. We have a new child, and I have to say goodbye."

"I'm afraid that's not going to be possible. From what I hear, there will be a considerable number of casualties right from the get-go. I need you here. Dismissed!" said Walton.

Frank was most upset. He needed to see Angela, if only to reassure her. He had a feeling of foreboding that he couldn't ignore, a feeling that something terrible might happen to him personally.

Before they had time to set up the new field hospital, orders came through ordering Walton's entire medical unit to move forward to the railroad junction at Manassas. Until recently, this had been a large supply area for the Union army, but its small guard had been overrun by Major General J. E. B. Stuart, known as "Jeb" to his men, and his advance cavalry unit. By the time the medics arrived, the town was full of half-starved Confederate troops who had been marching hard for many days over the hills. They were all over the town, ransacking the houses, blocking the roads, and sleeping in many of the buildings. They were searching for anything the Union troops had left behind— food, weapons, tobacco, maybe even some boots to replace their own worn-out ones. They had arrived in the morning. By the evening of the next day, they had disappeared, carrying as much as they could hold. Frank's unit had been told that the Union forces were better supplied in all areas than the Confederate army, and here was the proof. What they couldn't carry, General "Stonewall" Jackson had to reluctantly order to be destroyed.

Frank felt uneasy when he was packing up the Union supplies. Once again, he was gripped by a sense of familiarity, especially with some of the makers' names on vests and socks, but he tried to put it out of his mind for now.

After they left, they heard from their scouts that General Pope, the commander of the Union troops, had reentered Manassas, hoping to surround the Jackson army. He was too late, though; he found the town completely deserted and stripped of anything useful.

On 28 August, the Confederates lined up by an unfinished railroad track. There was a convenient bank to crouch behind, hiding the men from sight and from enemy fire. It was a natural defensive position.

In front, and some way from the track, was another line called the Warrenton Turnpike, along which could be seen a small group of Union soldiers. They were marching into an ambush, unaware that a large army was hidden behind the mound. The Confederates waited until their quarry had nowhere to run, and then they attacked. The Union men were taken completely by surprise, and the whole group, including their commander, Brigadier General Rufus King, were either killed or captured and then taken prisoner.

General Pope soon heard of the ambush and sent his men to attack the Confederates. The ruse had worked, for this had been Jackson's intention all along. His men were so well dug in and protected that they had a considerable advantage, one which they would have lost by advancing. Instead, they had lured the enemy in, to their destruction.

Chapter 33

Walton had arranged for his hospital unit to set up their tents about five hundred yards behind the lines, which would be near enough for the stretcher bearers and walking wounded to reach it, but far enough away to be out of the reach of artillery fire.

Frank was kept very busy day and night, doing his best by tending the Confederate wounded, as well as the odd Union man who had somehow found his way to the hospital. He could only sleep for short periods and was repeatedly awoken by new arrivals, which he attended to immediately and without once complaining. So diligent was he in his labours that he was once again becoming known as a saint. It could easily have been used in a derogatory manner, as a put-down, but every man who used the nickname meant it sincerely. The Union men were especially grateful, as they had not thought their enemies would treat them at all well, but Frank attended to the troops of both sides without a trace of favouritism.

One Union solider, Edward Berry, had a head wound. Frank said jokingly, "This medicine I'm giving you was captured at Manassas, did you know that? I've had to bring it all the way here, just to give it back to you!"

"It sure is a strange war," said Berry. "A lot of the men, including me, are beginning to wonder just why we're fighting at all. But I have to button my lip when there are officers around—they'd have me shot for that sort of talk. I just wish I could get home to my wife and our farm."

"Yeah. I'm missing my wife too. And we've got a new baby daughter. Amelia, she's called. I've only seen her twice since she was born. God, I miss them," Frank said. "Anyway, where are you from?"

"Maryland, near a little place called Rockville. Ever heard of it?"

"I've heard of Maryland. Near Washington, right?"

"That's right," said Berry. "And when this war is over, I want you to come and see me. I owe you my life, Frank. Take this photograph, and bring it with you. That's my wife, and our farmhouse is in the background. I'll write a message on the back. Make sure you bring it with you. My family will be glad to see you, even if I'm dead."

Berry quickly scribbled some words on the picture and gave it to Frank, who put it in his coat pocket.

"Thanks, Edward. I'll do my best to visit. Now you can help me by going round and giving the men some water." Frank watched as Berry complied.

As he went to his other duties, Frank saw the Union man helping a badly wounded Confederate soldier take a drink, and he smiled to himself. The two men would have been shooting at each other earlier in the day.

Meanwhile, the backlog of injured soldiers was mounting up. Some were lying in ditches, some were on open ground, and others had taken cover in the woods. These men were soon to suffer at the hands of a particularly callous man, the unpopular General Pope, who seemed proud of his hard and unforgiving reputation. He ordered his unwilling artillery units to fire into the trees where the wounded men had taken cover, causing further unnecessary deaths and exacerbating some already horrific injuries. Pope was never disciplined for this act. He explained to an inquiry that he believed the enemy had been using the wounded as a shield.

On 30 August, General Stonewall Jackson reorganised his troops and filled in the lines where the men had been thinned out by gunfire. General Pope then made a further mistake. When he thought the rebels were starting to retreat, he attacked the Confederates head-on, sending wave after wave of men against them. The defenders were holding their position against their attackers. However, towards midday, they began to run short of ammunition, and in some cases had run out completely and were reduced to throwing stones at the enemy. On the other hand, the Union troops were exhausted after being on the attack for one and a half days, and they had suffered many hundreds of casualties. They were led by a general they didn't respect and who had no respect for them. He had repeatedly ordered them to charge at heavily fortified positions in searing heat, and their morale and enthusiasm were fast ebbing away.

At the very worst moment for the Union troops, they were attacked by General Longstreet, who led his men in a devastating counter charge against them at the same time as his artillery opened fire. General Lee had rightly calculated that Stonewall Jackson's men could no longer hold out, having almost completely run out of ammunition, so he had called in reinforcements.

Frank, emerging from the hospital tent for a short rest, saw the Union soldiers break ranks and begin to run away as fast as they could. At this point, a runner brought Walton a request from a major in the attacking Confederate force, asking him to send a small group of medics forward to follow them and to help with the wounded. They were advancing as fast as they could, but it wasn't fast enough. They were so tired that they failed to surround the Union troops, allowing them time to set up a defensive position at Henry Hill House. This brave action let the bulk of the Union men escape towards the fortifications around Washington by crossing Stone Bridge over the Bull Run River.

Frank was ordered to make up the medical party. Together with two orderlies, he moved forward to the edge of the fighting at Henry Hill House, treating the wounded along the way. Troops from both sides were now scattered about, forgotten in the melee of the advance. The battle raged on around him for hours and only slowly died down as the troops left the area. The fighting eventually stopped completely, and a strange quiet fell over the battlefield. Then, one by one, the birds began to twitter. Their summer songs could be heard again, as though they were making a point of reclaiming the land for nature. The birds seemed to be singing out that the madness of man had passed and gone away.

CHAPTER 34

Frank's unit was ordered to continually move along the lines, following the various battles as the war progressed. It was always the same routine. First, would come news of an impending action, and then the hospital would have to pack up and move to the appropriate area. Meanwhile, the remaining patients were sent or transported to the base hospital. Usually, any fighting would be finished before the field hospital was ready. Once, in fact, it was all over before they even arrived.

Wherever they went, they were overwhelmed with casualties before they were ready, but they still had to treat the wounded as best they could. Sometimes it would take a week just to get to every soldier, and even then, treatment was of the most basic kind. This slow response gave plenty of time for infections and disease to set in, causing a large percentage of the men to die prematurely.

For Frank, this was most upsetting, as he could see that, with a few basic provisions and proper cleanliness, many premature deaths could have been avoided. The captured Union supplies from Manassas had been used up long before, though, leaving little more than a drink of water, some soothing words, and the brutality of field surgery to be used to treat the soldiers.

As summer became autumn, the Confederates appeared to be doing very well. They had victories across West Virginia at Chantilly, Harpers Ferry, and Blackfords Ford. Each time, they were led by General Lee; each time, they won the battle. Of course, these actions meant more moves for Frank and the medical unit. Every move meant they were getting further and further from his home in Richmond. It was now four months since he had seen Angela and Amelia, and it looked like it could be another four months before he would see them again.

On 17 September, the Battle of Antietam took place. The Confederates were defeated there by Union forces under General McClellan, but there were devastating losses on both sides. In fact, it was the bloodiest day in American history, with 12,410 Union troops and 11,172 Confederates dead, wounded, missing, or captured. Perhaps, because of the horrific numbers, McClellan had not pursued the rebels with any enthusiasm. President Lincoln was said to be furious, but it really made little difference—the Confederates would never advance that far into Maryland again.

Frank, too, was horrified and couldn't help thinking about how Angela and her mother would be taking such news. They would, he thought, be devastated that so many young men had lost their lives, perhaps even some among them who were their friends. This was all taking its toll on Frank as well. In addition to the mental turmoil he was suffering at the sight of such unrelenting slaughter, the supply lines were long and slow moving, causing food shortages on top of their other problems. Unlike the Union's railroad system, the Confederate railroad network was very poor, with all lines terminating at Richmond and each one using a different-gauge track. This meant that supplies had to be unloaded from one train and then loaded onto another, causing further delays. By December, Frank had lost around twenty pounds from his already lean frame, his uniform was now filthy and torn in places, and he looked worse than some of the injured men he was supposed to be looking after.

Things continued to get worse for the Confederates, as news came in from other areas of the western theatre. General Grant seemed to be able to outthink and outmanoeuvre the rebels at every turn, inflicting defeat after defeat.

On 12 December, the hospital unit was ordered to move to Fredericksburg, where a major battle was expected to take place imminently. The remaining injured patients were quickly dispatched to the rear, and then they were on the road once again. They barely had time to pitch their tent at the new site before the battle commenced at dawn. The commander of the Union troops at this battle was General Burnside, a man with a thick black moustache and tremendously bushy sideburns, and he had a reputation for being as stubborn as a mule. He sent wave after wave of men against the well-defended Confederate lines, with depressingly predictable results. General Lee's men shot them down like the gentry would shoot pheasants. The Union army suffered a huge percentage of casualties; but, for once, the Southerners took very few in comparison. When informed of the disaster, President Lincoln insisted Burnside be released from his duties immediately. The Confederates had won a great battle.

In the east, it was a different matter. General Sherman's Union troops were advancing steadily to the south. While they were celebrating their victories in the west, the people of the Confederacy did not seem to realise the danger this posed. If Sherman continued on his present path, the capital would be encircled, and the war would then soon be over.

As winter became spring, Frank's health began to improve. There had been a lull in the fighting, and a proper supply line had been established. Decent food was provided, the first in many weeks. With that food came fresh troops, medical supplies, new weapons, and lots of ammunition.

The hospital unit was still following the war in the west, but there were only skirmishes and chance engagements until the Battle of Chancellorsville began on 1 May. There followed five days of intense fighting. Once again, General Lee was victorious, with many more Union troops killed and injured than Confederates. This time, it was the unfortunate General Hooker who was replaced in the Union forces. General Grant was brought in, and he now took over command of all the Union forces. Grant was the most highly regarded of all the Union leaders, and he was told in no uncertain terms by President Lincoln that he had to stop General Lee. The future of the Union and, thus, the whole country, depended on him doing so.

General Lee was known for his situational awareness, his daring, his flair, and his flexibility. General Grant, on the other hand, had far greater nerve and a dogged determination that his predecessors lacked, and he was well respected by his men. No number of casualties or Union setbacks would deter him from his ultimate goal of taking Richmond.

Each time he got back to the hospital tent, Frank was exhausted, but there were still many more hours of work ahead. Every time he managed to go for a short sleep, he would be unconscious the second his head touched the pillow. He would invariably be awoken soon after, to attend another emergency, and it would seem to him as if no time had passed. The days passed in a blur, with the only respite the occasional movement of the hospital, which had to be as close to any battle as possible without endangering the doctors or patients. This had been Frank's life for nearly a year now, and he had not had one break to see Angela and the baby.

In early June 1863, General Lee began moving his forces northwards again, but without his cavalry, who were having their own battles in and around Culpepper, Virginia. On 16 June, Lee's men crossed the Potomac and drove into Pennsylvania. On 28 June, General George Meade was appointed by General Grant to take charge of the Union forces in this area, and he took up a defensive position to the west of the small town of Gettysburg while he waited for cavalry reinforcements which arrived on the afternoon of 30 June.

On 1 July, the Battle of Gettysburg began. Early in the morning, General Lee decided to launch a full-scale attack on Meade before more reinforcements could arrive. Against fierce defensive fire and despite the usual heavy casualties, the Confederates forced the Union army back to Cemetery Ridge, to the north of the town. Lee considered that the battle had begun well for him and that they had won the first day.

As the sun rose on the second day, Lee continued his attack, even though Meade had received more reinforcements overnight. This time, as the fading light brought the fighting to an end, it was an even bloodier day than the one before. Out of a total of fifty thousand killed, injured, missing, or taken prisoner in the entire battle, more than nineteen thousand occurred on this day alone.

As usual, Frank was sent out to do what little good he could, along with two parties of orderlies to help bring the walking wounded back to safety. Frank was tending soldiers of both armies, paying little attention to where he was. As he was treating a soldier who'd had one of his legs blown off, he realised he was behind the Union lines when an irate corporal in Union uniform came rushing over to him.

"Here's one of those swine who killed my brother!" the corporal yelled and raised his rifle.

He brought the rifle down hard on the side of Frank's head, and Frank collapsed onto the bloody stump of the leg of the soldier he had been treating. The man let out a scream of agony. The pain was too much for him, and he died at the same moment as Frank passed out. Luckily for Frank, the corporal's comrades pulled him away before he could inflict any more damage, and all three Union men ran off to join their retreating comrades.

Chapter 35

It was dark when Frank regained consciousness. His head was throbbing mightily, and he was too weak to stand. He dragged himself towards a small wooden outbuilding which revealed itself in the moonlight. Once inside, exhaustion took hold again, and he collapsed into a long and dreamless sleep. The battle raged on even as night fell, but eventually it became too dark to fight, and the sounds of fighting faded away. Only the cries of the wounded broke the silence.

On the third day, the Confederates attempted to consolidate their advantage by using more than 1,500 artillery guns against their enemy. When they charged following the barrage, they were cut down in large numbers by devastating defensive fire from the Union lines. All the artillery fire had little effect, and the strong defence weakened the rebels so much that they were unable to do any damage to the Union position. It became clear to General Lee that his gamble had failed, and his exhausted soldiers were forced to retreat back into Virginia. The Battle of Gettysburg would be recorded in history as a win for the Union and the turning point of the Civil War. Frank slept through it all.

When he woke, it was half-light, and all was quiet. To his astonishment, instead of getting brighter, the sky was getting darker. The only explanation was that he'd been so deprived of sleep that, when it did come, he'd slept for nearly a whole day. It was too dark now to do anything, and despite his ravenous hunger, there was no food in the barn. Therefore, he had all night to gather his thoughts and consider his next move.

He looked back over the last few days and wondered how he'd get back to the hospital. Suddenly, he realised he could remember back much further—back to before meeting Angela, back to Elizabeth, the only name from his recent past that he could recall, and back to his days in England. At last! He'd taken a savage blow from the Union corporal, but it was the biggest favour anyone could have done for him. In the light of the moon's rays beaming into the barn through the wooden slats, Frank could see tools and clothes hanging from pegs on the walls. He looked down at his ragged uniform, and it dawned on him that he shouldn't be in the army at all—he was English and shouldn't be on either side. He should be writing about the war, not fighting it.

After a long night spent ordering his thoughts and weighing his options, he decided that his only course of action was to leave the area at first light. He took off his uniform and hid it under a pile of sacks. He quickly pulled on the farm clothing he had found: ill-fitting trousers, a shirt that was far too big, and a torn jacket. He made sure he had removed everything he needed from his uniform, and then he stepped outside.

As he walked through the battlefield, there were dead and dying men everywhere. The smell of gunpowder was still hanging in the air, now mixing with the sickly sweet smell of death. Despite his previous duties as a medic, Frank knew he could do nothing for any of these men on his own. The army would have to look after itself.

In his poor clothing, together with his gaunt appearance and skeletal frame, Frank himself almost looked like a walking corpse. This, he thought, would suit his present circumstances well. The last thing he wanted was anyone stopping him and asking questions. A tramp would be ignored, he hoped. He was deep in thought as he left the carnage behind. He now knew that he had a wife and, quite possibly, a child in Washington; he must make his way there. On the other hand, there were Angela and Amelia back in Richmond, also his wife and child, wondering what had become of him.

He would have to put these problems out of his mind for now and concentrate on the immediate future—getting out of the area undetected.

It was a dangerous journey, as he tried to avoid human contact of any kind, so he moved warily from tree to ditch and slid around barns and houses, until he eventually reached the road to Washington. He kept to the side of the road, ready to dive for cover the instant he saw anyone. It was tiring work, but as night began to fall, he came to a railroad track and waited until a slow-moving freight train started to pass. He ran alongside one of the trucks, grabbed an iron railing that guarded a small set of steps, and hauled himself up. He clambered up the steps and found the truck was carrying wooden planks with a label giving their destination as Washington. So far, luck had appeared to be on his side.

The journey was not a long one, but it was slow and uncomfortable. Even so, the night was warm, and he slept intermittently, awoken every time the train screeched over some points or rocked about at a particularly bumpy section of track. The train slowed at one point to barely above walking pace, as though the driver believed the track might have been tampered with. Finally, they pulled into a large freight yard. A clock in a nearby church tower struck eight. As he looked about him, Frank was sure he'd never been to this part of Washington before. He got down from the truck and started walking towards a roadway he could see at the far end of the yard. Just then, he heard a shout from behind him. As he turned round, he saw a soldier with his rifle raised and aimed at him.

Frank instinctively ducked under the nearest railroad wagon. As he did so, there was a loud bang, followed by the sound of a bullet ricocheting off one of the metal wheels of the wagon. He crawled out from under it, into the next aisle between the lines of trains, and ran as fast as he could towards the road.

Just as he reached it, he ran headlong into a large man wearing a sergeant's stripes on a Union uniform. Frank's momentum forced all the wind out of the man as they collided. As the man fell, Frank went down with him. Before the sergeant could recover, Frank pulled the rifle from him and brought the butt down on his head. With a groan, he passed out and lay spread-eagled on the ground. Frank quickly looked around him and then set off down the road at a trot. He was still carrying the stolen gun, and he'd knocked out a soldier. Both of these were serious offences and would probably mean a death sentence if he got caught.

He saw a horse saddled up and hitched to a tree just ahead. It was obvious the rider had gone into the house that stood nearby. As he drew nearer, Frank kept himself hidden. He soon saw a soldier and his girl sitting in a swing seat on the veranda of the house. They were kissing each other with great enthusiasm, a situation that Frank took full advantage of. He ran out from his hiding place, quickly untied the horse, and jumped up onto the saddle. He trotted off down the road, making as little noise as possible, but he wasn't quiet enough. Despite his caution, he heard a shout from behind him as the soldier looked up for a moment and saw his horse being stolen. Frank spurred the horse into a canter, then a gallop. Stealing a horse was another hanging offence—he was certainly racking them up today!

He tried to make himself a little less conspicuous by throwing the rifle into a small river as he crossed a bridge. He was approaching a busier part of town, and he could see a number of pedestrians and other traffic ahead.

The day was off to a busy start, with everyone making their way to work, and early shoppers out buying the day's provisions. He reined his horse in and dismounted, leading the animal the last few yards to the road. Frank undid a whip that was tied to the saddle and gave the horse a quick slash across its buttocks. The startled creature lurched forward and ran off down the main street, scattering the people before it. Some carters tried to catch it by the bridle, and they soon brought it to a standstill. Frank walked towards them and heard the men discussing the matter among themselves. They were looking for a name on the saddle and wondering how much they would get as a reward for returning it to its owner.

"Here's a name," shouted one of the men to his friends. "Mr John Shafter, and his address is here in Washington. I should get a dollar or two for this beauty."

"Hey, wait a minute, buster. We all helped to catch him; we should all get a share!"

"Right, right. Just my little joke. We'll all go together. Come on, men, what're we waiting for?"

While they continued talking, Frank headed towards the centre of the city. He gradually started to recognise different areas and sought out the office from where he used to send his battle reports to England. As he looked in the window, other memories began to come back. He now remembered that he had lived not far from here and that he used to meet up with an Irishman at a nearby bar. Names of people, including his own, and of places were still eluding him, but he was now sure that everything would return in time.

Frank checked his pockets to make sure he still had his money. Before he did anything, he needed some respectable clothing and somewhere to clean his filthy body. Washing was easy enough, as there were horse troughs aplenty. He soon cleaned himself up, removing some ground-in dirt and blood from his hair, as well as a disgusting smell from his body. He drew plenty of curious looks while he was performing his ablutions, but luckily nobody questioned his actions. Further down the road was an outfitter's shop, where he bought a shirt and a pair of trousers. A coat would have been nice, but he had to be very careful with his money for now. Besides, the weather was warm enough for him to be able to do without one.

Now he had to find his old drinking buddy and somehow concoct a plausible story to explain his absence of more than two years. He dared not tell the truth. Firstly, it all seemed too far-fetched to be true. Secondly, any mention of his having helped the Confederates would have him locked up.

He looked around again. It all seemed so familiar! He looked across the road, and then it clicked. This was easy now. He crossed over and turned left at the next junction, and there was the bar, its faded blue sign just as he remembered it: "The Bell—Coffee House and Bar."

It was still early, but there was one man with a beer sitting alone in a corner, a roughly dressed Irishman who recognised him instantly.

"As I live and breathe! I never thought I'd see you again, Firth! Where have you been, my boy? Everyone thought you were long dead."

"Not dead, just missing."

"What happened? You went off with that neighbour of yours to Bull Run and never came back. They said your body was found, and that was it. We thought you were dead," the man said, starting to gabble and repeat himself in his excitement.

"It's wonderful to see you, but you're not going to believe what I have to tell you. I've had a truly dreadful time, and I promise I'll tell you one day, but you're the first friendly face I've seen since I've been back. I'm desperate to see my wife."

"Sure, and she's gonna be fainting when she sees you, Firth, my lad," he laughed.

As he was about to get up, the man stopped him by bringing his hand down on Firth's arm. "Can't you tell me what happened to you? You can't leave me wondering till the next time I see you. I think you owe me an explanation— and some money, now I think about it."

"Money?"

"Aye. For that last story I got you. You didn't pay me."

"Next time I see you, I promise. But now I really have to go. There is one thing, though."

"Oh?"

"Look, this is going to sound a bit odd, but I need you to tell me my surname. What is it?"

"Are you having a laugh, boy?" he asked, incredulous.

"I'm deadly serious. Firth what?"

"Brown. Firth Brown. And I'm Joe Higgins, in case ye'd forgotten that too. We're in Washington, by the way, in the great nation of America. Anything else?"

Firth smiled at him with gratitude. "Thanks, Joe. Now one last thing."

"Another last thing? Go on then," he said, ready now for anything.

"Where do I live?"

"Ha! Ha ha ha ha!" he guffawed. "Now I've heard it all. What the hell has happened to you?"

"I'm serious, Joe. Just tell me, and I'll be on my way."

"You live on East Sixth Street. I don't remember the number, but it's a white painted house between G and H Streets," he said, shaking his head in disbelief.

"Thanks, Joe. I should be able to find it. I'll see you in a day or two." Firth held out his hand, which, after a second's hesitation, Joe shook with a smile.

"Be sure you do. I can't wait to hear this story of yours. And don't forget my money."

CHAPTER 36

Firth got up and moved towards the door, turning round when Joe shouted to him.

"Firth! Firth! Be careful when you see your wife. I've seen her a few times, and she's still wearing the widow's black. She's still grieving for you, my boy. You'd better be ready. Mind you, once she's over the shock, I'm sure she'll give you a good seeing to tonight, eh?" He added with a leer, "For once, I envy a bloody Limey!"

Firth said nothing, just waved as he left, and headed towards his house. He already knew he had a wife here, but now the reality of his situation hit him hard. He was a bigamist, which, while it might not mean a death sentence for once, was still a pretty serious offence. Who would believe he had married both women in complete innocence and honesty? And there was at least one child involved, maybe two. As he carried on walking, he began to wonder if getting his memory back was such a good thing after all. The more he found out about himself, the more complicated his situation became. He thought of both his wives, and he was sure he had loved and married them both in total innocence. As he approached the house, he wondered if this was such a good idea, but he knew he had to face up to his problems for the sake of everyone involved.

He opened the little wicker gate and went up to the front door, took a deep breath, and banged the knocker. He heard steps from inside, and the door opened. He suddenly realised that he had not rehearsed a story or an explanation. He would just have to let events take their course.

The maid, Martha, he now remembered, looked at him anxiously. "Can I help you, sir?" she asked.

"Hello, Martha," Firth said quietly.

The girl's hand flew to her mouth. For a moment, Firth thought she was going to faint. "It can't be!" she said as she reached out to touch him, just to make sure she wasn't seeing things. She ran back into the house as Firth heard another voice.

"Who is it, Martha? Who's at the door?"

A young woman dressed all in black appeared from one of the rooms, holding the hands of two young children, one black and one white. She had a look of disbelief on her face, and her jaw dropped. She was unable to say a word. The children stood staring, too young to comprehend what was happening.

Firth held out his hand to his wife, but she backed away.

"Elizabeth, please," he pleaded, adding quietly, "I know this must be an awful shock for you. It must seem impossible that I've come back, but you must let me explain."

Elizabeth just stared at him, unsure if she could believe what her eyes were telling her. She made a visible effort to gather herself.

"You'd better come in. Martha, take the children," she instructed the maid.

"Are they both yours? Er, mine?" he asked awkwardly.

Elizabeth looked at him curiously. "Of course not. If you look closely, you'll see that one of them is black. That's Martha's child, Elijah, and this is Emily—your—that is, our daughter."

The child giggled, then ran off and hid in the safety of Martha's skirt. This strange man was too much for her. Despite him longing to hold his daughter and his wife in his arms, he knew he had to explain himself first. The confidence he had acquired since regaining his memory was beginning to slip away.

"I lost my memory, Elizabeth, at Bull Run. I was shot in the head," he said and parted his hair to show her the scar. "I've been wandering the country, not knowing who I was or where I'd come from. It's been dreadful. I've just drifted from farm to farm, doing odd jobs to earn a little money".

Elizabeth said nothing, but there were tears in her eyes.

"A few days ago, I had another accident. It was nothing as like as serious, but I banged my head again, and my memories started to come back. I've been desperately trying to piece it all together ever since. It's still not all there yet, but I'm sure it will come."

"Firth, my darling, I had no idea. We all thought you'd been killed. Mr Peters said you'd left him to get close to the fighting, and he never saw you again. Then, a week later, I got a visit from an officer who said that you'd been found dead in a wood. Look, he brought me all the things they found on your, er, body." She laughed nervously at the absurdity of the situation.

Elizabeth reached into a drawer and laid out the contents on the table. They were all his things, that was for sure. His wallet containing a little cash, his press card, a fob watch, and a photograph of his wife.

"I can't explain it, Elizabeth. When I woke up, I was in a ditch with two other bodies, and I had a thumping headache. I was lucky my head wound healed up so well, but I couldn't remember a thing. And now I'm back," he said.

He held out his hands to her. Elizabeth held them and drew him closer. They hugged each other and then kissed. Firth knew his story had been accepted at face value.

"Look at you," she said, looking him up and down. "I can see it's been hard for you. You've lost a lot of weight. When did you last have a good meal?"

He shrugged, adding, "Later, I'm not hungry."

He kissed her again.

"I've missed you so much, Firth. I thought my life was over without you."

"Well, you won't be needing this stuff anymore," he whispered and began removing her widow's garb.

They both desperately wanted to make love, but now that Firth had unburdened himself, his months of deprivation were making themselves felt again. He had been through so much since leaving Richmond. The trauma of countless battles, the terrible injuries and suffering he had witnessed, the return of his memory, and the difficulties he had endured while trying to return to Washington. All this was taking its toll. He was literally falling asleep on his feet. He felt himself sinking to his knees and was unable to stop it. He was already deep asleep as he fell to the floor.

He slept for the whole day and the following night. When he awoke in a lovely, warm, soft bed, the sun was shining brightly, and he felt better than he had for months.

He was refreshed and vital, but absolutely famished, and his throat was as dry as the desert. Most importantly, his mind was clear, and all his memories were intact, he was relieved to discover. He now thought of them as he would, say, a photograph or an item of jewellery—something valuable but that is taken for granted, and that, unless guarded, would be easily lost.

He sat up with effort and soon decided that was enough for now. The room started spinning, and he couldn't even sit straight without swaying, so standing was out of the question. He flopped back down and tried to call out, but his throat was so dry that little more than a croak came out. Just then, he heard voices outside the door.

"Do you think we should try to get the doctor to see him again?" he heard Elizabeth ask Martha.

"No, ma'am. Give it another day. He's breathing well. I expect the poor man is just worn out with all he's been through."

"I'm worried, so very worried. I've only just got my beloved Firth back. I couldn't bear to lose him again. I'm so afraid of losing him, Martha. It would break my heart if he were to die."

"He ain't gonna die, ma'am. He just needs time and love, that's all."

"I hope you're right," Elizabeth said quietly.

"I am right, ma'am. Just you wait and see. He's a strong young man. In a few days, he'll be up and about, laughing and joking like he used to. Nothing will keep the master in bed for long. He was always so full of life."

Firth smiled, and he took pleasure in remembering his first days in America, when he'd been footloose and carefree.

He'd had an eye for the ladies and, he thought modestly, a certain charm. He remembered too that he could be selfish and sometimes heartless, but that was all in the past. He forgave himself these misdemeanours, with the thought that most men would break a few hearts before they settled down with the one they loved. Some, though, went on doing it all their lives and never really grew up. In his case, through no fault of his own, he had two wives, each with a child. How on earth could he make both of them happy?

Elizabeth came into the room and saw that he was awake.

"How are you feeling?" she asked.

Firth let out a croak. "Water," he tried to say as he made a drinking gesture with his hand.

"Of course! You must be parched. I'll be right back."

She left the room, and Firth could see her talking to the maid again. She soon returned with a large pitcher of ice-cold water.

Firth grabbed the pitcher and drank straight from it. He guzzled it down as fast as he could.

"Firth, take it slowly. There's plenty more where that came from."

Just then, Martha came in with a big bowl of steaming-hot beef stew.

"This'll put the energy back in you. You've been asleep for ages, and it looks like you haven't eaten either, so enjoy this."

Firth put down the nearly empty pitcher and inhaled the aroma of beef coming his way. His tummy started rumbling, and his hunger went into overdrive. It was a real effort to stop himself from wolfing down the food unchewed, but he made himself behave. Elizabeth had experienced enough shocks recently without him causing her to think he'd changed into some sort of caveman. Nevertheless, he thought the food was the best he'd ever tasted, and after the first few mouthfuls, he told her so.

"Your voice has come back as well, I see. Take your time over that, Firth. You don't want indigestion now, do you?"

"I never thought food could taste this good. Are all your meals like this?"

"Every time—and don't you forget it," she said with a smile.

Firth emptied the bowl in record time and asked for some more. While Elizabeth went to refill his bowl, he suddenly felt heavy-lidded again. He didn't fight it, and sleep overtook him once again.

When he next awoke, Elizabeth was there, sitting on a wooden chair next to his bed, and there was a full pitcher of water on the cabinet.

"Hello, sleepyhead," she said, smiling at him. "You've been snoring away quite happily, so I didn't want to wake you. At least you've got a little more colour in your cheeks now. You truly looked like death earlier."

She was an attentive nurse, and her gentle care, some good food, and her encouragement all combined to speed his recovery. His next big hurdle was meeting his child, Emily, whom, except for their brief encounter on his arrival, he hadn't seen.

"Where's Emily?" he asked. "I need to meet her."

"Do you think you're strong enough? She can be quite a handful," Elizabeth said.

"The sooner the better. She must have asked you about me."

"She never stops. Just a minute then. I'll go and get her."

Firth made an attempt to tidy his hair and put a smile on his face.

Elizabeth was soon back, holding the hands of the two children, one on each side, and Martha followed them in.

"Hello, Emily," said Firth.

Emily looked at her mother. The child seemed unsure what to do next.

Elizabeth brought her over and sat down on the bed. She took Firth's hand and said, "This is your daddy, darling. He's been away for a long time, but now he's home. Aren't you going to say hello?"

"Hello," said the child hesitantly.

Firth and Elizabeth kissed each other as Emily watched. Her mother obviously trusted this man, so she would too. She climbed onto the bed and put her face next to Firth's. She wanted to be kissed too. Firth was finding it all highly emotional and had trouble holding back the tears. He wrapped his arm round his little girl and kissed her.

He made a great effort to compose himself, though, because both Martha and Elijah were still watching. Martha was embarrassed, but Elijah seemed to be rapt.

Elizabeth beckoned them over.

Firth held out his hand. "Very pleased to meet you, Elijah."

Elijah slowly took it, smiling broadly when Firth shook his hand up and down.

"I'm so pleased things have worked out for you, Martha. Are you happy here?"

"I sure am, sir. I don't know what I would have done without you and Mrs Brown. We are very happy here, sir."

Firth's recovery continued steadily over the next few days. The doctor called and told him he was suffering from mental exhaustion, as well as the more obvious physical fatigue. He insisted Firth stay in bed for a further few days and undertake only the lightest of physical activities for at least two weeks.

Firth tried to do as the doctor instructed, but he was becoming increasingly agitated. He had to see Joe again, for a start. He also needed to get a message to Smythe at *The Manchester Echo* to see if he still had a job, he had to see Daisy Swinton, and he had to work out a plan of action concerning Angela and Amelia.

One thing at a time, though. As soon as he was able, he went to the bank to see the state of his finances. He was pleasantly surprised to see that a small but regular amount had been paid in every month from England until a year ago, and a much-larger and steadily increasing amount was transferred every quarter from Daisy. She had been as good as her word, and Firth was overcome with gratitude. There was a healthy balance, as Elizabeth had obviously been living quite frugally, presumably because there was no certainty of future income.

That will all change now, he thought. He withdrew fifty dollars and left the bank. *Next stop, the Bell, for a visit with Joe Higgins.*

He now remembered that Joe was a little more than just his drinking partner. He recalled details of their business together, mainly that Joe was the source of the information on which he had based the reports he sent to England. This was what he owed the money for, but some details still eluded him. He needed to speak to Joe to help him fill in the missing pieces of information.

Firth went to the Bell, but there was no sign of his friend, so he asked the barman whether Mr Higgins would be in today.

"Who?" was the barman's reply.

"Higgins," Firth said. "Usually sits over there." He pointed to Joe's favourite seat.

"Oh, him. Couldn't say either way, buddy. Do you want a drink?"

"Why couldn't you say? How about if I buy a drink. Could you say then?"

"Look, buster. He's not here. Maybe he's gone away. I don't know. I'm not his goddamn mother, am I?! Now, what'll you have?"

"I'm an old friend of his. We used to sit over there, don't you remember?" Firth asked, managing to keep his temper in check.

"I'm not paid to keep tabs on people! I'm paid to tend the bar. I keep myself to myself, and that's why my face hasn't got a mark on it. You'd do well to follow my example."

Firth realised he wasn't going to get any useful information from this surly character, and so he left the bar. As he made his way along the road, a man fell into step beside him.

"I know where he is," he said.

"Where?"

"Times are hard, mister. Nothing comes for free anymore."

"How much do you want?" Firth asked.

Firth looked sideways at the man, who was a few inches shorter than he, a weasely little fellow with poor clothing hanging from a thin frame. He coughed between each sentence he uttered and was generally down on his luck. Firth was reminded of himself not so long ago.

"I can't pay you much. It's Joe I owe money to, and I only need to see him so I can pay him."

"It'll still cost you two bucks. I ain't tellin' you nothin' without a proper reward."

"Two dollars! I'm not that desperate. I'll give you half a dollar," Firth said with a take-it-or-leave-it tone.

"Come on, mister. A dollar, please," the man whined. "That'll buy me a good hot meal."

"Well, you certainly look like you could do with one." Firth reached into his pocket and held a coin out towards his informant.

As the man went to take it, Firth closed his fist, enclosing the coin. "Information first, if you don't mind."

"He's staying with a woman on the top floor of a big blue house on Fayette Street. There aren't too many houses on that road, so you won't miss it."

"How do I know you're speaking the truth? If this turns out to be a wild goose chase, I'll find you again, and I'll crush what little breath you have out of your body. Understand?" Firth said with as much menace as he could muster.

"It's the truth, honest. What would be the point in lying? Just don't tell Joe you got it from me, will you?"

Firth nodded and gave the man the dollar coin. He watched as he disappeared back down the street. He was about to call out, as he realised he hadn't a clue where Fayette

Street was, but it was too late. The man had vanished as quickly as he had appeared.

It took an hour, and he had to ask a few passers-by, but he eventually found the blue house. It was an imposing double-fronted building with a large and ornate front door. The house had once been owned by a merchant family of considerable wealth, but its present owner had partitioned it into single rooms for rental. Firth knocked and waited. There was no answer, so he tried the handle. He was surprised when the door opened, and he stepped inside to a large hall. There was still no sign of anyone, so he started up the stairs.

He knocked quietly at the only door at the top of the stairs. Again, there was no reply, so Firth tried the handle. As it wasn't locked, he slowly pushed open the door. It opened into a large, untidy room with clothes all over the floor. A double bed could be seen at the far end, and there was someone asleep in it, snoring peacefully.

"Hello, Joe," Firth said loudly.

The figure moved like lightning, and a long rifle barrel appeared above the bedclothes, pointed directly at him.

"Stay very still, mister. Who the hell are you, anyway?"

"Calm down, Joe, it's only me, Firth, your old buddy."

The bedclothes flew back and revealed two naked figures. Joe's companion, a rough-looking middle-aged woman, sat bolt upright and stared at Firth. She made no attempt to cover herself.

"Who is this fellow, Joe? I thought we were going to have some time to ourselves, honey. Can't you get rid of him?" she asked.

"Let me speak to him. I'll just be a minute."

The woman gave him a "you'd better" look and rushed off into a little room next to the small attic window.

"You nearly got yourself killed there. Next time, you'd better knock instead of just barging in on a man. What d'yer want, anyway? And who told you where I live?"

"Cheer up, Joe. Why are you so miserable? It's not like you, especially with a girl in your bed."

"Not anymore she's not. And probably won't be again if this keeps happening."

"You can put the gun away too, if you don't mind."

"Sorry. Yeah. I owe money to some folks. You can't be too careful, you know."

"How much do you owe?"

"Fifty bucks. And I can't pay," he said mournfully.

"I can help you out, Joe, if you'll let me. Tell me who they are and where I can find them. I'll pay them off for the time being, but you've got to promise me not to borrow anymore. Can you do that?"

"Sure, I can do that. I only borrowed it so I could pay the doctor. I caught something from my last girlfriend. The rotten cow never told me she was dirty. Don't worry; I'm not planning on catching anything else."

Firth raised his eyebrows, questioning this last statement. He nodded in the direction of the room where the woman had gone. "What about her?" he asked.

"You shut yer mouth, yer bastard. I've known Ruby for years, and she's a good, clean woman," Joe said in a low voice. He wrote the name and address of the moneylender on a piece of paper and handed it to Firth. "Why are you helping me out like this?"

"I owe you, don't I? This will wipe out my debt to you, and then some. I'm going to need a bit more information, and I want you to keep quiet about it. Come down to the Bell at twelve o'clock, and I'll buy you a drink. See you later, Joe."

Firth left the house, noted the name and address on the piece of paper Joe had given him, and sought out the moneylender. He was easy to find, working out of another bar, McTavish's.

He was a nasty-looking character, sitting at a table flanked by two hefty men whom Firth took to be bodyguards. The man with the money must have a lot of enemies, as he was in a dangerous business.

"Mr Philpott?" asked Firth.

The man regarded him from deep-set eyes under bushy eyebrows. "Who are you?" he growled.

The two bodyguards were staring at Firth, and he felt distinctly uncomfortable.

"I'm a friend of Joe Higgins. I believe he owes you some money."

"I don't talk business with strangers."

"I've come to pay off some of his debt."

"Some? How much?"

"I can pay you twenty-five dollars now. The rest will be paid within a month from today."

Philpott continued looking at Firth. After a moment, he said. "That will be acceptable, Mr …?"

"English. Frank English," Firth said. He had no intention of telling this man who he really was.

"Of course it is." Philpott laughed. "What else with an accent like that, eh, boys?"

His bodyguards joined in the false laughter, but their eyes didn't leave Firth for a second.

Philpott gave Firth a receipt for the money. "Nice to do business with you Mr English. He has thirty days to find the rest."

"Thank you, Mr Philpott. Good day, gentlemen."

Firth left and hurried home. He was glad to get out of the place in one piece. *Joe must have been desperate to borrow money from someone like that,* he thought.

It was time to meet Joe again, so he headed off to the Bell. Joe was sitting in his favourite chair, waiting patiently for a drink. Firth went straight to the barman and ordered them a beer each. The barman made no mention of their earlier encounter; indeed, he made no gesture of recognition at all, which Firth found rather strange.

"Hi, Joe. Get this down you, I'm sure you're thirsty after last night's exertions," Firth joked.

"It's just as well you're me friend, Firth. I'll say no more," Joe said with a note of warning in his voice.

"Calm down, Joe. Look, I've been to see Philpott, and I've bought you some time. You've got a month to come up with twenty-five dollars, which is everything you owe him now."

"I thought you said you were going to pay him off?"

"No, Joe. If you search your memory, you'll remember I said I'd get him off your back for the time being. Twenty-five dollars more than covers what I owe you, but you can earn the rest by helping me out."

"Some things never change, do they? What do you want?"

"Well, it's simple really. I want you to bring me up to date on the war. I need to know what's happened since Gettysburg and what the situation is now. Can you do that?"

"Sure, I can do that very easily. I can tell you right now that the Confederates are on the run. After Gettysburg, Meade's men chased them back across the Potomac, and they've been retreating ever since. Looks like they're gonna chase them all the way to Richmond."

"And then?"

"Well, if they take Richmond, the war will be over, won't it? You can't command an army without a headquarters, can ye?"

Firth sat and digested this. He somehow had to get to Richmond to see Angela and Amelia, but how?

"Thanks, Joe. I've got to go; I've got a lot of work to do."

"What about me money?"

"You'll get it; don't worry. I'll need chapter and verse next time, not just the headlines. See you soon," Firth said.

He headed home, deep in thought.

CHAPTER 37

"All that fresh air looks like it's done you a power of good," Elizabeth remarked when he got home.

Firth, however, had different matters on his mind. "Were there any letters for me from England while I was away?" he asked.

"There were one or two," she said and went over to a desk in front of the window. She opened a drawer and pulled out a bundle of envelopes neatly tied together with a piece of blue ribbon.

"You've kept them? What do they say?"

"Firth, they're addressed to you. I haven't read them. I kept them because I hoped—" Her voice trailed away. "I don't know what I hoped. Here you are. They're yours, so you can read them whenever you want."

"Well, if you don't mind," he said, taking them, "I've got a lot of catching up to do."

"I'll leave you to it."

Firth quickly went through the pile. It seemed there were only two senders: Smythe from *The Manchester Echo*, and his father. The most recent one was from his father, dated 18 February, more than six months ago. Those from Smythe had stopped more than a year before that.

He wrote first to his family, who, like Elizabeth, had been convinced that he was killed after getting too close to the fighting at Bull Run. There was nothing he could do but to reassure them that he was in full health, and then give them an idea of what had happened. A full explanation would have to wait until he saw them, whenever that might be.

He read through the letters from Smythe. The first few demanded to know why he had stopped sending reports, coupled with threats of firing him. Next, he gave Firth an ultimatum—start reporting again, or he would send out someone to replace him. There then followed one terminating his employment and stopping his pay. Lastly, there was one letter that had been opened. It was addressed to "Mrs F. Brown". It expressed his, Smythe's, and the paper's condolences to his widow for her husband's sudden and untimely death. Firth was touched that Smythe had taken the time to write this—he wouldn't have thought it was in the man's nature to have any sympathy for anyone, except, maybe, himself.

Firth settled down to write to his editor, explaining his injury and subsequent memory loss. He promised a report in the next few days and pleaded with him to give him back his job. As an enticement, he said that, as well as battle reports, he could give details of life behind the Confederate lines, surely something of great interest to his readers.

Firth had to hope that this would be enough and that they would recall the replacement reporter. He sent the letter the next day, but he knew that it would be at least a month before he got a reply.

One day, he sat down with Elizabeth, to find out more about what had happened while he'd been away.

"How are things between you and your father now?" he asked.

"I knew he didn't like you, Firth, and when you told me about those horrible men who had tried to kill you, I had a suspicion he was involved somehow. Whenever the subject was mentioned, he'd leave the room, or just try and change the subject. One day, after you'd gone missing, I confronted him about it. He was outraged that I should question him, then he said I was better off without you. When I asked why, he said you had tricked him out of thousands of dollars. I asked him how, and when he started talking about the factory in Philadelphia, I knew he was involved in trying to have you killed. I said as much to him, and he went mad—started ranting and throwing things. I was so scared. I was going to leave the room, but then, he started staggering about, clutching his chest. Then he fell over, so I went to him, but I couldn't help him; I didn't know what was wrong. The doctor said it was a heart attack, and there was nothing anyone could have done. Mamma still lives in the house, and at least she has been left well provided for. He was a very wealthy man."

"Your mother must have been very upset."

"Not as much as I would have expected. She once told me he'd changed and wasn't the man she'd married. She'd never admit it, but I think she's glad he's gone. He was a horrible old tyrant—she's really come out of her shell over the last year or so, and now she does lots of work with the local women's groups helping the soldiers, and also works helping at the church. She seems, dare I say, very happy now that the shock has worn off."

"Well, I'm very pleased to hear it. We must invite her over soon; I'd like to see her again. You mentioned Philadelphia a little while ago."

"Yes?"

"I must go there. I have to see Daisy, to thank her for keeping up her end of our deal, and to see how the factory is doing. I thought I'd go next week for a few days. Will that be all right?"

"You'd better come home this time—I'm not going through all that again. I have seen Daisy once, to tell her you'd been killed, so be careful when you see her, won't you?"

The next morning, Firth stepped off the train at Philadelphia's Broad Street Railroad Depot. As he walked through the station to the street, everything became familiar to him. He almost expected Lew Todd to trot up in his carriage, then he remembered their final meeting. He knew now that he had fully recovered.

It didn't take long to walk to Mulberry Street. As he turned into the road, he was greeted by a busy scene. There were four carts standing at the side of the road, each waiting their turn to be served by the factory. The one being tended to at the moment was being loaded by four men. They were lifting heavy-looking wooden boxes, each about five feet long, onto the flat bed of the carriage. Firth was gratified to see the factory doing so well. He went in the same entrance he'd used the last time he was here. The internal layout had changed from what he remembered. Instead of walking straight onto the factory floor, he was confronted with a receptionist at a desk, a wall behind her showing photographs of, he presumed, the factory's products displayed by satisfied customers. They were mainly pictures of men with guns of varying types, but there was also one of a steel tube chair and one of a bicycle, a contraption Firth had no desire to try for himself.

"Good morning," he said to the woman at the front desk, a Miss Leadbeater, according to the plate in front of her. "I would like to see Miss Swinton, please."

"Do you have an appointment, sir?"

"No, I haven't, I'm afraid. If you tell her Mr Brown is here, I'm sure she'll see me."

"Yes, sir. A moment, please," she said and disappeared into the factory.

It was some minutes before she reappeared, looking a little flustered.

"Miss Swinton won't see you, sir. She says you should make an appointment in the usual way, and I also need to know your business, sir."

"I knew this was going to be difficult." Firth took out his pen and wrote a short note. "Give her this, would you?"

"I'm sorry, sir. You'll have to make an appointment."

"Look, young lady, I am her business partner. Give her that, now, or I'll forget my manners and find her office myself."

"Just a moment, sir," she said, taking the note reluctantly.

This time, the woman was back a lot more quickly. "She's coming, sir" was all she said.

A smart and prosperous, but angry looking woman followed the receptionist a few seconds later. She was about to start talking when she saw Firth. She stopped in her tracks, and her mouth fell open.

"Firth! Good God! What …?! You're supposed to be dead!" she said, shocked.

"Well, here I am, large as life," he said, smiling, and held out his hands to her.

She stepped forward and took them. She looked him up and down, and then hugged him.

The receptionist was watching all this with great interest—she wasn't used to her employer displaying such emotion, and this was the first she'd heard of a partner, alive or dead!

"This is a real surprise. You'd better come through," Daisy said, recovering well. "Miss Leadbeater, I'm not to be disturbed for anything, understand?"

"Yes, ma'am."

Daisy lead Firth through the factory, which was as busy on the inside as it was on the outside.

"Looks like you're doing well," he shouted above the noise.

"You bet we are. Business has really taken off," she said as they entered her office.

Daisy closed the door, and the noise level reduced considerably.

"That's better," Daisy said. "Come on, then, let's hear it."

"I'll start at the beginning, shall I?" Firth said and began to tell his story. He wanted to tell her about Angela and Amelia, but even though he trusted Daisy completely, he couldn't bring himself to tell her. He did tell her about his working for the Confederate army, but he stressed that his role was as a medic, not a fighting soldier.

Daisy, of course, was incredulous and would have dismissed his story as a fantasy had she not known Firth so well. She believed every word.

For her part, Daisy had an equally difficult, if not quite such an exciting time.

On her first day as the new owner of the factory, Mr Kearney was sitting in his customary place in his office. He had not believed at first that a woman, especially one as young as she, would be running the place. After convincing him that she was indeed the rightful owner, Kearney had agreed to stay on indefinitely as an advisor and consultant for as long as she felt she needed him. They had become good friends, and he still came in two or three times a week. He'd been a great help in soothing bruised egos among the workers, who had never worked for a woman and never expected to, and he had helped secure their existing contracts with Colt and Remington for high-quality gun barrels.

Firth said he'd seen the photographs at the reception and mentioned one of a man standing by a multibarrelled gun unlike anything he'd ever seen before.

"That's Mr George Gatling," she said. "Each gun has eight barrels, and it fires by cranking a handle on the side. It loads automatically, and it can fire three hundred rounds a minute. Imagine that! Anyway, the barrels get real hot, much hotter than a rifle, and only we can make them strong enough to withstand the heat."

"Three hundred? It sounds terrifying."

"Gatling says it'll help shorten the war, because no one will want to fight against such a lethal weapon. I have my doubts about that, I must say. Anyway, it's bringing in lots of work and lots of money."

"That's wonderful, Daisy. And what about your father? He must've been livid when he found out we'd snatched the factory from under his nose."

"I told you I could handle him, didn't I? He disowned me at first, but when old Burkett died, his biggest source of income dried up. He was too proud to come to me for help, but I could see what was going on. I've helped him out by giving him a third of my earnings from the factory. It leaves me plenty, and he can live comfortably on what he gets. I think he's ashamed at having to be supported by his daughter, but not ashamed enough to refuse it. He wouldn't dare disrupt the factory now. He'd be cutting his own throat. I think it would be a good idea if you stayed away, though; I don't think he'd be very pleased to see you."

"Don't worry. I've no intention of going anywhere near him. It's you I came to see, and to thank."

"Thank? Whatever for?"

"For being an upstanding woman and for keeping your word. Elizabeth would never have survived my absence without the money."

"That was our agreement, was it not?"

"Yes, but—"

"But nothing, Firth. I keep my promises."

"You've really grown up in the last two years, Daisy. You look the part, and you act the part. I can see the place is safe in your hands."

"Thank you," she said with a smile. "There's too many waiting for me to fail. It feels good to have someone on my side, for a change. How long are you staying for?"

"Well, it's been a long time, hasn't it? I'd like to stay for a few days if I could. I'd like to get a better understanding of everything here."

Daisy was pleased he was showing such interest, and she put aside a few days for them to catch up. She arranged a room for him at the Continental, the best hotel in town.

CHAPTER 38

When he returned home, Firth found that Joe, too, had been busy. As well as his usual information about the various battles, he told Firth that President Lincoln was to make a major speech at Gettysburg, on 19 November. When Joe told him what the subject was, Firth was determined to be there at all costs.

He'd also had a letter from Smythe, at last, reinstating his job. He seemed uncharacteristically delighted to hear of Firth's resurrection. He said that as soon as he had Firth's agreement, he would recall the replacement reporter, who had never had Firth's knack for being where the action was, and whose reports had a distinctly second-hand flavour to them.

If only he knew! Firth thought.

Smythe went on to say that Firth would henceforth be known as "Our North America Correspondent", and his pay would be doubled to one pound per week, plus expenses, to reflect his seniority and new position. He closed by asking if all this was acceptable.

This was great news, and it certainly was acceptable. It cemented Firth's financial future, at least until the end of the war, and meant that he could continue reporting. Firth told Elizabeth of all the developments and of his intention to go to Gettysburg.

"Don't worry, though; the fighting finished there a long time ago. I've heard that the president's going to make a speech there, dedicating a new national cemetery for all the soldiers who've died in the war. It'll be a big occasion, and it'll be reported all over the country—and beyond! I've got to be there," he told her.

He hired a horse for the occasion and set out two days before the speech was scheduled. It was an easy journey, but parts of it were grim. There were many reminders of what had taken place at intervals along the way, more so on the second day. Battle sites with their shell craters, trees that had been shorn of their limbs, destroyed barns and farmhouses, lots of abandoned weapons, and still-unrecovered bodies of horses and men littered the landscape. Fortunately, the corpses had all rotted beyond the point of putrefaction and had been picked clean by scavenging animals. Little was left now except white bones and the ragged tatters of uniforms of both armies.

As he neared Gettysburg on the afternoon of the second day, the number of people increased markedly, all of them there to hear the president make his speech. Firth's first priority was to find somewhere to stay. He knew all the hotels in the centre of town would be long since filled, so he took his horse on a tour of the outskirts. After two rejections, he found a small inn with equally small rooms. The room cost him an outrageous five dollars for two nights. The proprietor had obviously taken the chance to cash in on the occasion, and Firth had little choice but to pay the asking price. He'd had his fill of rough sleeping. Besides, it was November now and far too cold to chance a night in a barn or shed.

I'm a man of means now, he reminded himself. *I deserve a little luxury now and again.* He did at least get breakfast included in the price.

The next morning dawned clear and bright, but surprisingly mild for the time of year. Firth had his breakfast and contemplated the day ahead. He wanted to leave early to get a good place so that he could hear the president clearly. He was intending to write down the entire speech as it was delivered; he wanted to send it verbatim to Smythe for him to edit as he saw fit. As he neared the podium, which was decked out in red, white, and blue bunting, with an American flag on each side of the speaker's position, he realised just how many people wanted to see the president. There were thousands of people there. Army uniforms made up a large contingent, presumably to provide security and to honour their dead. The whole occasion was, after all, for the army's benefit.

There were also large numbers of press men, mainly distinguishable by their writing pads and curiously similar way of dressing. Then, there were traders selling everything from food, to clothing, to miniature American flags, and copies of the forthcoming speech as well. He bought one and tucked it away in his pocket. He'd never heard of this practice before and was rather sceptical. He thought he'd still try to write down the speech in case it varied from this advance copy. If everyone knew in advance what was going to be said, why bother saying it in public?

Like an invisible blanket, a silence spread across the crowd until there was not a sound to be heard. All heads turned to the right, where a train of horse-drawn carriages could be seen approaching. The silence was replaced by an expectant buzz. The president stepped out of his carriage and paused to greet a few people standing by the steps of the podium. All went quiet again as he took his place at the lectern, an unmistakable figure, with his trademark top hat, bushy beard, and frock coat. He put both his hands on the rail in front of him and looked at the crowd for a moment. Firth could feel the charisma of the man radiating out in every direction. At just that moment, everyone in the crowd felt that the president had looked directly at each of them for an instant and that, somehow, he was about to address each of them personally.

He then began to speak in a strong clear voice that reached every corner of the vast gathering: "Fourscore and seven years ago, our Fathers brought forth, on this continent, a new nation, conceived in liberty, and dedicated to the proposition that all men are created equal …"

Firth tried to listen and write at the same time, but he was soon captivated by the president's oratory. He was glad now that he'd bought his advance copy of the speech. As the speech drew to a close, he found himself transported back to the last time he was at Gettysburg. He realised he must be very near the spot where the Union corporal had clubbed him. He could see the barn where he'd slept until he was well enough to move on. Otherwise, the whole area was unrecognisable. It wasn't just that the bodies had been removed—there was nothing but the new memorial to suggest that this had once been a battlefield. It had only been four months, but the combined effort of man and nature had returned the whole area to its former glory.

Firth spent one more night in his hotel, writing his report and making plans for the coming months. He didn't want to leave Elizabeth alone for any great length of time, but the war looked like it would drag on for a long time yet. Luckily, he had Joe, a man who needed a purpose in life.

Chapter 39

On his return journey, Firth again passed the debris of war and realised it was only Gettysburg that had been cleared, purely for the benefit of the president's dedication of the new cemetery. Every other battlefield, going back nearly three years, must still be as it had been left after each battle.

Elizabeth was again overjoyed to see him, even though he'd only been away for a few days. He was certain now that he had to follow his plan and persuade Joe to help him.

When they next met, Joe told Firth of the Mine Run Campaign. Mine Run Creek, just south of the Rapidan River, was where General Lee had halted his retreat, late in November. For nearly a week, Meade's men made exploratory pushes into the Confederate lines, looking for weak points and seeking to gather information in preparation for an attack.

Unfortunately for Meade, it was late in the year, and a harsh winter was settling in. He decided to postpone any further advances until the weather improved.

Firth had become convinced that the war would be over soon, especially when he heard of Lincoln's plan to issue the Proclamation of Amnesty and Reconstruction, which was designed, apparently, to help heal the rift between supporters of the North and South by pardoning their "existing rebellion" if soldiers of the South joined the Union.

"Joe," said Firth, "I want to give you a job."

"Oh, yes?" Joe inquired, with a note of suspicion.

"Yes, I want you to follow the army southwards and report back to me with real eyewitness reports. It's just what I need for my newspaper articles."

"Follow the war? Are you mad? You nearly got yourself killed doing that. I'm quite happy here, thank you very much."

"Look, Joe, I'd go myself, but I can't leave Elizabeth again. Do this for me, and I'll pay the rest of the money you owe to Philpott. You'll be in the clear. On top of that, I'll pay you three dollars a week in expenses. It's not a fortune, but it'll be enough to pay your way. What do you say?"

"I'd rather take me chances with Philpott."

"Really? Well, the debt's due three days from now. I hope you've been saving hard."

Joe was silent for a short while. "I don't have any choice, do I? When do you want me to go?"

"Look on the bright side, Joe. If it carries on like this, the war could be over in a few weeks."

"Yuh. Or a few years, or maybe twenty goddamn years."

"We'll meet once a month at a place I know that's about halfway between here and Richmond; that way, you won't have to travel too far."

"Big of you. And Philpott?"

"I'm a man of my word, Joe. I'll go and see him and pay him off. You'll promise to go when I say?" Firth asked, holding out his hand.

Joe shook it reluctantly.

"Deal," he said.

Firth paid Philpott, as promised, and sent Joe off in late March. It was still bitterly cold, but nature was beginning to reassert itself. Flowers were blooming everywhere, and the farm animals were bringing the next generation into the world.

In the meantime, after several battles, General Sherman's forces had captured one of the Confederacy's major supply towns, Meriden, Mississippi, causing severe shortages of supplies to the Southern army, which was already on the back foot. Things were looking grim for the rebels, as the superior number of men and better supplies finally seemed to have tipped the scales in the Union's favour.

Although the Confederates were still being pushed back, there were no big engagements for Firth to report on, so he started sending reports reflecting on the position the rebels found themselves in, giving his opinion that, if Richmond fell, the whole Confederate state would collapse.

Firth received a terse letter soon thereafter, telling him that he had exceeded his remit by giving his private views. The article, however, had been published unedited because Smythe had been away on a shooting holiday.

Sympathy for the South had decreased in Manchester, and Lancashire as a whole, because the mills had started getting their cotton from other sources. Even so, neither Smythe nor his readers believed that the Confederate army would be defeated. Public opinion was slowly beginning to change, though, especially now that Prince Albert, who had always been against slavery, had ironically become such a popular figure following his death.

Finally, a major engagement took place between General Lee and General Grant, between 5 and 7 May 1864. The advancing Union troops battled in an area that was soon to become known as the "Wilderness", a large area of thickets and small trees. The undergrowth made it difficult to use firearms, so a great deal of hand-to-hand fighting took place, resulting in some horrific injuries and a considerable number of casualties on both sides. General Lee won the battle; however, in doing so, he lost some ground and also one-fifth of his army. The North had plenty of reserve troops, while the South had no more men to spare. Therefore, to lose 20 per cent of the army was devastating.

Joe related all this to Firth on one of their meetings but said that he dared not venture into the battleground until many hours after the fighting had ended, as it was too dangerous. The undergrowth was so thick, the soldiers mostly had no idea whether they were attacking friend or foe, and anyone there could easily have got themselves killed. Instead, Joe relied on information from wounded soldiers who had managed to get out of the battlefield, often by crawling on their hands and knees for many hours.

On 8 May, the battle of Spotsylvania began. Fighting raged for nearly two weeks, but General Lee finally halted the Union's advance on Richmond. General Jeb Stuart also played his part by stopping Sherman's forces just six miles from the city, but then came the devastating news that Stuart had been mortally wounded on 11 May, at the Battle of Yellow Tavern. He was a major loss for the Confederates. Commander of the cavalry, and a very capable and highly regarded leader, he had been much feared by the Union troops. General Lee, too, had been most upset when he heard of Stuart's death. Stuart was irreplaceable, and this was a doubly serious blow for the Southerners, for he was the man who was responsible for training new recruits to the cavalry.

The next big engagement was at Cold Harbour, during 1 to 3 June, when the Union unleashed a series of attacks on Lee's men. The fighting was brutal and bloody, but the Union army failed to dislodge the Confederates. Attacks on other parts of the Confederate defence lines around the city were also beaten back. By mid-June, Grant concluded that his only option was to lay siege to the city.

By that point, Smythe had stopped writing to Firth to scold him, which seemed to suggest that even he was beginning to think that the South could lose the war. Consequently, Firth became ever bolder with his reports.

The news was unrelentingly bad for the South. The siege of Richmond continued, despite attempts by Lee to break it. He made several diversionary attacks on Union forces, including one at Monocacy on 9 July. There, the rebels met a defensive force of six thousand men who stopped them advancing any further; in doing so, they saved Washington itself. The strong defence at Monocacy gave time for reinforcements to arrive in the capital, and they forced the Confederates to make an early withdrawal.

As the siege of Richmond continued, General Sherman was also making excellent progress elsewhere for the North. He was, by the summer, marching through Georgia, burning the large houses of the rich estates as he proceeded, and destroying plantations, crops, and communications. On 2 September, the Union men forced the Confederates, commanded by General Hood, out of Atlanta, the second-biggest industrial town in the South.

Firth wrote a long article for the *Echo* about this great loss. He pointed out that industrial production in the South had been comparatively small even before Atlanta fell, and now it would be impossible for the Confederate states to make up the shortfall. He predicted that the final defeat would occur within twelve months.

Smythe may not have liked Firth's views, but as a good newspaperman, he recognised a scoop when he saw it. He sent Firth a copy of the paper, something he'd never done before. He had put a big black headline at the top of the front page. It read, "War over in America within a Year"; underneath, in smaller letters, "Our North America correspondent predicts victory for North in Civil War within twelve months". Smythe stressed that these were the views of his reporter, not his own views or those of the paper.

Firth sat down with Elizabeth one day and told her of his thoughts on the latest developments. He explained that he intended to be there at the end to witness the final surrender of the Confederates. It was his duty to his newspaper, he said, and he didn't expect to be away for more than a few days. He hoped he had given her enough time to get used to the idea, as she still didn't like him leaving for any length of time.

While the siege continued, Firth was becoming more and more worried about the fate of Angela and Amelia. He had no idea what had become of them, but surely the longer the siege lasted, the worse things must be. By seeing them, he would be admitting adultery, and that could mean a prison sentence—not to mention the devastating effects on both Elizabeth and Angela.

But, no matter the dangers, he had to see them, and so he planned to visit the house as part of his job of reporting the fall of Richmond.

He tried not to let his gloomy mood affect the stories he was sending to England, but there was little to report about the war other than the siege. He realised he was still going to need a job once hostilities had ceased, so he sought other stores that might be of interest to the *Echo*'s readers.

He covered the presidential elections. On 8 November, he told of Lincoln's reelection, confirming the people's approval of his conduct of the war and their confidence in an eventual victory. He also reported the president's inauguration, on 4 March 1865. In return, he received a letter of praise from Smythe, who seemed to approve.

Soon after the inauguration came news that the Confederates were finally starting to weaken as the siege tightened its stranglehold on Richmond. Joe had rushed back to Washington to tell Firth that the end was imminent. Firth was extremely grateful to him. He'd fulfilled his brief beyond expectations, and Firth released an equally grateful Joe from his obligations, on the spot.

Firth said his goodbyes to Elizabeth and Emily and took a seat on the next coach. He was more than usually affectionate to them, as it was not a journey he was looking forward to undertaking.

"Just come back to me this time, my darling," said Elizabeth. "The war's nearly over now. Just make sure you don't get shot by some trigger-happy rebel firing at you out of spite. They won't realise you're a British reporter."

CHAPTER 40

Firth arrived outside Richmond on 1 April 1865. General Grant was expected to enter the city at any time now. The Confederate forces, led by General George Pickett, were totally beaten. Many of the troops had either died or surrendered at the last battle, at Five Forks, forcing General Lee to abandon Richmond and Petersburg on 2 April. The departing army set the cities ablaze, filling the sky with smoke and exploding shells.

The Union troops quickly moved in, to occupy both cities, but it was slow going. Firth followed the army into Richmond as closely as he dared. On more than one occasion, he was told to fall back and not get too close to the front-line soldiers. All the destruction made him terribly worried about Angela and their daughter. It was almost as if he were returning home, a similar feeling to when he went back to Elizabeth after Gettysburg. Would he always have this feeling of going home in both Richmond and Washington? To both Angela and Elizabeth? The difference was that, this time, he could remember his family, and he longed to see them.

The Union troops reached Richmond city centre the next day and started putting out fires and restoring order.

Firth managed to persuade a junior officer that his reports were more than necessary; they were vital. The world had to know that the war was ending, after four long years, and that the Union was in sight of victory.

He was given an armband with the stars and stripes of the Union flag on it, so that the Union troops wouldn't mistake him for a Confederate left behind to undertake a rear-guard action. With the help of a sergeant, Firth also managed to acquire a Union cap, to which he pinned a badge with the words "Official Army Reporter" on it. This wasn't strictly true, of course, but the helpful sergeant pointed out that it would mean he wouldn't have to give explanations everywhere he went. He was also given a small five-shot pistol, for his own protection.

Firth wandered through the deserted streets of the defeated city, headed towards the Coolings' house. As he turned to walk up the garden path, he saw that the front door was open. It was very quiet, with no gardeners, servants, or anyone else to be seen. It looked as if the whole street, like the rest of the city, was deserted. Perhaps Angela, Amelia, and Mrs Cooling had fled, along with the rest of the inhabitants of the city.

He listened at the door, but there was no noise from inside. He waited a while longer, but there was still nothing, so he gingerly ventured into the house. He slowly and methodically searched the ground-floor rooms, but they were all empty, and also undamaged. As he put his foot on the first step of the stairs, there was a noise from above. Firth froze on the spot. His instinct was to run away as fast as he could. He swallowed down his nervousness and drew his weapon. He crept into the dining room, where there were some long velvet curtains he could hide behind. He felt absurd hiding like a child afraid of an imaginary monster. Besides, what if Angela was making the noise? What would she say if she pulled back the curtain to find him hiding there?

He pulled himself together and left his hiding place. As he again moved towards the stairs, he heard a man's voice. It was gruff and hard, but quiet at first. It got louder and louder, and now Firth could also hear a woman's higher-pitched voice pleading with the man. It was Angela's voice, Firth realised with a start. He was relieved to hear her, and he turned to leave. But, then, he heard the cry of a young child.

"Mamma! Mamma! What's happening? What's he doing to you?" he heard the child cry, and then the sound of the child sobbing.

Firth stopped in his tracks. He looked up the stairs. Something was very wrong here. He abandoned his caution and bounded up the stairs. He was only halfway up when he saw the body of Mrs Cooling. She was lying on the landing, with blood soaked into the front of her dress. It had run down from a wound in her neck and had started to drip onto the top stair. Her eyes were still open, and for a moment, Firth felt she was looking at him. He was about to go to her aid when he realised she was dead. Her eyes had the curious lack of vitality that he had seen all too many times before. He made certain by feeling for her pulse, but there was nothing.

Then, Angela spoke again. "Don't worry, Amy," she said, her voice shaking slightly. "You go into your room and wait for me. I shan't be long."

It seemed to Firth that she was trying to coerce the child into doing as she said without causing her any further alarm. Amelia knew something was wrong, but she did as her mother told her.

Firth quickly and silently retreated down the stairs as the door of the main bedroom opened. A small girl of about three years appeared and stopped outside the door, looking curiously at her grandmother.

"Mamma," she said hesitantly.

"Amelia, go to your room. Now! I'll see to Grandma in a moment. And close the door. I'll be with you shortly," Angela told her, a rising note of desperation in her voice.

Amelia did as she was told, closing the door as she disappeared into her room, sobbing quietly.

As Firth silently climbed the stairs again, he could hear the man clearly. He realised with horror that he knew the voice. It was that bombastic, bullying man who lived in the house opposite: Rumbold. Firth remembered the man's silly, immature daughter and how Angela had saved her life. It all came back to him now, the details tumbling into his memory like small stones poured into a bucket. He also remembered warning Rumbold to leave Angela alone.

"You will let me have my way, girl!" Rumbold said angrily. "You were happy to make love to me when I had my money and my position."

Firth could hardly believe what he was hearing.

"Oh yes, happy as well to take my money to keep you in this house after your husband died. Did he die?" Rumbold taunted her. "Maybe he just ran off—deserted you and deserted the army. Now you think you can say no to me, just because you feel like it. I won't have it, I tell you!"

"Frank didn't leave me or desert from the army. He was better than that, and a better man than you'll ever be. You didn't even go to war. Look at you. Enough money and influence to keep out of it. That makes you a coward in my book!" shouted Angela.

"A coward? Why you—" And then came the sharp crack of a hard slap.

Angela continued in a lower voice. "We never made love. I let you have your way with me because I had to. Think about it—my mother was ill, and my child needed a home to live in. I'll never give in to you again. You've killed my mother, and the war is nearly over. If you've got any sense, you'll leave before the Union soldiers find you. They'll have a few questions for you, I'm sure."

There was silence for a moment, as Rumbold digested her words, then Angela pushed further. "All your money is in worthless Confederate bonds, and your house is worth nothing now that the city is burning. Who'll want to live here after this? Go now, while you've got the chance," she urged him.

"You little slut! You're trying to trick me! I'll kill you, and I'll kill your little brat too!" bellowed Rumbold.

Firth had heard enough. He crossed the landing and opened the door of the bedroom. Angela's eyes widened in shock, and Rumbold turned to see what she was looking at. In his hand was a large pistol. He froze for a second when he saw the man he knew as Frank English.

"You! But you're dead!" he said stupidly.

Rumbold raised the gun and fired it at Firth. It was a poorly aimed shot that whistled past him, grazing his arm and tearing a hole in the sleeve of his coat. Rumbold retreated into the room and slammed the door shut to keep Firth out.

"What's he doing here?" he demanded. "Have you been hiding him all along?"

"Angela," called Firth. "It really is me. Listen to me, Rumbold. I warned you once before to leave her alone. You've chosen to ignore my advice, but I'm a fair man. Go now, but this is your last chance. If you don't, I'm going to come in there, and I'm going to kill you."

"I don't think so, English. I've got your wife here, remember."

Firth knew he had to end this quickly. He ran across the landing and charged into the bedroom door. It flew open and crashed back hard against the wall. He saw Angela cowering in a corner. Her dress was ripped down the front, and one of her breasts was exposed. As intended, he had taken Rumbold by surprise. He had his back to Firth, the gun pointed at the floor.

Angela's face was a mass of conflicting emotions: joy as she recognised her husband, and fear as Rumbold started to raise his gun to fire at her. Firth had no hesitation in firing his own pistol before Rumbold could fire his. The sound of the shot was covered by a huge blast from Rumbold's gun. Firth's bullet lodged in the man's shoulder blade, and he staggered forward. Despite his quick action, Firth had been too late. Rumbold's bullet had hit Angela in the chest, and blood was running through her fingers.

Rumbold was still on his feet, and he turned to face his attacker. He tried to raise his heavy gun, but his strength was failing him. He shot, but he missed Firth, and the bullet lodged in the wall behind him. Firth aimed his gun at

Rumbold's body as the big man lumbered towards him. He pulled the trigger from less than three feet away. The effect was devastating. Rumbold staggered back from the impact, his face contorting in agony as the bullet slammed into his chest. He fell to the floor, blood seeping from his wound.

Firth kicked the gun away from his hand and rushed over to Angela, but he knew there was very little he could do.

She was fading fast but managed a few last words. She reached up to his face and ran her fingers down his cheek. "I knew you'd come back, Frank. I knew it." Her breathing was becoming shallower, but she managed one last sentence. "Amelia," she said. "You must take her with you."

"I promise," said Firth, choking back his tears.

He didn't know if she heard him, as her eyes were now closed, and her breathing had stopped. Firth couldn't move for some time, overcome as he was. He sat with Angela's body in his arms, tears rolling down his cheeks. He had made a promise to her, and now he had to act on it. Poor little Amelia must be frantic with worry after all the noise, and now a deathly silence.

He gently unwrapped his arms from Angela and laid her on the floor. He got up, stepped over Rumbold's corpse, and left the room, closing the door behind him. He stepped carefully round Mrs Cooling's body, gently knocked on the door to Amelia's room, and then went in. Amelia was cowering in a corner.

"Don't worry, darling. It's all over now, but I'm afraid that man has hurt your mamma and grandma very badly. I'm your mamma's friend, and she wants me to look after you now. So, come on, we have to go," he said.

Kneeling down, he held out his arms to her.

"What's your name?" Amelia asked.

"It's Firth. And you're Amelia, right?" he asked gently.

"Yes, but Mamma calls me Amy."

"Amy it is then. Shall we go?"

The child hesitated for a few seconds, but then she decided she had to trust this stranger. She came to him slowly at first, then flung herself into his arms.

Firth hugged her, finding the tears were threatening to start again.

"Where's Mamma?" Amy asked.

"She's dead, Amy. Do you know what that means? Mamma and Grandma are both dead." He thought it best to be honest and tell her the truth, although doing so also seemed brutal with a three-year-old child.

"Mamma, Mamma! Where's mamma?" Amy whined and started to cry.

Firth lifted her into his arms and walked towards the stairs, avoiding Mrs Cooling's blood, which was still spreading.

At that moment, he heard a noise from behind him. He turned to see Rumbold lunging towards him, a wild look on his face. Blood was running down his front, soaking into his waistcoat, and a ball of pink frothy bubbles had appeared at his mouth. As he charged forward, Firth quickly stepped out of the way. Rumbold tripped over Firth's outstretched foot and fell headlong down the stairs. He made no sound as he fell; he hit the floor headfirst and stopped moving. Firth knew he was dead this time. His head was at an entirely unnatural angle to his neck, and blood was creeping across the floor. As the effect of the adrenaline in his system wore off, Firth realised his arm was throbbing badly, and there was a lot of blood too. All his exertions had opened up the old wound.

"Where's Mamma?"

"She's dead, darling. We have to go," he told her again.

Firth could see that Amy was not going to leave without seeing her mother first. Against his better judgement, he took her into the main bedroom. "We'll see Mamma, Amy. You can say goodbye to her, and then we have to go, all right?"

They went into the bedroom, and Firth took Amy over to the corner where Angela's body lay. He gently lowered Amy to the floor and watched as she went to her mother. The little girl was sobbing quietly but didn't turn away. She knelt down and gently stroked Angela's cheek, whispering something to her. Firth looked for a bandage for his arm while she was busy, and he found a shirt, possibly one of his own, in a drawer. When he was satisfied that the bandage would hold for a while, he returned his attention to Amy. She was very dignified. For a moment, she seemed to behave like a grown-up little lady. She took one last look at Angela, then came back and wrapped her arms round his legs, once again a child.

"Amy, we have to go now. It's not safe here. Have you said goodbye to Mamma?"

Amy nodded and asked, "Where are you taking me?"

She was still unwilling to move.

Firth wanted to tell Amy that Angela was his wife and that she was his daughter, but the words stuck in his throat.

"We're going to my home, Amy, where it's safe, but we must hurry on; more bad men may come and hurt both of us. When we get to my home, you'll meet my wife and my daughter (he almost said, "My other daughter"), Emily. My wife loves little children, and I'm sure she'll want to look after you."

The mention of a lady to look after her, especially one with another child, finally seemed to have the desired effect. Amy allowed herself to be picked up without another word. They went out onto the landing, where he once again cautiously stepped round Mrs Cooling's body.

"Bye-bye, Grandma," said Amy.

Perhaps she really had understood something of the reality of the situation. As he reached the bottom of the stairs, he had to step onto Rumbold's inert body before reaching the floor.

Firth closed the front door behind him and lifted Amy onto his shoulders, then hurried off towards the railroad station. His arm was still throbbing, but the bandage seemed to have done its job and stopped the flow of blood, and he could manage the pain for now. As they reached the station, it got considerably busier, but there were very few civilians. The whole area was teeming with Union troops brought in to take control of the city.

As he approached the station entrance, the same young lieutenant who had given him the armband came over to him.

"So, you got a bit more than just a story, I see. And who's this little lady?" he asked, then more seriously added, "I'm sure your paper doesn't want a mascot, fella, so come on. Who is she, and where are you taking her?"

Firth could see that the man was suspicious, and rightly so. He would have to satisfy him quickly, or he could be held up—and even have Amy taken away from him. Luckily, she had both her arms wrapped round his neck and showed no signs of wanting to leave him.

"I live in Washington with my wife and daughter, Lieutenant. This is Amy, my wife's niece. Her mother's been killed, and she was alone in the house, so I thought it best to take her home with me."

Firth could see the man was still sceptical. He tried to speak to Amy.

"Where's your mamma, little girl?" he asked in a none-too-gentle voice.

Amy didn't reply, but tears welled up in her eyes, and she buried her face in Firth's shoulder.

"Here are my papers," Firth said, handing them over. They included his press credentials and a photograph of Elizabeth and Emily. They seemed to allay the lieutenant's doubts, but then he noticed the wound in Firth's arm.

"You're hurt. You ought to get that seen to by the medical unit," he said.

"I will when I get to Washington. I really just want to get Amy here to safety; she's had a terrible time."

"Well, if you're sure."

"I think so, yes. Now look, do you think you can tell me how to get to Washington? Which train do I get?"

"There's a hospital train going straight there from platform three. The tracks have been repaired already, so there'll be no stopping. Come with me; I'll make sure you get a seat."

The lieutenant led them through the crowded station to a train which was filling up with bandaged and bloodied men, mostly walking wounded, but also many on stretchers.

"Have you got the authority to get us a seat?" Firth asked.

"Of course I have. I'm the officer commanding the station, and I say who gets on which train."

"That's wonderful, sir. We're both greatly indebted to you."

The officer held a door open for them, and Firth climbed aboard. They were in a compartment with four soldiers who had various injuries. One was wearing a bandage round his head, two others each had one of their arms in a sling, and the fourth was holding a pair of crutches in front of him. None of them said a word to him as he sat down; they just stared.

The lieutenant gave orders for a nurse to bandage his arm properly after the train departed. Firth shook the officer's hand and thanked him again for his help. No sooner had he closed the door than the train gave a jerk that signalled its departure. He looked down at Amy on the seat next to him, but she was already asleep. Firth relaxed for the first time since arriving in Richmond.

EPILOGUE

On 9 April 1865, at the Appomattox Courthouse, General Lee formally signed the surrender of all the Confederate forces to General Grant, but Firth wouldn't be there to see it. On his arrival in Washington, he walked with Amy to his house, pointing out things of interest on the way.

They turned into East Sixth Street, and then into the path to his house.

"Ready?" he asked Amy.

"Ready," she said, nodding enthusiastically.

Firth knocked firmly on the door and waited until Martha opened it. She saw Amy and looked at Firth with a question in her eyes, but said nothing except to call her mistress. Elizabeth quickly appeared and took one look at him before flinging her arms round him.

"Firth!" She quickly ran her eyes over him and the child. "What's happened to you? What's wrong with your arm? And who's this?" The questions came tumbling out.

Firth laughed. "One at a time, Elizabeth. This is Amelia. She likes to be called Amy. Amy, this is my wife, Elizabeth."

"Hello," Amy said, looking at the ground.

"Hello, Amy. It's very nice to meet you," Elizabeth said, kneeling so that she was at the girl's height.

Elizabeth gently tilted Amy's head back until their eyes met, and they smiled at each other.

"Amy's mother was killed in the chaos in Richmond, and she was all alone. I couldn't just leave her behind. Anything could have happened." Firth paused long enough for Elizabeth to feel sorry for the child, but not long enough for her to worry about the implications.

"It's awful in Richmond, Elizabeth; you have no idea," said Firth. "Most of the citizens have left the city, there are looters everywhere, ammunition dumps have been blown up, and half the city is in flames. I couldn't leave her to fend for herself."

"Bring the little one in. We'll take care of her until we can find out who she belongs to. She must have relatives somewhere."

She took Amy by the hand and turned to go inside.

Firth gave a silent sigh of relief. He knew Elizabeth found young children irresistible. Once Amy had entered the household, there was little chance of her ever leaving. After all, she had no close relatives except himself.

He then introduced Amy to Emily and Elijah. In the way that only young children can, they seemed almost instantly to become best friends. As the years passed, they became inseparable.

By 1881, Amy—"my daughter from Richmond", as Firth thought of her—had become a beautiful young woman and was engaged to a local lawyer.

He saw Angela in the way she talked, smiled, and inclined her head, and in lots of other little details. Sometimes Elizabeth commented that Amy looked a little bit like him, but he just laughed and said it must be because they spent so much time together. If Elizabeth had any suspicions, she kept them to herself. Firth considered himself a lucky man. He loved his wife and family, but he would never forget Angela and for this reason he had a special place in his heart for Amy.

Firth was eternally grateful to Elizabeth, but he could never tell her or Amy the truth. That would be a secret and a burden he would carry with him to his grave.

Lightning Source UK Ltd.
Milton Keynes UK
UKHW041936080819
347643UK00002B/10/P